James Macaulay

Across the Ferry

first impressions of America and its people

James Macaulay

Across the Ferry
first impressions of America and its people

ISBN/EAN: 9783337252588

Printed in Europe, USA, Canada, Australia, Japan

Cover: Foto ©Andreas Hilbeck / pixelio.de

More available books at **www.hansebooks.com**

FIRST IMPRESSIONS OF

AMERICA AND ITS PEOPLE.

BY

JAMES MACAULAY, M.A., M.D., EDIN.,

EDITOR OF THE "LEISURE HOUR."

London:

HODDER AND STOUGHTON,

27, PATERNOSTER ROW.

—

MDCCCLXXI.

"It is said that the expression of regret in the preamble of the treaty, at the escape of the Alabama, 'under whatever circumstances,' is 'without precedent, and eminently calculated to shock the sentiment of diplomatic propriety.' But then, we fear, it is without precedent for two nations to resolve upon making up differences so grave without resort to arms, in the manner prescribed by Christianity, and constantly adopted in private life. If this noble resolve be called national humiliation, let us glory in the reproach ; and if saying now what ought to have been said ten years ago lowers us in the estimation of Europe, let us hope that Europe will, before long, rise to a higher conception of international fellowship."—*The Times*

CONTENTS.

CONTENTS.

ACROSS THE · FERRY.

CHAPTER I.

INTRODUCTORY.

IT is a long sail across "the ocean ferry" from England to America. But though the broad Atlantic separates the two countries, the nations are near. Not only are we immeasurably nearer to our kinsmen over the sea than to our neighbours across the Channel, but in language we are as near to them as Somersetshire is to Yorkshire; nearer in modes of thought and habits of life than Midlothian to Middlesex.

Anything beyond " First Impressions " it would be presumptuous to give as the result of a brief visit, and an apology is due for the publication even of these, when there are so many books on America.

Washington Irving long ago said with regret, that, " notwithstanding the constant intercourse between England and America, there is no people concerning whom the British public have less pure information, or entertain more numerous prejudices." It is the same still. Ordinary books of travel do not give a fair idea of what is most important and useful to know about America. I have read many of them, and have found some of the most recent and most popular the worst and most misleading. Books on Mormonism, or on "Spiritual Wives," may be attractive to idle readers, but we do not look to them for a true account of national life or character. The reader of such books would receive the impression that the country was full of social lawlessness and disorder. But such evils are mere specks on the fair face of the nation ; and a traveller may be for months in the United States, except he goes in search of what is foolish and repulsive, without hearing the subjects of which some writers have made so much ever mentioned, or, if mentioned, only with regret and condemnation.

I find it also a common thing in conversation, as in books, to take the worst points in American character, or the worst specimens of the American people, and contrast them with whatever is best in the old country. There is a remark of Dean Swift worth noting, who said that in describing national character we do not refer to the froth at the top nor the dregs at the bottom, but the great body of a nation. Of the froth and the dregs of American society we hear much in books and in newspapers, but less than we ought of the sound substance of a people numbering more than the population of Great Britain.

The papers in the "Leisure Hour," upon which this Volume is based, attracted more notice in the United States than the writer ventured to expect, having written them only for the information of readers on this side the water. They have been largely quoted and freely commented on in American papers and magazines, and some of the leading journalists have been pleased to approve their spirit, and to express a wish for their publication as a separate book. On the other hand, some English critics objected to the report as too favourable. To this my answer is, that many writers on America seem chiefly to have sought to amuse their readers by accounts of the national faults and foibles. They have given caricatures, not portraits. I should like to know what idea would be given of the English national character, if our bad and weak points were alone presented, as has been too much the practice with writers on

America and its people. The faults and weaknesses of American life and manners are on the surface, and are patent to all observers. A nation which has grown up to be our own equal in less than a century, may be expected to exhibit some of the faults of youth as well as the vices of maturer life. But the great and good elements of national character are not seen or understood by those who write or speak in disparagement of America. To present these is my main purpose, in the assurance that fuller knowledge will lead to better feeling.

The intelligent Briton who, newly arrived in New York, prepared for his first walk down Broadway by buckling on a belt with dagger and pistols, is a fit representative of the current notions about America. Many suppose that every stranger goes about in constant peril from revolvers and bowie knives. I was told by Bishop Simpson of the Methodist Episcopal Church, that he had been in the habit of travelling thousands of miles every year in every part of the Union, and he had never once seen a pistol or a knife produced in car, or boat, or public conveyance. Angry disputes may arise in drinking saloons and other places, but violence of this kind is not unknown in London, and in any seaport town or great city of Europe. This is but a sample

of the ignorance about American life and
customs, prevalent even where better information might be expected. Few of our newspaper writers, for instance, have any true
knowledge of the States. The extent to which
the public mind was misled during the war,
was apparent to all who knew the real state
of affairs. In our public and private schools
little is taught about the United States. Of
the history of the Republic for fifty years
before the election of Abraham Lincoln and
the civil war, few of our public men knew
anything, and even now more is known in
east-end workshops than in west-end clubs.
Brooklyn, Baltimore, St. Louis, Chicago, Cincinnati—how many English readers know
which of the States these cities belong to ?
Yet they contain together above a million and
a half of inhabitants, and each of these States
is greater than the second-rate powers and
kingdoms of the old world.

During the Indian mutiny, there was an old
chief who resolutely refused to join in the
rebellion. Pressed to give his reasons, the
only answer that could be got from him was,
"I have been in England." In like manner,
but on higher grounds, every Englishman who
has been in America ought to be an advocate
of peace and good feeling with the United

States.   It is not merely that he has seen the
power and resources of the great republic, but
he has been among a people one in race and
in language, with the same history and literature, with social institutions founded on the
same Common Law and the same Bible.   No
two nations are so closely allied in sympathy
and interest.   The points of agreement are
many, deep-rooted, and of long standing; the
points of difference are few, superficial, and
but of yesterday.   A century has not yet
passed since the Declaration of Independence.
There are men alive who knew Franklin and
Washington.   Our Sir John Burgoyne, whom
we lost but the other day, was the son of the
General Burgoyne whose army surrendered at
Saratoga.   There has been time for misunder-
standings and quarrels, but there has not been
time for the people of the two countries to
forget their common origin, or to lose their
mutual respect and affection.   The very resentment displayed when any cause of offence
arises is like the feeling when wrong is done
by friends or brothers, always far more keenly
felt than injuries by strangers.   The sensitive-
ness, too, on the part of the Americans to
what is said or done by England is a proof of
deference and love to the old country.   They
would bear ten times as much from any other

nation. They care more for the good opinion of England than of all the world besides.

But this bond of brotherhood may be strained too far. We cannot always count upon this feeling of friendship. A new generation is rising up, with new aims and new interests. Even if the old American feeling remained undiminished, the vast increase of foreign elements in the population must be taken into account. They have not the same restraints of love and goodwill to England. American statesmen cannot disregard this foreign element in national opinion. Nor would it be wise in English statesmen to disregard the altered circumstances of America. The conduct of England during the great rebellion left a deep feeling of resentment in the United States. It is felt that a great wrong was done, and that reparation is due. They say that the sympathy of a large and influential part of the English people was with the Southern States, and encouraged them in their rebellion. They say that the American Government did not obtain the moral support and co-operation that they justly expected. How far they are right in these opinions may be questioned, but the existence of a sense of wrong is undoubted. It is the duty as it is the policy of the English nation to remove this feeling, and to admit the wrong where it can be proved. The Americans look for generous spirit more than for pecuniary recompense. But even if their claims were measured by pecuniary results alone, it would be wise to close the controversy. Far larger sums have been paid in past times by England in subsidies to petty German potentates than would now suffice to regain the goodwill of a great nation, in alliance with which we need not fear the world in arms.

The Washington Treaty has already done much to restore this international good feeling. The language of goodwill and mutual compliment which in former days used to distinguish festive speeches had a somewhat conventional sound. It is otherwise now. The old animosities and jealousies are clearing away. The irritation of a century cannot be extinguished in a year, but a new epoch of fraternity has begun. The liberal relief sent from this country to the sufferers from the Chicago fire was but a response to the generous help to our Lancashire during the cotton famine. Such interchanges of fraternal feeling reach the heart of both nations, and show the time to be near when

> " Love will tread out the baneful fire of anger,
>   And in its ashes plant the tree of peace."

CHAPTER II.

THE OCEAN FERRY—INCIDENTS OF THE VOYAGE.
THE ATLANTIC IN CALM AND STORM.

I WENT on board the Cunard steamer
"Scotia," at Liverpool, on Saturday, the
13th of August, at 10 A.M., sighted the American shore at noon of Monday, the 22nd, and was
at anchor in the Hudson river, off Jersey city,
at 8 P.M. of the same day. We were detained
seven or eight hours at Queenstown, Cove
of Cork, waiting for the last mail from England *via* Holyhead; but setting against this
the gain of time in going westward, about an
hour a day, the voyage was nearly nine days
and a half. The distance from Liverpool to
New York is about 3,060 miles, more or less,
according to the course taken. Old travellers
talk lightly about the "ferry," but to those
who, like myself, cross the Atlantic for the
first time, every detail of the voyage has its
interest, and some practical points may be
worth noting for the benefit of others.

During the summer months the number of passengers is so great that it is advisable to secure a berth a long time in advance. It is well, also, by a letter to the chief steward, to secure a good place at the table, which is retained throughout the voyage. The nearer to midship the better, both as to seats and sleeping berths, provided the latter are not too near the noise of the engine, or the still noisier "donkey engine," which is at work every four or five hours, heaving up the ashes from the furnaces. The outside cabins are the best for light and ventilation. It is rare in summer to have the comfort of a whole cabin, or state room, as it is called. The berths are in pairs, and have room for only one to dress at a time. The "Scotia" being a favourite ship, every berth was filled in its August passage, and the tables in the fore as well as the after saloon were crowded.

Of the Cunard ships, which sail from Liverpool every Tuesday and Saturday throughout the year, some do not carry steerage passengers. The rates of cabin passage to New York by the Cunard ships are, first class £26, second class £18; return tickets 250 dollars, and 150 dollars, gold, according .to the current rate of exchange. By steamers carrying steerage, the fare is 15, 17, and 21 guineas, according to accommodation ; return tickets 150 dollars, gold. This includes a plentiful and even luxurious table, but without liquors.

There is ample choice of good steamers to all the great American ports. To New York, the Inman, the Guion, the National, " White Star," and Allan lines have well-built and well-appointed vessels, with fares from 21 guineas down to 6 guineas for emigrants. There are also French and German lines. By sailing ships the fare is as low as £3 10s.

I was recommended to the " Scotia" as a paddle boat—in fact, the last of the paddle-wheelers of the great transatlantic lines. The motion is said to be less disagreeable than that of screw steamers. All the recently built ships have the screw, and the machinery of the others has been converted. Economy of fuel and of space caused the change, the paddle boats requiring half as much coal again as the screws. The " Scotia" lays in for every voyage 1,900 tons of coal, the daily consumption being about 150 tons. But, besides its paddle-wheel machinery, this is, or was, the largest steamer on the Atlantic, 4,000 tons burden, and nearly 400 feet in length. It requires a rough sea to disturb the steady movement of a ship of this size. The only inconvenience in moderately rough weather is that the spray of the paddle-wheels is blown upon the deck, and keeps the after part of the ship in a dripping state.

There was not even this discomfort in the outward voyage. The weather was superb, excepting one day of fog, followed by a night of chopping sea, as we neared the great bank of Newfoundland. Each day was bright with sunshine, and each night clear and brilliant A light north-easterly wind filled the sails, tempered the summer heat, and crested the blue waves with white foam. On several nights were beautiful displays of the aurora borealis, and on others the ship ploughed through water flashing with phosphorescent light. Whales " blowing " far off, and shoals of porpoises gambolling near the ship, gave occasional enlivenment to the monotony of the sea. Not more than two or three ships were sighted throughout the voyage. The rare occurrence of vessels gives a striking illustration of the vastness of the ocean, even when the course is more direct than that taken by the " Scotia." At seasons when ice is not dreaded, the most northerly route is preferred, sometimes even sighting Cape Race, on purpose to diminish the risk of meeting vessels. The danger of collision, or in spring of encountering icebergs, makes fog the chief source of anxiety. During our foggy day the lookout was doubled, two of the officers being also at the bow, and the captain keeping his post near the compass on the bridge. From this his orders were conveyed by electric wires to the engine-room and the wheel-house. The speed was not slackened, the only precaution being the frequent sounding of the deep-toned fog-whistle. The remark was made that, in case of striking an iceberg, the only difference between going at half speed and full speed was, that in the former case the ship would go down in a minute, in the latter in half a minute! Nothing else could injure the " Scotia," and it was the business of other vessels to look out for themselves. Towards night the wind rose and cleared away the fog. Early next day the pilot-boat hove in sight. We were then about 200 miles from land. The first pilot that meets a ship being taken, the pilot-boats push far out to sea, and are often cruising about for ten or even fifteen days. They belong to associated pilots. Not long before, an adventurous boat was rewarded by putting a pilot on board each of three European steamers, above 300 miles from shore. The payment is by regulated rates, according to the tonnage of the ship, with an increase when the pilot goes on board out of sight of the farthest lighthouse or the coast.

In general routine, the arrangements of all steam-vessels on a voyage are much alike. Landsmen soon come to understand the mysteries of the watches and the ship bells. The correction of time by the observation taken at noon, the heaving the log, and the report of the course, were topics of daily curiosity. It was pleasant at night, after the bell struck, to hear the "all's well" ringing out clear, like a muezzin call. The order and discipline on the Cunard ships are as perfect as in the Navy itself.

We were two Sundays on board, on each of which divine service was held. It was pleasant to hear "the church-going bell," and to see the crew mustered in their Sunday best. The saloon was crowded as far as the seats allowed, and groups of passengers were within earshot at the doors and windows. The captain read prayers—the usual morning service, with the special forms for sea, and a petition interpolated in the Litany for the President and magistrates of the United States. A sermon was read, but it was only a rhetorical discourse, apparently one of old Blair's sermons. The captain of the "Scotia" always conducts the service himself, to avoid, it is said, the difficulty that might arise from the claims of ministers of divers sects or communions. The captain was well supported by the doctor of the ship, who acted as clerk and precentor.

Of Captain Judkins, long commander of the "Scotia," and commodore of the Cunard fleet (since retired), many amusing anecdotes are told, which I withhold because I have heard some of them associated with other names. Thus it was the captain of another ship, and not of the "Scotia," who said in reply to an old lady who, off the Newfoundland banks, asked if it was always foggy there, "Don't know, ma'am; don't live here." It was just such an answer as the old Commodore might have given ; a bluff John Bull of a man, in appearance and in manner, and no doubt regarded as a typical English sailor by the thousands of Americans who have crossed with him. The other officers of the ship were also men of long-tried efficiency. The chief engineer, Waddell, for instance, had been above thirty years on the line. The purser, Fleming, and the boatswain, also a Scotchman, were veterans in the Cunard service. From men like these, who had crossed the Atlantic hundreds of times, I had many interesting recollections of voyages and of voyagers. The ship's company, officers and seamen, engineers and stokers, stewards and attendants, not forgetting the cooks, numbered fully two hundred, all told.

There were about 250 passengers. In the fore-saloon, which received the overflow of the larger state cabin, we had a curiously miscellaneous assembly at table. There was a group of ecclesiastical dignitaries, a Canadian Archbishop, a Mexican bishop, and several of the American bishops, returning from the Œcumenical Council at Rome. There were other clergymen, including the senior bishop of the Methodist Episcopal Church, Bishop Simpson, who had attended the Wesleyan Conference held last summer at Burslem. We had an English M.P., and the Chamberlain of New York, T. B. Sweeny,—Bismarck Sweeny, as he is called from his political influence. There were American officers who had fought through the Civil War, and American merchants from every part of the Union. An unusually large number of American families were returning home in consequence of the war on the Continent. With such a company there was opportunity for obtaining much useful and interesting information. I learned more about various regions of America in a week than long reading could have conveyed. It was not now that I first valued the society of travelled Americans. I had met them at home

and abroad, in all conceivable circumstances.
No devouter pilgrims visit the holy places of
the East, or wander with truer enthusiasm
through classic lands.   In our own country,
the American is always more than " the intelligent foreigner."   Some of them know more
about our island than the majority of Englishmen.   It is not only at Abbotsford or Stratford-on-Avon that you meet them.   If you see
a stranger ruminating on the island of Run-
nymede, or pencilling his name on Cowper's
summer-house at Olney, or deciphering the
inscription on the Covenanters' Tomb in the
Greyfriars' churchyard at Edinburgh, he is
likely to be an American.   I know few greater
treats than wandering with an intelligent New
Englander through the old sites of " Haunted
London."   A voyage even of only a week
gives time for pleasant intercourse with such
associates.   The days passed all too quickly.
I saw with regret the last of the glorious sunsets
in the west, towards which we were steering,
and look back with pleasant memory on the
truly social and republican club that broke
up in New York harbour, never all to meet
again.

But an Atlantic voyage is not always such
a pleasure sail.   I came back in the " Scotia "
in October, during tempestuous weather, when

few of the passengers were in the mood for talk or recreation. There was no playing at rope quoits or shovel-board this time; and the plates of the diners, few and far between, had to be secured to the tables by a double fence. The equinoctial gales were supposed to be over, but we had heavy head winds against us all the way, and at last came in for part of the weather which proved fatal to the "Cambria." A storm at sea is the time for deepening the sense of human helplessness, and for strengthening the feeling of dependence on Him who is mightier than the waves of the sea. Next to this trust I was helped to quietude by the coolness recorded of Captain Scoresby in his Life, which I found in the ship's library. During a storm in the Atlantic he occupied himself, with the coolness of an old sailor and a Christian philosopher, as he was, studying the size and force of the Atlantic waves. Mounted on the paddle-box, and holding on to the railings, during a violent north-west gale, he watched the waves, and the following is the general result of his observations :—

Highest altitude	43 feet.
Mean distance between each wave .	559 „
Width from crest to crest . . .	600 „
Interval of time between each wave .	16 seconds.
Velocity of each wave per hour . .	32½ miles.

" This," he says, " is the measurement of a
rough Atlantic sea, not of the highest possible
waves." He writes as if he regretted he had
not the chance of observing a stormier sea !
I was glad to get safely back again to *terra
firma* on old England.

During the outward voyage it was strange
to reflect that while we were tearing along at
the rate of fifteen knots an hour, the latest
telegrams from Europe were being flashed
deep down under us with lightning speed. We
had left just after the opening of the war.
" To Berlin" was still the cry resounding on
the Parisian boulevards. The first shots had
been fired, and the Imperial Prince had received his " baptism of blood " at Saarbruck.
It looked as if the French armies were to cross
the Rhine and invade Germany. The last
papers received at Queenstown threw doubt on
the easy triumph of the French, though the
mitrailleuses were said to have "mown down
the enemy like corn " in the first engagement.
Throughout the week, blank of news, the
prospects of the belligerents were keenly discussed. From some ship on its way to Europe
we might have got tidings of what was going
on in the old world, but no ship came near
enough for signals. As we approached the
American coast, the first sight of the pilot's

boat, always welcome, was eagerly expected, in order to relieve the anxious curiosity about the war. Great was the excitement when the pilot, after a few moments' conversation upon the paddle-box with the captain, threw down a New York newspaper among the crowd on the deck. I happened to catch the paper, and was immediately required to mount a bench and read aloud. The large capital headings were first proclaimed, amidst cheers and counter-cheers from French or German sympathisers. The first great battles had been fought, but the result was still doubtful; at least the brief headings told nothing decisive. Then the details of the telegraphic despatches were read, till the reader was hoarse and gave up the paper to another speaker of more stentorian voice. "What's the price of gold?" "What are Consols?" "How is Nancy?" A volley of such questions having been answered, the crowd broke up into knots of conversation and discussion. Sympathy seemed pretty equally divided. There were only two or three Frenchmen on board, and many Germans. The English were neutral, but the majority of the Americans and of the Irish cheered when the news appeared hopeful for the French success. It was altogether a curious scene, and prepared me for what I witnessed during my stay in America of conflicting voices and sympathies concerning the war.

CHAPTER III.

THE HUDSON RIVER—AMERICAN STEAM POWER
—THE ELECTRIC TELEGRAPH—CANALS—IM-
PRESSIONS BEFORE LANDING.

WHEN the excitement caused by the arrival of the pilot, with the news from Europe, had subsided, we found ourselves steaming along the southern coast of Long Island. In due time we sighted the point of Sandy Hook, from which the arrival of ships is telegraphed to New York. Opposite Sandy Hook, with its lighthouse, is the outer bar of the bay or harbour, still eighteen miles from Battery Point, the southern extremity of Manhattan Island, on which New York City is built. There are two ship channels, which admit at high water vessels of the greatest draught, the " Great Eastern " having repeatedly crossed the bar. We steamed slowly up for Sandy Hook, towards " The Narrows," about two-thirds of a mile in width, where the bay or harbour ends, and we enter the inner har-

bour. The bay is alive with steamers and sailing vessels, and surrounded by villa-crowned
heights, with strong forts at all hands. Off
Staten Island the quarantine officer boarded
us, after repeated signal guns had been fired.
It was too late to pass the Custom House
that night, so the " Scotia " anchored in the
Hudson River, off the Cunard dock in Jersey
City. Some of the passengers, whose homes
were near, went ashore, but the majority spent
the night on board.

My first impression of America was the
result of the late watch that night in the
Hudson River. The glancing lights on the
water, and the distant illuminations on the
shores all round, with brilliant lime-lights on
the heights over the ferries, gave proof of
our being near a busy hive of life. These
Americans know how to use steam, was my
first mental remark. Steamers of all sorts and
sizes were moving about in the bay. Fussy
little tugs were hurrying hither and thither,
others slowly dragging up great merchant
ships. Several of the large river steamers
passed near. One of them, a celebrated Long
Sound boat, which plies between New York
and Boston, seemed as long as the " Scotia,"
and had an imposing appearance with the
light flashing through the saloon windows

from stem to stern. Forests of funnels were
in the slips along the shore. Not far from our
ship, the Jersey ferry-boats were crossing at
short intervals throughout the night. These
ferry-boats are to New York what the bridges
are on the Thames. There is a broad roadway in the middle of the boat, on to which
horses and vehicles of every description drive
till the space is filled, the sideways being left
for foot passengers. The traffic on some of
the ferries, especially between New York and
Brooklyn, is enormous.

This first impression as to the " steam-
power " of America was strengthened where-
ever I went, on land or water. I have no
statistics, so as to draw comparison with our
own or other countries, but everywhere on the
rivers, or the great lakes, in the factories, on
the roads, and even in the hotels and stores,
the steam-engine was always at work. I wondered how much the operative and productive
power of the population is multiplied by this
energetic employment of steam. The people
of Russia, or of Spain, may be told off against
equal numbers in the United States; but when
we multiply the numbers by the steam-power
in each country, we cease to wonder at the
rate of American progress. And this is only
one of the ways in which the energy of the

national character is hurrying to unprecedented greatness.

The use of the electric telegraph afterwards suggested similar reflections. The whole country is netted with wires. The tall mast-like telegraph posts form a conspicuous feature in the streets of all the towns. Every office and hotel and great store has its telegraph bureau. The newspapers far exceed our own in the extent of their telegraphic arrangements. During the war the despatches from Europe often doubled in length those of the *Times.* Letters appeared in the *New York Tribune* and *Herald* as long as those of " our own correspondents " sent by ordinary post to the London newspapers. The European news of the previous day is thus read in San Francisco and New Orleans. I saw a curious example of the use of the telegraph in the Exchange at Chicago. As the clock struck twelve, the rap of the president's hammer stilled the tumult of the corn speculators and other "operators" in the crowded hall, and the latest prices of funds and stocks were announced. The closing prices of corn in Mark Lane were known in Chicago even before the same hour at Manchester. The difference between Greenwich time and New York time, and the times of different places

on the vast continent of America, gives rise
to curious complications in the mind as to the
chronology of telegraphic news.

Another curious instance I may mention of
the use of the telegraph in the details of even
indoor life. In the hospital at Cincinnati, I
saw a bureau in the hall in charge of a smart
coloured boy. Wires centred in this office
from all the wards, and every hour the tem-
perature in each ward was telegraphed by the
head nurse, and entered by the clerk, for
the inspection of the medical superintendent,
whose room was adjoining. In many private
as well as public establishments the telegraphic arrangements are equally complete.
The Americans know how to make the most
use of electricity as well as of steam.

In all mechanical contrivances for applying
science to the uses of life, their ingenuity and
skill are remarkable, as their Patent Museum
at Washington attests. They are at least
abreast of England in such matters, and
before all other nations.

We went ashore after breakfast the next
morning, in a steam tender, to the Cunard
wharf. The Custom House examination was
not troublesome. A schedule had been previously signed on board ship, including a declaration as to the objects liable to duty.

Another schedule required answers as to country, occupation, and as to whether it was the first entrance to the State of New York. The Custom House officers wore no uniform, and as they stood in line to be told off for each passenger as the schedule was presented, they had a motley look. I thought at first they were a row of touting commissioners for the hotels, kept in order and quietness by the police regulations. The baggage was spread out in a long shed for being claimed and examined. Hackney coaches, hotel carriages, and baggage cars were outside the gates. There was no crowding or bustle, but the fares demanded seemed excessive, generally being two dollars for a coach. This was the beginning of experience as to the high rates of hackney vehicles in America. There are no one-horse cabs, but two-horsed carriages like our old hackney coaches. A dollar an hour is the regular fare, but it is rare to get off under two dollars for a course. The hotel coaches have a fixed charge, which is included in the bill. Or the passenger may consign his baggage to the agent of an " Express " company, and make his way on foot or by omnibus. The "express," however, often involves delay in arrival for many hours.

While waiting my turn in the Custom House shed, I saw alongside the slip a boat or barge laden with grain, which was being lifted into a granary or "elevator." This name is from the mode of elevating or lifting the grain, by a series of iron buckets moving by steam. A similar machine is in use among us for lifting sand or soil in the deepening and cleaning of harbours. The vast development of railway traffic has thrown into shade the canal traffic of America, which is, however, of great magnitude and importance. Here was an illustration on my first landing. This corn barge had brought its cargo from the far west, coming by canal to Albany, and thence down the Hudson. I afterwards saw the great works at Albany, where the Erie Canal joins the river. In other parts of America I saw the extent and skill of canal engineering. From the shores of the great western lakes, produce is taken eastward to the St. Lawrence by a canal, with a series of locks outflanking the falls of Niagara. From Chicago a great ship canal is in progress, which will carry the produce of the west down the Mississippi to New Orleans.

CHAPTER IV.

NEW YORK OR NEW CORK?—CELTIC AND OTHER
NATIONALITIES—A FEW WORDS ABOUT THE
CENSUS.

I S it New York or New Cork that I am in?
The porter who carried my baggage from the
steam-tug to the Custom House wharf was an
Irishman. The Custom House examiner was
an Irishman. The harbour men in the boats
and lighters were shouting in Irish brogue.
The hackney coachman who drove me to the
hotel was Irish. The drivers of the omnibuses
are unmistakable Paddies. On the staring
signboards of the stores are familiar Irish
names. The chambermaids and servants in
the hotels are Irish. The Irish Chamberlain
of New York told me that "the Irish vote"
is about 40,000. No wonder that the Irish
have their share, or more than their share, in
the offices and good things of the city. But
while there are Irishmen at the council board,
and in Fifth Avenue mansions, the masses of

the Celtic population occupy the poorest parts
of the city.　Five Points, the Seven Dials of
New York, owes its squalid notoriety to the
Irish population.　The servile work of the
Northern States is done by the Irish, as much
as the same work in the Southern States is done
by the negroes.　At the same time, it is a rare
thing for an Irishman not to improve his condition in the New World.　Even in New York,
where the least industrious and enterprising
of the emigrants prefer to remain, instead of
going to the west, there is a large proportion
who live in plenty and comfort.　The " levelling
up " of good wages and of education, affects the
Irish along with the native Americans.

Between the two races there is not much
sympathy or good feeling.　The Irish go to
America more to escape poverty in their own
country than with any clear notions about the
land of their adoption.　Many of them look
with longing regrets to their early homes.　I
was amused one day with the remark of a
labourer in talking about his work and wages
and way of life.　He had been saying that work
was plenty for a single man, but that it was a
hard fight for " thim with families."　" And
there's little of pleasure here," he added; " I
could get more fun out of half-a-crown at a fair
and the loike in the ould country, than out of

three dollars in this place ! " It used to be said that though the emigrants retained their habits and their religion, the children, by attending the common schools, and by association with the people, would become good American citizens and good Protestants. This is not now the case. The influence of the Roman Catholic Church over its members is more generally retained. The number of Catholic schools is largely increasing, and the "Christian Brothers," a trained order for supplying teachers, are indefatigable in their labours. The result is that the Irish are becoming more and more a separate and compact power in the Union. Their aggregate vote, under the bidding of their priests and politicians, can be counted on, especially in New York. Hence, too, the success of Fenian agitation, hatred to England for its alleged oppression of Ireland giving an additional bond of union. But for the ignorance which thus makes them a prey to professional agitators, the patriotic remembrance of the old country would be a noble feature of character. This is expressed in one of their songs, " The Lament of the Irish Emigrant " :

" They say there's bread and work for all,
And the sun shines always there ;
But I'll not forget old Ireland,
Were it fifty times as fair."

Taking advantage of this feeling, political craft has made popular another Irish song, " The Wearing of the Green " :

" Oh, Paddy dear, and did you hear the news that's going round?
The shamrock is forbid, by laws, to grow on Irish ground !
No more St. Patrick's Day we'll keep, his colour last be seen,
For there's a cruel law agin' the wearing of the green !

    *   *   *   *   *   *

When the law can stop the blades of grass from growing as
    they grow,
And when the leaves, in summer time, their verdure do not
    show,
Then I will change the colour I wear in my cabbeen ;
But till that day, plaze God, I'll stick to wearing of the green.

But if at last her colours should be torn from Ireland's heart,
Her sons, with shame and sorrow, from the dear old soil will
    part ;
I've heard whispers of a country that lies far beyond the sea,
Where rich and poor stand equal in the light of freedom's day.

Oh, Erin ! must we leave you, driven by the tyrant's hand ?
Must we ask a mother's blessing, in a strange but happy land,
Where the cruel cross of England's thraldom never can be
    seen,
But where, thank God, we'll live and die still wearing of the
    green?" ·

Remembering how much songs and ballads not only express but intensify and perpetuate national feelings, the popularity of these songs in America is worthy of note.

One other favourite song I must refer to because it illustrates what I said about the want of good feeling between American and Irish.

It is common in advertisements for servants in New York, as in London, to append, " No Irish need apply." These words grate rather harshly on the ear in a land where all are supposed to be " free and equal." Hence another song, of which the following are the closing stanzas:

" Sure, I've heard that in America it always is the plan
That an Irishman is just as good as any other man ;
A home and hospitality they never will deny
The stranger here, or ever say, No Irish need apply.
But some black sheep are in the flock—a dirty lot, say I ;
A dacint man will never write, No Irish need apply!

Sure, Paddy's heart is in his hand, as all the world does know,
His praties and his whisky he will share with friend or foe ;
His door is always open to the stranger passing by ;
He never thinks of saying, None but Irish may apply.
And in Columbia's history his name is ranking high ;
Thin shame upon the knaves that write, No Irish need apply !

Ould Ireland on the battle-field a lasting fame has made ;
We all have heard of Meagher's men, and Corcoran's brigade ;
Though fools may flout and bigots rave, and fanatics may cry,
Yet when they want good fighting-men, the Irish *may* apply ;
And when for freedom and the right they raise the battle-cry,
Then the rebel ranks begin to think, No Irish need apply."

There are other nationalities apparent besides the Celtic.* I see Dutch Reformed Churches, and names of places and people reminding me

* The census of 1870 showed that nearly one-tenth of the population were born either in Ireland or Germany, Ireland having contributed 1,855,779, and Germany 1,690,533. The largest number of Irish reside in New York, where there are 528,806. Of Germans in New York there are 316,902. The Germans are most numerous in the West, the Irish in the Eastern States.

3

that New York was once more New Amsterdam than New Cork. There is still enough to re-call the days of Rip Van Winkle and of Died-rich Knickerbocker. But the modern German element is strongest. I see German names everywhere, German läger-beer saloons, and German newspapers. The German vote is 30,000 already, and is increasing in greater ratio than the Irish. I believe that in New York there are more Germans than in any city of the Fatherland, except Berlin and Vienna. The Scandinavian races are also largely repre-sented. In by-streets I came upon colonies of Italians, and other continental birds of a feather, flocking together. The coloured people also prevail in certain localities. As to the Jews, their number may be gathered from the fact that there are above twenty synagogues. All this suggests that New York can scarcely be regarded as a typical American city, and that due allowance must be made, in speaking either of the civic government or the habits of the people. It is all the more to the credit of American character and energy, that the great foreign element, amounting fully to half of the whole population, is held in check by, and is gradually becoming more and more assimilated to, the institutions and public opinion of the country of their adoption.

The census was being taken while I was in America. Local politics in New York caused more than usual anxiety and excitement as to the results. The enumerators (about 350) were nominated by the Marshal, Sharpe, appointed by the United States Government. The returns in some of the wards were somewhat startling. In one district, chiefly inhabited by Irish, hundreds of votes had been given for years to the democratic ticket more than there were voters, according to the census. In the tenth electoral district of the sixth ward the total population, men, women, and children, was returned as 870. The vote for that district, last fall, was 707 ! The republican party supported the Marshal ; their opponents denounced the enumeration as unfair. From the correspondence in the papers it appeared that there were some grounds for complaint. A letter, for instance, from Mr. Sidney E. Morse, formerly editor of the " New York Observer," stated that he had expected to be furnished with a schedule to be filled up with the fourteen persons in his house on the 1st of June. The schedule never came, and on inquiry it was found that the census taker had called one evening and taken a verbal report from a black servant. On going to the Marshal's office, Mr. Morse found his schedule containing six instead of fourteen names ; and

almost every entry, as to name, age, occupation, and property, was an error.

Many similar complaints being made, there
can be no doubt that the census was imper-
fectly taken.   After much discussion, it was
resolved by the city authorities to take an
independent enumeration, upon which the
Government ordered the census to be retaken.
By striking an average a fair approximation
to the truth may be obtained, but the census
returns under these circumstances can have
little value for exact statistical purposes.

Apart from political grumbling, the pride of
progress caused much dissatisfaction with the
result of the census.   Not only New York, but
almost every one of the largest American cities,
expected and claimed a greater population than
the returns showed.   The following table gives
the population in eleven of the largest cities,
with the corresponding numbers in 1850 and
1860 :—

Cities.	1850.	Increase per cent.	1860.	Increase per cent.	1870.
1. New York	515,547	58	813,669	14	927,341
2. Philadelphia	408,762	28	562,529	$16\frac{1}{4}$	657,159
3. Brooklyn..	96,838	115	266,661	$48\frac{3}{4}$	396,661
4. Chicago ..	29,963	$264\frac{1}{4}$	139,260	219	348,709
5. St. Louis..	77,860	$106\frac{1}{2}$	160,773	$94\frac{3}{4}$	313,013
6. Baltimore	169,054	$25\frac{1}{2}$	212,418	$30\frac{1}{4}$	276,599
7. Boston ..	186,881	30	177,840	41	250,701
8. Cincinnati	115,435	$39\frac{1}{2}$	161,044	36	218,900
9. San Francisco ..	24,776	63	55,802	$164\frac{3}{4}$	150,361
10. Washington	40,001	$52\frac{3}{4}$	61,122	79	109,358
11. Pittsburg..	46,601	$5\frac{1}{2}$	49,217	$77\frac{1}{4}$	87,215

In the case of Boston, between 1860 and 1870 a number of outlying villages were annexed to the city, making its population larger in proportion. The San Francisco population reported for 1850 was really that resulting from a census taken in 1852. The most remarkable increase in population is that shown by Chicago, which was the eleventh town on the list in 1850, the eighth in 1860, and the fourth in 1870. Brooklyn, which was the sixth in 1850, is now the third. St. Louis, the seventh in 1850, and also in 1860, became the fifth. Baltimore and Boston in 1850 were the third and fourth cities, in 1860 became the fourth and fifth, and now are the sixth and seventh. Chicago by its disaster in 1871 has fallen behind St. Louis, but is likely to recover its place before another census.

CHAPTER V.

MANHATTAN Island, upon which New York is built, is a long strip about thirteen miles and a half in length, with an average breadth of a mile and a half. The whole area is about twenty-two square miles. The Hudson River separates the western shore of the island from the mainland, on which stands Jersey City. On the other side of the island is East River, dividing it, or rather connecting it with Long Island, on which Brooklyn stands. Between New York and Brooklyn, ferry boats maintain constant communication, the boats running to and fro day and night. From the southern extremity at Battery Point, the City of New York is compactly built for about six miles. On the east side the buildings reach, irregularly, four miles farther to Harlem. On the other side, beyond Sixtieth Street, the buildings are less continuous, running into the scattered suburban residences of Manhattanville and Washington Heights. The Central Park occupies a large space in the midst of the island. It is any-thing but central with regard to the busy part of the city, nor is it likely that the northern end of the island will ever be densely peopled like the southern district. Long before reaching the park the city has a straggling, unfinished look. The streets are laid out, indeed, beyond the hundred and fiftieth, but with intervals of unoccupied and sparsely-built ground. Here and there, between blocks of imposing houses, are groups of rough wooden huts, where Irish squatters herd with their poultry and pigs. These huts are perched on the bare rock, which in many places crops up to the surface, even south of the Central Park.

I had been advised to go to the Metropolitan Hotel, in Broadway, as being a thoroughly American house. Entering my name in a book at the office, and securing a room, I went out for my first stroll in New York till my baggage arrived.

Broadway is like no other street in the world, and, taken altogether, it is perhaps the finest. Thackeray said so, and most travellers will agree with him. The lower part, from the Bat-tery and the Bowling Green to the Park at the

City Hall, is thronged with business life. Above
Canal Street there is a succession of splendid
shops, huge hotels, and other public buildings,
more imposing than any one London street
can show for the same distance. Above Tenth
Street the ladies' shopping ground begins, the
roadway filled with carriages, and the pavements crowded with promenaders. For these
three miles, Broadway is a scene of ceaseless
excitement.

The number of omnibuses is very large.
From the hotel window I sometimes noted the
traffic, and never counted less than five omnibuses pass in a minute, often twice as many.
There is a perpetual procession of them,
moving slowly up and down ; and, by the way,
on different sides from ours. In America, as in
France, the rule of the road is to pass on the
left, not on the right. There are no conductors
to the omnibuses.   The driver opens the door
by slackening a strap, and is stopped by pulling
the strap, which is held under his foot. Payment, ten or twelve cents for all distances, is
made on entering, through a hole in the roof.
The driver's notice is called by a spring bell,
which he takes care to sound if any passenger
neglects to pay promptly.   The omnibuses are
all painted white or yellow, with showy pictures
on them ; some, however, artistically executed.

There is a seat on either side of the driver, but
none on the top, where it is too hot in summer,
and too cold in winter. A great cotton um-
brella is in summer fixed above the driving-
box. The crowd of drays, waggons, and other
vehicles is equal to that of Cheapside or the
Strand. At the chief crossings, policemen are
posted to regulate the traffic. I continually
admired the sagacity of the horses, and the
cleverness of the drivers. It was really difficult
steering, with such crowded way, and so many
cross lines, including street tramways. Yet
there never seemed difficulty or confusion. I
am bound also to say that never but once did
I witness a squabble between drivers. I was
struck with this, remembering the frequent
quarrels and the volleys of abusive language
which our carmen and cabmen too often indulge
in. There is a society in New York for the
prevention of cruelty to animals, but its operations are very limited, so far as horses are concerned. In general they are kindly treated,
and not overworked. I went to several stables
and found the arrangements excellent. Many
of the stables are above the ground level, being
reached by an ascending slope, so that they
are kept dry as well as thoroughly ventilated.
At work the whip is little used compared with
the voice. The intelligence of "the lower

orders," as we call them, has influence even in the treatment of dumb animals. The drivers of the business vehicles are mostly Americans, of the coaches and omnibuses mostly Irish, but I saw no difference in the usage of their cattle.

The streets are generally very badly paved. Even Broadway is in this respect inferior to most of our London streets. This neglect is more painfully evident in the off streets, and the river sides are in sad want of proper quays and embankments. Excepting the space near the chief ferries, the coast line of Manhattan is in a discreditable state. On the Hudson River side the piers and wharves are formed of rough wooden piles, often dilapidated and grimy with sewage and tide refuse. Crowds of barges and boats line the wharves, the oyster boats alone forming a floating suburb, while every form and size of sailing craft and river steamers crowd the river. Opposite the tall warehouses and rude sheds on the East River side are vessels laden with provisions for the commissariat of the city, with great ships at anchor bearing foreign produce. The vast traffic of the Erie Canal supplies its quota of boats, bearing flour and grain from the far west. The markets—Washington Market with its irregular town of wooden sheds, and Fulton

Market, the Billingsgate of the New World—
are scenes of busy excitement. The old ship-
yards have a deserted, desolate look, but the
iron foundries are alive with industrial noise
and activity. When there are embankments
and wharves worthy of the wealth of New
York, the water-sides of the city will present
an aspect as grand as the commerce is vast and
various.

Striking inland from the lower shores of the
East River, we come upon the worst regions of
the city. The noted locality of Five Points is
as much improved from what it was formerly
as is the locality of our Seven Dials. But in
the lower parts of the city are crowded streets
of the poorest kind, made up of what are called
tenement houses, crowded with inhabitants.
These tenement houses are more like what may
be seen in the Wynds of Glasgow, or the Closes
of Edinburgh, than any London buildings.
Here the Irish most do congregate, and the
lowest of the American population. At night
these places are scenes of disturbance, which
keep the police on the alert, and give to New
York its character of a disorderly city.

Returning to the Broadway pavements, the
gay shop windows afford constant amusement.
The sign-boards are generally more conspicuous than in London, and gilt letters of

enormous size give the idea of French rather
than English commercial life. The tobacconists' shops have big wooden painted figures,
a typical Yankee with lank hair, tail-coat, and
light pants, or an Indian girl, or Lord Dundreary, or Sir Walter Raleigh, corresponding
to the kilted Highlandman once common in
London snuff-shops. Drinking-shops and oyster saloons, down steps, are rather too frequent.
Every now and then we come to magnificent
buildings which would be architectural ornaments in any capital. The interiors of the
stores are often very imposing. Conspicuous
beyond all is Stewart's dry goods' store, the
largest retail establishment in the world. It
occupies the ground of a whole square or block
between Ninth and Tenth Streets, and from
Broadway back to Fourth Avenue. The eight
floors of this building, would, on a level, cover
about fifteen acres. Including the sewing girls,
with their machines on the upper floor, I was told
that eighteen hundred persons were employed
in this store.

But I must not indulge in recollections of
the various streets of New York, with their
wonderful diversity of interest. The Fifth
Avenue, the Bowery, Wall Street, Chatham
Street, and a score of others, all have points of
varied interest for strangers. Many of the side

streets have trees, especially acacias, and the recently-introduced Œlanthus, which flourish well, though I saw in many cases fine trees perishing from stupid neglect, space not being left in the pavement for the increasing growth of the trunk. I noticed this especially in the streets near Washington Square, and on the other side of Broadway, as Bond Street. The names of the streets are painted on the lamps at the corners. Post-office receiving boxes are also attached to these lamp-posts. The building material of New York is chiefly brown stone and brick, but there is a large proportion of marble and granite to be seen. One thing I specially noticed, that the basements are far more carefully constructed than in our London houses. Even in low-lying streets like Canal Street, the arrangements are all that could be desired for health and business convenience. In London, while looking in at shop-windows, one is saluted with pestilential odours from the open grating above the dark subterranean ground. In New York the ground floor is usually light and wholesome. With our skill in glass and iron-work, a great improvement could surely be made in the basement floors of our business streets. I suspect, however, that the land and property laws partly account for the more careful building in New York. What

interest has a tenant in London to erect a
building to last much beyond the term of a
lease, when the building then becomes the property of a ground landlord ?   *Sic vos non vobis
ædificatis.*

CHAPTER VI.

FROM the "New York Directory," a copy of which was chained at the office desk of the hotel, I gleaned some interesting facts about the past changes and present condition of the city. It is a huge book, with numerous pages of advertisements, almost equalling in size our "London Directory" before a supplemental volume was required for the surburban districts. The volume for 1870 was the eighty-third of the series. The first was published in 1786, a comparatively small volume. There was no publication in 1788, but since that date the issue has been annual, and with increase of bulk, till it includes above 190,000 names and addresses. The increase of 1870 over 1869 was 3,962. In keeping with American keenness in business, the top of every page is occupied by an advertisement.

The Directory shows that the same changes have taken place in the business region of New

York as in our own City. Forty years ago in
Wall Street, the Lombard Street of New York,
many families resided in the upper floors of the
houses. There is now not a single dwelling-
house, but the whole street is given up to
business offices. There are only 120 numbers
in the street, but 2,320 names, representing
firms or heads of families residing elsewhere.
In the streets adjoining Wall Street there is the
same crowding of business addresses. Broad
Street, from Wall Street to the East River,
with only 144 numbers, gives 1,210 names;
Beaver Street, 95 numbers, has 590 names;
Nassau Street, 1,570 names; William Street,
1,405 names; and the small space of Exchange
Place, 715 names; bankers, brokers, attorneys,
merchants, and commission agents crowding to
the centre of commercial activity. Broadway
has 8,500 names, densest at the southern or
city end of its long range. The Directory also
reveals in a general way the kind of population
in other parts of the city. Thus the First
Avenue, nearest the East River, has 2,765
names; the Eighth and Ninth, on the other
side of the island, have 2,370 and 1,925
respectively; while the Fifth Avenue, with its
spacious houses and wealthy residents,* gives

---

* The following estimate of incomes and expenditure is given
in a New York paper. Of families that spend between 25,000

only 665 names and addresses. Madison Avenue, outvying the Fifth, has 295 houses, and not a single hotel or store.

In the front of the Directory are some curious pages. One contains a list of the names and addresses of duly qualified nurses. Another list, extending over several pages, gives stores and dwellings the names of the occupants of which were refused. There are between six and seven hundred of these, large numbers of the stores being liquor-shops, oyster-saloons, and variety stores. The dwelling houses are particularised as, on the basement, first-floor front, second-floor back, and so on,—useful information, no doubt, for the police, as many who refuse to give names are likely to have special reasons for the refusal.

In the crowded business streets, not in New York only, but in all the great American cities, I noticed, more than among us, the large num-

and 30,000 dols. a year, there are about a thousand in New York. It would be impossible to ascertain the exact amount, but the above figures can be relied on as a very near approximation to the fact. It is easier to give a close figure as to the families spending between 50,000 and 60,000 dols. a year. There are about sixty or seventy such families. Our figures would stand thus : 10,000 or 13,000 families that spend 10,000 dols. a year ; 1,000 spend 20,000 to 30,000 dols. a year, and sixty or seventy 50,000 dols. a year. On Fifth Avenue it costs 25,000 dols. to live respectably. In this sum we do not include the rent of the house, which would certainly swell the amount to 30,000 dols.

4

ber of names with one address. In the same
office many men have " desk room," or will
even pay rent merely for having a safe, or
compartment of a safe, in the office, with the
name painted on the door. Names are also
conspicuously painted between the steps on the
common stairs. I noticed also in the working
parts of the city it was common to have rooms
"with the use of steam power," one engine in
the basement having gear attached for many
separate workshops.

Within a limited space there is perhaps
greater bustle and activity than could be witnessed in the same area in any capital in the
world. But taking New York as a whole, a
few days' exploration will show the stranger
that with all its suburbs it is a small place
compared with the vast and teeming region of
the British metropolis. Away from the business
centre and off the great lines of traffic, the city
has a quiet air compared with what may be
seen in many of the London suburbs. There
is most bustle in the streets along which run
various lines of street tramway cars. The lines
of some of the great railways run through parts
of the city on the level of the street, not raised
on an arched elevation as are our London lines
on their way to the termini, or depôts, as they
are called in America. In a side street in New

York, in my first ramble, I saw a long train of "freight cars," ready to start for the west. Painted in large letters on one of the cars was the announcement "straight through to San Francisco," a journey of 3,000 miles. The vast system of railway communication, and indeed of passenger and goods traffic to every part of the world, is one of the things that surprise a stranger. In all the hotels, and in numerous public places, there are bureaus, with conspicuous advertisements, for the sale of tickets, with coupons not only to every part of the United States, but to all regions of the globe. Thus you can buy a ticket with coupons for Boston, Niagara, Chicago, Omaha, Salt Lake City, San Francisco, Japan, Hong Kong, Calcutta, Bombay, Alexandria, Marseilles, Paris and London, Havre or Liverpool, and so back to New York. On board the "Scotia" there was a party of travellers from Boston, including several young ladies, who had thus made the tour of the world. The Americans certainly travel more than any other people, and on more unbeaten tracks. Of their own railway travelling I must reserve what I have to say for a separate chapter.

Reserving also for special description the common schools, hotel life, and other social features, I may here note a few miscellaneous points that struck me as novel or peculiar in my first rambles. In New York the tramway-cars traverse all the main thoroughfares except Broadway. There seems no limit, as in the omnibuses, to the number of passengers. They crowd in clusters on the platforms at the end, and stand in the centre between the seats. If there are regulations as to the numbers licensed to be carried, they are not enforced. Giving up seats to "ladies" used to be universal, but the gallantry was so seldom met by even a sign of thanks, that men now often leave "the fair sex" to shift for themselves. At all events, the deference to "ladies" is not so marked in New York as it used to be. The markets seem well distributed, well ordered, and plentifully supplied. The abundance of fruit and of vegetables is apparent. A large trade for the supply of the city brings wealth to the growers in New Jersey State. It was curious to see the "old apple-women," with their well-piled boards, at the corners of the streets,—only selling peaches instead of apples. Ice is in summer another cheap and common luxury. Iced soda-water is a universal drink, not bottled, but drawn from a tap, and flavoured with a variety of syrups. There are not many itinerant vendors in the streets, like our costermongers with their barrows. In Broadway, there are sellers of pictures and photographs, and of Mexican tonquin beans. The principal shopless traders are the newsboys and the shoeblacks—a numerous horde, of much the same class as in our own cities. Street beggars are not allowed, and of musicians and other street performers there are few. Two or three barrel organs, however, I heard in back streets, and two or three juvenile German bands. The windows of stores and offices in the great thoroughfares are not closed with shutters, but the gas is left burning, a practice which gives greater safety as well as cheerfulness to these streets by night.

The hearses and mourning coaches strike the eye of a stranger. The hearses are light, elegant vehicles, with plate-glass top and sides, through which the ornamented coffin is seen. Black horses are not essential. The interments are all now extramural, in cemeteries.

The prices of almost every article in the shops seem high ; but since the war, everything is in an exceptional state, heavy duties and taxes being imposed, in the laudable and successful effort to reduce the national debt. Board in the chief hotels is nearly double what it was before the war, and prices generally have risen in the same proportion. Much distress has been inevitable among the poorer classes, but it may be hoped that this is only temporary.

I may here set down what I have to say on American dress. I speak of the people at large, not of the "upper ten thousand," who follow the fashions as imported from Europe. In all the large towns there are French *modistes*, and the native dressmakers have as good taste as their foreign rivals. Among the vulgar rich, especially in New York, there are to be seen outrageously loud exhibitions—Parisiennes out-Parisienned. The clever poem, "Nothing to wear," well expresses the reckless extravagance of female dress among certain classes. But, on the whole, I have never seen more elegance and good taste than in the walking dresses of American ladies. The men also follow the European fashions in dress. There was a merchant tailor on board the "Scotia," a German, of the Broadway, who had been purchasing stock in London. He had got for himself a complete outfit of the latest fashion in every article of clothing. He showed me Poole's bill, and he had paid Poole's prices, and would gladly have paid more, for the patterns to his cutters. But in speaking of dress I am not referring to the followers of fashion. The national tendency towards carelessness in costume is shown in many ways. The first speci men of an American from shore was the pilot who boarded the " Scotia." His dress gave matter for study and reflection. He had nothing of the look of a sailor. He had a chimney-pot hat, and a tweed suit—coat, vest, and trousers—all of different patterns. An Englishman, walking through the White House, was asked if he would like to see the President, " I won't trouble him," he replied ; "besides, I have not come prepared to be presented." He referred to his dress, but was set at ease by the answer, " We don't think about that here ; " and so he went upstairs, and " interviewed " the President. It is common to see a minister in the pulpit in black cravat, and with coat of most unclerical cut. In the Court of Common Pleas in Philadelphia, I saw a judge, not of middle age, and who looked younger from having none of the externals of office. Around him were the counsellors, all wigless and robeless. The scene was as if a set of lawyers' clerks in Chancery Lane were burlesqueing a trial. Yet Judge Ludlow is respected as an able lawyer, and the proceedings are as weighty · as if surrounded by all the bumbledom of office. Such is the power of habit in lessening what Bishop Butler called "the influence of externals."

At funerals, too, black is not universal, often not general, and I saw the drivers on mourning

coaches with coats of various colours. Few
officials, either of the government or of companies, have any distinguishing dress. One
might think at first there was aversion to
anything like livery or the badge of servitude.
Yet there is no principle in the thing, for the
police and the postmen, as well as the army
and navy, have uniforms. The carelessness as
to dress is only part of the national spirit of
independence. I often heard the words used
proverbially, " It isn't the clothes, but the man
in the clothes." It is with dress as with rank,
it is " but the guinea's stamp,"

"A man's a man for a' that."

CHAPTER VII.

SUNDAY IN NEW YORK—RELIGIOUS AND

CHARITABLE INSTITUTIONS.

M Y first Sunday in America was spent in New York. I was surprised at the outward observance of " the day of rest." In the morning after breakfast, going out on the balcony of the hotel, I saw none of the week-day bustle of the Broadway. The omnibuses were not running. Groups of well-dressed children and teachers, on their way to the Sunday-schools, were almost the only occupants of the pavement. Except a few carriages at the doors of the hotels, not a vehicle was in the street. Walking out, I found the street cars running, but the public-houses and shops were closed, except those of tobacconists, fish-mongers, and a few others. In the afternoon there was certainly more of the aspect of a continental Sunday, but this was to be expected in a great city, especially with so large a pro-portion of foreigners in the population. The

Germans gave concerts in the evening for the wounded in the war, and other inroads appeared on the old American strictness of Sabbath-keeping. In every land there are too many who do not know they have souls, and only care for the body's welfare, but the proportion is less among the American than the foreign part of the population. When the church bells rang, the streets were thronged with church-goers. Grace Church, at the top of the Broadway, where I went, as being nearest, was well filled. I had inquired about several popular preachers, but found they were absent, and in most cases their churches were closed.

This closing of churches in New York during the summer is a feature worth noting. It is confined to the upper part of the city, in wealthy and "fashionable" quarters; and also to the Presbyterian and Congregational churches. The Episcopal and Roman Catholic churches do not follow the evil custom. It may sometimes be necessary to close an edifice for repairs or alterations, and the summer season may be the most convenient for this purpose. But it looks bad to see churches "closed for the season," like theatres or places of amusement. Even though the regular sitters may be mostly absent, the house of prayer should be open, and the pulpit supplied, for those who

may be willing to avail themselves of the opportunity of attending. It was mentioned with
approval in the papers at the time that in a few
of the richer churches, such as Dr. Gardiner
Spring's in Fifth Avenue, and Mr. Northrop's
in West Twenty-third Street, services were
held without the intermission of a single
Sabbath. I saw also, from advertisements, that
eminent divines and eloquent preachers were
officiating at Saratoga, Newport, and other
places of fashionable summer resort. A season
of rest and change is as necessary for ministers
as for people, but they might have left substitutes
in their churches. Those which were open were
well filled—even down city, in business parts—
with the small resident population.

Such is the power of caste and fashion, even
in the service of God ! A lady residing near
one of these rich churches told me that during
" the close season " some of her neighbours
shut up the front of the house and do not go
out on Sunday, that they may not be thought
to be " out of the fashion" by being in town in
summer.

On returning to New York in October I
found the churches reopened, and special services were held at the commencement of " the
fall." There was also an interesting evening
meeting of ministers, for exchanging their

summer experiences, and uniting in prayer for
the coming season. Here are a few sentences
from Dr. Irenæus Prime's report of this meeting in the " New York Observer " :—

" It was curious and interesting to notice
that nearly all had been preaching, and some
of them every Sunday. Scarcely one had been
making a business of resting from labour, and
it is a question on which they were divided in
opinion, whether there was more to be gained
in the summer by letting the mind be fallow, or
by giving it moderate exercise. One of the
ministers said he had written six sermons during
his vacation, and had written them all in the
morning before breakfast! This was a great
feat. It was proof of good health, energy,
economy of time, and considerable perseverance.
He was the only one who made such a report,
and I rather think the rest thought he would
have done better to let such work alone, when
he went away to play.

" For play is quite as much a duty in its season as work. It is good for boys, and men are
grown-up boys, and need play more than they
did when young. Their studies are attended
with cares, anxieties, perplexities, and dis-
tractions, that wear the nervous system, and
make recreation a necessity of health and life.

" City ministers are the most overworked men

I know of except city editors. But let a man be a city editor and a minister too, and he must be a man of iron frame and wiry nerves who can bear the constant strain without giving way. It is the duty of the pastor to take a season of perfect rest, for a few weeks at least, every year.

"Some of the ministers had been *down* East *up* in Maine. Another had been up the Hudson River, fifty miles from New York, over the mountain below Cornwall, back of Butter Hill, a genuine wilderness still, where there are lakes lying a thousand feet above the river, and streams abounding in trout, where successors of the disciples in fishing may find occupation of the most delightful kind. Other pastors had been on little farms of their own, tilling them with their own hands; and when they were gathering in their harvest they were reminded of that appropriate text placed on the beautiful tablet to the memory of the late Rev. Dr. Potts, in the University Place Church,—'He that goeth forth and weepeth, bearing precious seed, shall doubtless come again rejoicing, bringing his sheaves with him.'

"Several had been summoned from time to time to the death-beds or funerals of their parishioners. Some of them had sickness and death in their own households. All the circle sympathized tenderly with the brethren who had been thus afflicted, and prayer was made for them that such sorrows as theirs might work out for them an eternal weight of joy."

All very excellent : only let the absent ministers, as a rule, leave efficient supplies to fill their pulpits and shepherd their parishes, and so avoid scandal, and effect good.

Another evil custom and "bad fashion" I observed, not in New York churches alone, but everywhere in the States, leaving the singing to a hired choir. Generally there were four performers besides the organist, sometimes more, and to them was delegated the "service of song," the whole congregation listening in silence. It was literally "praise by proxy." All churches were alike in this ; even the Methodist Episcopal congregations were mute during the singing of the stirring hymns of Charles Wesley. Not more than two or three times did I hear hearty congregational praise. At Mr. Ward Beecher's church the singing was general, and in one or two other places, but commonly this part of the service was a dreary performance. I spoke about it to ministers of different denominations, and they all expressed regret, adding that it was "the custom"—a custom surely more honoured in the breach than in the observance ! Singers and musicians are a

troublesome race under all circumstances, but
the choirs of American churches have got the
better of pastors and people in a lamentable
degree. The curious thing is that the singing
in the Sunday-schools is well attended to, and
the musical talent of the people is well cultivated,
yet in the highest of all exercises it is hushed
into silence—by custom. The heartiness of
praise is often a test and measure of spiritual
earnestness. It is found to be so in times of
revival. The converse may not be true, for in
some of the churches with most life in the pulpit, and most devotion in the people, the choir
singing is specially notable. All the more
reason is there for the ministers who admit the
fault to throw off the tyranny of fashion, and
restore the good custom of congregational
praise.

New York is often spoken of as a very
wicked city. There is, no doubt, much vice
and crime in a place with more than a million
of inhabitants, including peoples from every
region of the world. There are many gambling houses and dancing rooms and drinking saloons in and behind Broadway ; and in
the lower part of the city there are frequent
scenes of violence and disorder, as in all seaport towns. But I saw little of the open and
shameless depravity which disgraces our London

streets.   Such scenes as are nightly witnessed
in our Haymarket and its purlieus, are not
tolerated in New York.   The disturbances
which drunkenness produces are confined to a
small part of the city.   Temptations to vice are
not at every step as in London, with its flaunt-
ing gin-palaces and public-houses.   On Sunday
especially, there is less drunkenness and riot-
ing than with us, the drinking shops being now
closed, because they were found to produce a
plentiful crop of cases for the police-courts every
Monday.   If New York is the worst of American
cities, it may be favourably contrasted with most
of the great towns of the old world.   And if it
is evil, there are active influences for good, ever
combating vice and relieving wretchedness.

There is no city in the world more distinguished by religious and charitable agencies.
Exclusive of the numerous institutions under
the care of the Commissioners of Public
Charities and Correction, costing over a million
and a half dollars yearly, exclusive also of
countless private charities in connection with
churches, there are about eighty charitable
organisations for dealing with every phase of
human need.   I might describe the ragged-
schools and home missions, the refuges and re-
formatories, the hospitals and asylums; but the
management and working of these beneficent

institutions are much the same in all places. A visit to the Bible House in Astor Place will give the stranger a gratifying view of the extent and variety of organisation for practical Christian work. This great block of buildings, taking its name from the Bible Society, which has here its head-quarters, contains the offices of a number of other religious and charitable associations. Of these I cannot here give details, but must not omit brief reference to two great institutions, the Bible Society in Astor Place, and the Tract Society in Nassau Street, which are in the New World what the parent societies are in the Old.

The American Bible Society is a worthy rival of our own British and Foreign Bible Society in the great work of diffusing the Word of God throughout the world. Besides the distribution of Bibles throughout the States and Territories of the Union, with its various races and nationalities, the operations of the society extend to every part of the globe where American missionaries are stationed. Last year the circulation of Bibles, Testaments, or portions of the Bible, was 1,330,640 volumes. The total number of volumes issued in fifty-four years has been 26,572,371,* up to the date of the last

* The British and Foreign Bible Society, instituted in London in 1804, twelve years before the American Society, has issued above fifty-seven million copies.

5

report.   The receipts in the first year, 1816-17, were 37,779,35 dols.   Twenty years later, in 1836-37, 83,259,79 dols.; in 1856-57, 441,805,07 dols., and last year, 1869-70, 747,058,69 dols. The foreign countries to which special efforts have been lately directed are Mexico, South America, Sandwich Islands and Micronesia, China, Japan, North India, Turkey, with its dependencies, Persia, and Egypt.   Most attention is given to countries where other societies are not specially at work.   But it is in the home work of the society that its operations are most interesting.   No region of the Republic is unvisited by the Bible Society's agents and colporteurs.   They follow the track of explorers and settlers in the remotest parts. The Freedmen of the south, the Chinese in the west, the immigrants throughout the Union, and the scattered tribes of Indians, are attended to by the Bible Society.   Nor are the " heathen " in crowded cities neglected, though few in number compared with the neglected poor of European cities, were it not for the constant influx of emigration.   In the hotels I almost always found a copy of the Scriptures placed in each room.   The universal diffusion of the Bible, its use in every school, and its general influence on society, accounts for the right direction given to American progress.

The American Tract Society also is a power
ful agent in this patriotic and beneficent work.
Like the parent society in England, it is a
catholic institution, embracing all sections of
the Christian Church, and having the same
object, the spread of the gospel by the press.
From large volumes down to small tracts and
leaflets, its publications have this one purpose;
at home and abroad, and in all languages and
races of men. During the year 1869-70, 339
new publications were issued, in English, German, Spanish, Portuguese, Swedish, and Ar-
meno-Turkish, bringing up the whole number
of publications now on the society's list to
4,569. Of these, 881 are volumes of various
size. Of the 339 publications of last year, 43
were volumes. It is right to note this, because
the magnitude and importance of the work of
the Tract Society, whether in London or New
York, are sometimes under-estimated, from
the conventional idea attached to the name
"Tract." In regard to the operations of these
societies, the word is really to be taken in its
old meaning of a treatise, whether in large
volume for the scholar and student, or in small
size for diffusing truth among the masses of
the people. Each work has its own field and
influence. While millions of light leaves
diffuse gospel teaching among the poor and

the young, thousands of weightier books spread the same truths among the educated classes. One of the recent publications of the American Tract Society is a splendid edition of Luther's Bible, with notes, which has had a large sale among the German people in the Union. Twelve other German books were issued during the past year, proving that the foreign element in the population is duly considered. The Tract Society also wisely attends to the field of periodical literature. Of the " American Messenger " there is an average monthly circulation of 170,250 copies; of the " Botschafter," or " American Messenger " in German, 37,058 copies ; of the " Child's Paper," 348,250 copies ; in the aggregate, 555,558 monthly. The total number of the three papers in the year is 6,666,700 copies. The society has branches and auxiliaries throughout the country, with depôts in the great towns, while an extensive system of colportage distributes the publications to remotest districts. The operations of this great institution, next to the Bible Society and the Sunday School Union, whose head-quarters are in Philadelphia, serve to leaven the people with that truth which forms the best element in national character. The flourishing state of these societies, aiding

the influence of the pulpit, the common school,
and the Sunday school, attests a high standard
of public opinion, in spite of all faults of political institutions or government.

CHAPTER VIII.

GOVERNMENT OF NEW YORK.

N EW YORK is governed by a Corporation, composed of Mayor, Aldermen, and Council, with Committees of Finance, Police, Law, Markets, Buildings, and other departments of civic administration. *Eadem Magistratuum vocabula*, as Tacitus said, when writing the names of Consuls, Prætors, and other ancient magistrates, in the times of Imperial Cæsars. The old Anglo-Saxon names reappear in New York, with which we are familiar in our own York or London. They are elected, too, by popular suffrage, yet every one speaks not of the government, but the mis-government of New York! Here is a sentence from the leading article in the *New York Tribune* of Sept. 30 of last year :—

" It has been often said, and probably truly said, that the great bulk of the population of New York do sincerely desire good government, and abhor knavery and peculation, and could

put them down if they were united against
them. Now, why can they not be united
against them ? How is it that in a great commercial community, composed, at least in
ninety-nine parts out of a hundred, of honest
and industrious men and women, living by
their labour, loving order, economy, and
honesty, eager for good justice, good police,
clean streets, and good gas, a small board of
knaves is able every year to secure the continued possession of the public offices, to the
misery and disgrace of the whole community ?"

How is it ? The "knaves" know how to
combine, while the "honest men" stand aloof
and grumble. Fancy a Cogers' Hall, or a less
reputable sort of discussion forum, having
grown into a great political organisation,
managing all the municipal elections in London ! Such is the Tammany Hall in New
York, the seat of the *imperium in imperio.*
Tammany Hall is a large place of meeting,
like our Freemasons' Tavern or Exeter Hall,
with ranges of offices for Managing Committees. From this centre of influence the whole
of New York is controlled. Every now and
then, as some new abuse or fraud comes to
light, there is a spasmodic attempt on the part
of the respectable citizens to throw off the yoke
of Tammany Hall; but "the Ring" is too

strong for the unorganised opposition.   For
instance, a " Citizens' Association " was lately
formed, for the express purpose of dragging to
light the misdeeds of " The Tammany Ring,"
and the City Hall.   An energetic manager
was employed, who, " terrier like," began to
tear the skirts and stick his teeth into the calves
of the principal robbers.   But he had no sooner
(we quote from the same article in the *Tribune*)
" become possessed of a few valuable facts, and
begun to promise to be really useful to his employers, than he was taken into the tax-office,
on a high salary, and may be seen there now
every day, seated among the very men he was
engaged to bring to justice.   Similar incidents
mark nearly every attempt at reform, so that
the plunderers now laugh openly at the efforts
of the public to break up the gang."   By distribution of patronage, by disposal of contracts,
and other jobbery, the Ring continues to retain
its power, and New York remains the worst
governed city in the Union.

There is, however, at length the prospect
of better days.   On the 9th of November, our
Lord Mayor's anniversary, the news came of
the overthrow of the political misrulers of New
York.   " The news," said the *Times*, in its
leading article, " will rejoice the hearts not
merely of all honest men and of all well-wishers to

the United States, but of the friends to popular government throughout the world. The elections have resulted in a complete defeat for the notorious ' Tammany Ring.' The city has been carried against this gang of public robbers by a majority estimated at from 18,000 to 26,000 ; and all their candidates, except one, have been defeated. The republicans have also wrested from the democratic party, of which Tammany was the centre, the control of New York State, and have secured a majority in the State Legislature. The significance and importance of these victories extend far beyond any party success. What they show is that the mass of the citizens in the chief City and State of the Union, have at length been aroused to the infamous corruption practised in their municipal administration, and that having been once aroused, they have been strong enough, in spite of a powerful political organisation, to assert the supremacy of honesty and law, and at once to overthrow a conspiracy which, in its municipal stronghold, was deemed almost unassailable.

" To appreciate these results, the reader must recall the position to which the matter had been · brought by the occurrences of the last two months. On the 4th of September a great meeting was held in the Cooper Institute, at

which all classes in New York were represented, to take into consideration the 'not
merely monstrous but fabulous' frauds dis-
closed by the vigour of the *New York Times.*
At this meeting, amid indignant enthusiasm,
a committee of seventy was appointed, whose
duty it should be to enforce all legal remedies,
to recover, if possible, the sums of money
fraudulently abstracted, and, finally, 'without
reference to party, to obtain a good government, and honest officers to administer it.'
This was a satisfactory step, and it has been
followed up by the opening of legal proceedings.

"It is of subordinate importance to inquire
into the causes of this remarkable result. The
broad fact remains, that the people of New
York have exhibited the power to rescue themselves from the control of the most unscrupulous
conspiracy which ever has abused popular institutions. It remains that the victory be prosecuted to its full results. The honest citizens
may now be sure of support, from both the
law and the legislature, in enforcing their
rights against their corrupt governors. Even
· 'Tammany judges' will quail, as one of them
has already done, before this unquestionable
expression of popular feeling.

"We shall now hope to see the investigation

already commenced prosecuted to the utmost, and an example made, once for all, of those corrupt practices which are the great scandal of American public life.''

Yet it would be hardly fair to speak of such abuses as American. Look at our own Corporation abuses, our Ecclesiastical and Charity and School Endowment abuses, and let us admit that poor human nature, with temptation and opportunity, will fall into similar maladministration and misgovernment whether in the Old World or the New.

To a stranger the misgovernment of the city may not be apparent, except in the state of the roadways. The water supply, the lighting, the scavengering, and other requirements of a great city, seem well attended to. The police are generally intelligent and energetic. Complaints of their being insufficient in number were met by a resolution to add a thousand men to the force, which would bring the number up to three thousand. Life and property are as safe in New York as in any capital in Europe,—as safe as in London itself. Except at times of political excitement, or when religious animosity is roused, as in the attempted procession of Irish Orangemen, the police easily preserve order. Until the accidental display of military force, called out to grace the obsequies of

Admiral Farragut, I did not see a soldier in New York.

There must, however, be ample grounds for the universal complaints as to the misgovernment of the city. Even in the administration of justice the Tammany Hall and Erie Ring influence is felt. The corruption of some of the judges is notorious,* and it is a common thing for prisoners to escape punishment from political influences being brought to bear in their favour. I heard of condemned criminals being for years in the cells, the governor not daring to carry out the sentence of death, in face of the threats of the political associates of the prisoners.

In a History of New York by the clerk to the Common Council, I find the following extraordinary statement: "The first entry in the records of the magistrates of this city is a prayer, which, having been inserted at length in their minutes, is supposed to have been designed by them to go down to posterity, and is therefore here given in full." I am not going to extract the prayer in full, but give a portion of it :—

* Mr. Ward Beecher, expounding the parable of the unjust judge, paused at the words "in a certain city," and said, "If it had been New York, this would not have been specific enough. There are so many unjust judges here, that the description would not have identified him."

"We beseech Thee, O Thou who art the fountain of all good gifts, qualify us by Thy grace, that we may, with fidelity and righteousness, serve in our respective offices. To this end enlighten our darkened understandings, that we may be able to distinguish the right from the wrong, the truth from falsehood, and that we may give pure and uncorrupted decisions; having an eye upon Thy word, a sure guide, giving to the simple wisdom and knowledge. Let Thy law be a light to our feet and a lamp to our path, so that we may never turn away from the path of righteousness. Deeply impress on all our minds that we are not accountable unto men but unto God, who seeth and heareth all things. Let all respect of persons be far removed from us, that we may award justice unto the rich and poor, unto friends and enemies alike; to residents and to strangers, according to the law of truth, and that not one of us may swerve therefrom. And since gifts do blind the eyes of the wise and destroy the heart, therefore keep our hearts aright. Grant unto us, also, that we may not rashly prejudge any one without a fair hearing, but that we patiently hear the parties, and give them time and opportunity for defending themselves, in all things looking up to Thee and to Thy word for counsel and direction."

In this devout and pious strain the whole
prayer is expressed, with earnest petitions for
the Divine guidance and help, " so that we
may be praised by them that do well, and a
terror to evil-doers."

Had I heard of this entry in the Council
Records while I was in New York, I would have
transcribed it as a historical curiosity.   Seeing
it in a book, I do not know what to make of it.
Is it a bit of quiet humour on the part of David
T. Valentine, clerk of the council ? or is there
veritably such an entry at the beginning of the
records ?   If the entry is ancient and genuine,
it ought to be rescued from its oblivion, and
painted in conspicuous letters on the walls of
the council chamber.

With the democracy of New York we in England might have no concern beyond study of
character, were it not for the mode of courting
the Irish voters.   It is Tammany Hall which
keeps alive the anti-English feeling which pre-
pares receptions for released Fenian rebels, and,
through them, foments discord between the two
nations.

CHAPTER IX.

THE CROTON WATERWORKS—THE BOWERY—
BROOKLYN—PLYMOUTH CHURCH, AND THE
REV. HENRY WARD BEECHER.

I HAVE referred to the water-supply. The New Yorkers are justly proud of their Croton Waterworks—a magnificent undertaking which throws into the shade every work of the kind since old Roman times. The water is brought from a distance of forty miles, over valleys and rivers, through rocks and hills, and gives a plentiful supply to the whole population of the city. The great reservoir in West Chester County is calculated to contain five hundred millions of gallons of water. The home reservoir at New York, thirty-eight miles from that at West Chester, covers thirty-five acres, and holds about a hundred and fifty millions of gallons. A third, or distributing reservoir, covers four acres, holding twenty millions of gallons. The distributing pipes are of iron, laid so deep as to be beyond the reach of the

severest frosts. The aqueduct is throughout a
noble piece of engineering, constructed of stone,
brick, and cement. The bridge crossing the
Harlem river is finer than any of our London
bridges, being 1,450 feet long, with fifteen
arches of 850 feet span, and 115 feet above
high-water mark. The source being higher
than the loftiest buildings in the city, there
is a constant supply of the purest water.
This vast undertaking was commenced in the
spring of 1837, and its completion was celebrated in October, 1842. The cost of the
work was £2,386,158. It is time for wealthy
London to undertake a work of corresponding magnitude for its teeming population,
and so displace the private companies by
which comparatively impure water is now
pumped up and doled out under the management of directors and shareholders.

I meant to have noted a few of the points
that most struck me in the great centres of
commercial and intellectual activity, southward
and eastward of the City Hall, and especially
the great newspaper buildings and offices
about Park Row. But space forbids. However, I must not pass from New York without
notice of the Bowery, which is even more than
the Broadway a characteristic street of the
Empire City. Here are no marble or granite

buildings, plate glass windows, and magnificent displays of goods to attract wealthy customers. Business is here done on a smaller scale, but with greater intenseness. Rows of little stores of every imaginable kind are mingled with mammoth " emporiums " and " marts " of furniture, ready-made clothes, and dry goods. The broad line of pavement is at places covered with stands, on which cheap articles are exhibited. Ticketing of prices is general here, and competition is keen. Some one has counted more than two hundred and forty distinct trades in the Bowery. There are also not fewer than a hundred taverns, oysterhouses, and refreshment saloons, most of which are crowded at night. But from morning to night the street is alive with bustle from end to end, while street cars are perpetually passing in the broad roadway. The contrast between Pall Mall and Tottenham Court Road, between Regent Street and Whitechapel, is no greater than that between the Broadway and the Bowery, but the peculiarity is that these two are parallel within a stone's throw of each other. The Bowery population is like that of our East-end, or Borough. The Bowery Theatre attracts audiences like our Standard or Victoria ; and altogether, in business, in amusements, in dress, and in language, the Bowery

6

is the place to see the democratic side of New York street life.

Brooklyn seems to a stranger as much part of New York as Westminster and the Borough are of London.   But the Long Island city has its own civic and municipal government, its own mayor and alderman, its own Courts and Boards.   By the Wall Street, Fulton Street, South, and three or four other ferries, there is perpetual traffic going on between the two cities.*   Every morning there is a rush from Brooklyn Heights towards the river.   First the workmen for the factories and stores, and then the clerks and merchants, crowd the boats.   The population of Brooklyn during the day is in the proportion of ten women to one man !   Somebody has called Brooklyn " the bedroom of New York."   The population is near 400,000, less than half of that of New York, but the proportion of private dwellings over stores and workshops is greater than in any other city of the size.   The general character, as well as the number of the inha-

---

* In Brooklyn, near the Ferry, I saw hundreds of sparrows boisterously enjoying themselves.   They have come to good quarters in America.   It is quite a rage in New York and Brooklyn to have houses built to entice them, like our robin-houses.   It is only four or five years since they were taken over and naturalised ; and they seem to be thriving like most other emigrants.

bitants, may be gathered from the crowded places of worship. It is called "the City of Churches." There must be above a hundred of them, some of them of vast size. In Plymouth Church, where Mr. Ward Beecher officiates, there are 3,000 sittings. Several other churches are almost as large, and most of them far more imposing in outward aspect. Brooklyn has many things notable besides its churches,—navy yard, docks, libraries, and public institutions. Prospect Park is as fine a piece of ornamental ground for its size as any in America, and there is no "city of the dead" more beautiful than Greenwood Cemetery. The views from the Heights are magnificent, but the most striking sight to my mind was the vast number of well-built mansions and comfortable villas in the streets and avenues of Brooklyn. There is plenty of space here for the population, and none of the over-crowding which in New York, as in the large cities of the Old World, thrusts the humbler classes of the people into unwholesome and cheerless dwellings. Brooklyn is a " city of homes " as well as " a city of churches."

To me, as to most strangers, the great attraction in Brooklyn was Plymouth Church, and its pastor, Henry Ward Beecher. I meant to say nothing about people I saw, as the

" interviewing " of notable persons has grown to be a nuisance, and is often destructive of frank and natural conversation. But it is otherwise with public appearances, and Mr. Beecher has to pay the penalty of fame, in being mobbed by travellers and described in their journals as one of the curiosities of the New world. One of the first questions asked in connection with New York is, "Did you hear Ward Beecher ?" Well, I did hear him, and will give some account of what I heard and saw at Plymouth Church.

It is a large, plain building, with double galleries,* capable of seating about three thousand hearers. Every seat seemed filled, and crowds of strangers thronged the doorways. By the friendly help of one of the office-bearers of the church I found access by a door near the pulpit, and had a seat in a good pew. I said " pulpit " by force of habit, but the preacher's post is an open rostrum or railed platform, with plenty of room for action and movement.

---

* At the last annual business meeting of Plymouth Church, at the close of 1870, the clerk reported the number of members to be 1,982, of which number 1,216 are women. The admissions in the year had been 173, baptisms 64. The pew rents produced 56,000 dols. ; church collections, 15,846 dols. ; collection for the schools, 1,611 dols., and for the poor, 1,500 dols., making a total of nearly 75,000 dols. The expenditure on the organ and choir amounted to 6,000 dols.

At one side of the platform was an ornamentally carved stand, made, I was told, of wood from the Holy Land, and supporting a flower vase with some lovely exotics. The aspect of the pulpit betokens the absence of conventionalism in other matters. ' There is a fine organ, which was playing when the minister entered. He wore no clerical garb, but, with collar turned down over a black necktie, and in ordinary dress, he stood up to open the service.

The service commenced with a chant, followed by a brief invocation prayer. Then there was reading of the Scriptures, and a hymn from "the Plymouth Collection," one of old Isaac Watts', "Loud hallelujahs to the Lord." Next, there was the baptism of three children, preceded by a chant, and followed by a prayer, in which reference was made to the ordinance just witnessed by the congregation. I give this portion of the prayer, as it was very touching in tone and very characteristic in diction :—

"Grant, we pray thee, that all households may be households of love. And more especially we pray, this morning, that thy dear servants who have come hither into our midst, and have, before their brethren, dedicated these children to the Lord Jesus Christ, promising to bring them up in the fear of God, and in the ordinances of the sanctuary, may never fail in their intentions. May they have wisdom and grace ministered to them, to bring up their children in the nurture and admonition of the Lord. May their children's lives be spared unto them. And yet, if it is best that they should fly away before the summer is over, we pray that they may fly as birds, and sing in the branches of the tree of life. And so may they sing that their bereaved parents shall hear by faith their call, and come toward them every day, step by step, sure that they are nearer to all that they have loved, and all that is gone before.

" If there be any in the congregation who are bereaved of their children, and whose hearts are touched this morning by the sight of these sweet faces, that bring back recollections of their own, we pray that upon them may rest the cooling dew of Divine comfort, and that God may be very near to speak consolation to them to-day.

" If there be any who are mourning over their children, and are anxious for them, and are pained or troubled in their behalf, help them, dear Saviour, to-day, to stand in the midst of their brethren and realise the faithfulness of a covenant-keeping God, and to cast their care upon Him. For why should we cast

those cares on God which are as the light dust
of the road, and withhold those cares which,
like the rocks, do crush us? May every one
know how to cast heart-cares, and inward
cares, and unspeakable cares, and sorrows, and
troubles upon God, who loves and cares for all
His creatures.

"And we beseech of Thee that Thou wilt
grant that children may grow up in right ways
in our midst, walking in the footsteps of their
parents, in so far as their parents are following
Christ. We thank Thee that there are so many
in our midst who have been taught to serve
Thee, and that there are so many who have
grown up in our sight and are walking in the
ways of virtue and integrity and piety. We
pray that Thou wilt grant a blessing upon
them, and upon their children, and upon their
children's children."

I remember in the "Diary of Queen Victoria"
she tells how she was affected on hearing a
Scottish minister pray for her and for her
children, in words not more earnest but more
unwonted than those of the book of Common
Prayer. "I felt a lump in my throat," the
good Queen says. And so that day in Plymouth Church many felt a lump in the throat,
and tears came to many eyes, when the minister,
with tremulous voice, prayed that comfort

might be brought to parents bereaved of children, " the sad memory of whose loss had been
recalled by the sight of those sweet faces."

The closing petitions of the prayer were
specially striking, and had the ring of noblest
Christian patriotism :—

" We pray for all the States in this nation—
especially for those that are new, and for those
that are struggling to lay the foundations of
future days.   Grant that schools and churches
may spring up everywhere, and minister to
them and sanctify them.   Grant that everywhere, all over this land, justice may prevail.
More and more may it be humane.   More and
more may it be the justice of love.   We pray
that Thou wilt make this great people, not
greedy of power, not avaricious of wealth, but
to desire truth, and purity, and righteousness,
and liberty, and intelligence, and piety over all
the earth.   May we be strong, not for de-
stroying, but for blessing.   Let us be rich, not
for luxury and selfishness, but for beneficence.
And may this great land, calling itself Christian, be Christ's indeed.

" And look upon the nations of the earth.
Oh, grant that the time may speedily come
when Thou canst afford to sheath Thy sword.
Grant that the day may so soon come of knowledge and of justice among men, that Thou

shalt not be obliged to chastise them with
burning flames. May wars cease, and the pro-
vocations and causes of war, and all nations at
last study the welfare of one another, and the
whole earth be redeemed."

A number of notices were given, whether
before or after the sermon I forget, one of
which referred to the annual meeting of the
American Board of Missions to take place in
the next week. Delegates to this meeting
were expected from all parts of the Union, and
Mr. Beecher made an earnest appeal to his
congregation to show generous hospitality to
the strangers, an appeal which I heard was
responded to in a way worthy of the pastor
and people of Plymouth Church. "My family
being absent," said Mr. Beecher, "I am unable
to receive visitors at my house, but let all who
are thus circumstanced do as I mean to do—
subscribe double to the fund for entertainment
of strangers."

The text was Galatians, chap. ii. 20. The
sermon was on "the Fatherhood of God," and
was an eloquent and forcible exposition of the
Divine attribute of love.

"Love is the ministrant force of the universe. It is that energy which lies behind all
phenomena; which creates law, and shapes
government, and administers them both. It is

that which lies behind all pain, and all sorrow,
and all suffering.   These things seem here to
spring from malign causes, because many men
think they do, to a very large extent; and
they are traced back and over to a demoniac
god, or to demons.   But according to the
teachings of the New Testament, God's central nature is love, and His government is the
issue of that love; and all the phenomena in
the universe, if they are traced back to their
source, will be found at last to have been co-
ordinated under this great central attribute and
element of the Divine character.

" Force and penalty are sent out by Love,
and are but its hands.   Justice and Indig-
nation are but so many surgeon-hands of love.
The whole play of light and shadow, of tears
and of groans, of sorrows and of turmoil, in
time, either have sprung from, or have been
permitted by, infinite central love, and at last
will be found to have been working in the '
cause of that love.   For God is love ; and God
is government ; and goverment is love ; and
all phenomena are infinitely blended or connected with it."

The least satisfactory portion of the sermon
was where Mr. Beecher attacked the " theologians," as he is too often in the habit of
doing.   To say nothing of the irreverence dis-

played in caricaturing the method of salvation, by these attacks Mr. Beecher is playing into the hands of deists and infidels, who reject the special revelation of the New Testament. The Fatherhood of God is an important truth, perhaps too much neglected by some theologians; but it is worse to go to the other extreme, and forget that He is also a Lawgiver and Ruler. For man, mere mercy might suffice, but in the moral government of the universe other Divine attributes have to be upheld, and the Christian atonement alone harmonises them all. The Gospel represents this as the highest manifestation of the love of the Father. To preach the Divine Fatherhood is good, but to separate it from the justice and holiness of God, and from the doctrine of the atonement, is dangerous preaching. It is "another gospel," all the more dangerous as coming in the guise of an angel of light and love. Mr. Beecher may have been repelled by "dry systems of divinity," but the works of Leighton, and Flavel, and others in the "golden age of theology," can hardly be unknown to him; and what does he think of Bunyan's "Pilgrim," and his "Come and Welcome"?

With more pleasure we turn to a passage of sound and practical teaching. The readiness of God to receive the awakened soul, and the folly of man trying to make himself more fit to appear before God, was thus illustrated:—

"When the eye of God rests on me, it rests on me as a mother's eye rests upon her child. And the parent does not love the child according to its deserts. The parent loves the child whether it deserves it or not. And it is God's nature to love just so. How many are there who, as a matter of experience, feel that? We think that, if we fix ourselves up a little, God will perhaps love us. A man is in deep distress, and there is a great heart in the neighbourhood (I hope there is at least one great heart in every neighbourhood), and he is told that if he will go and tell that great heart what his mistakes have been, and what his misfortunes are, that great heart will certainly relieve him. And instantly he begins to think of himself, and to fix himself to go to that great heart, covering up his rags the best way he can, and hiding his elbows so that they shall not be seen, and putting a little touch on his shoes that are clouted and ruptured, and then goes in. But do you suppose it makes any difference to that great heart to whom he goes, that his clothes are a little less dirty, or that they have a few less patches on them, or that his shoes are a little less soiled or torn? It is the man behind the clothes that the benevolent heart thinks of.

It is not what the needy man is, but what the benefactor is, that determines what he will do. Why does he take that man into his compassion, and say to him, ' Come again ' ? Does he do it because of what he sees in the man, or because of what he feels in himself? "

The idea of the man " fixing himself up a little "—a thorough American phrase, by the way,* represents expressively the vain attempt of the sinner to make himself more worthy of receiving Divine mercy and grace.

It is said that when he left college, Beecher had no thought of the ministry. He had a roving disposition, and his love of adventure led him with two companions to the Far West on a sporting expedition. In the backwoods the sermon of a Methodist preacher arrested his conscience, and led to his conversion. Selling his rod and gun, he got a horse, and went about among the backwoodsmen, preaching the Gospel which had brought gladness to his own soul. For three years he continued this evangelistic life, and there acquired the homely, forcible style of illustration which still distinguishes his preaching. His first settled ministry was in a little wooden church in a wild district of Indiana. But he was not long left

* They talk of fixing a room, fixing a dinner, fixing a fire, and so on.

to be as one crying in the wilderness. Since
his call to Brooklyn he has been one of the
foremost men in the Union, the press carrying
the influence of his voice far beyond the crowds
who hear it week by week, and sending the
echoes round the world.

How far the foregoing story of his conversion
and first commencement of preaching is true, I
know not; but I heard the following bit of autobiography from his own lips in this sermon :—

"It is love which melts the heart, it is love
which encourages hope, it is that which inspires
courage, it is that which cleanses. Fear does
but very little. Fear may start a man on the
road to conversion, but fear never converted a
man. Truth does something. It shows the
way, it opens a man's eyes ; but simple truth,
mere intellection, never converted a man. No
man's heart ever grew rich, no man's heart
ever had a God-touch in it, until he had learned
to see God as one whom he loves. It was that
which broke my heart. It was on an early
spring morning. Oh, how full of music were
the woods, as I remember them, that lay beyond
my father's house on Walnut Hill, at Lane
Seminary ! But of all the notes of birds that
sang in the trees on every hand, there was not
one which sounded sweet in my ear. How full
on that morning was the sky of little fleecy

clouds that ran hither and thither, sent on errands of nameless joy! And yet there was no beauty in them to me. I was borne down; I was sad; in a thousand ways I was orphaned and godless; until, suddenly, as the result of some readings and discussions preceding, I was raised to a conception of God as a Being of whose nature the inevitable and chief characteristic was love; who loved because that was existence to Him; who poured out His love upon all, whether they would see it or not, and whether they would take it or not.

"In other words, when I had a God whom I could call Love, universal, infinite, ineffable, from that moment I said, 'I can worship God. I can worship, not power, not threat, but Love. I can worship a God who deals with men as a father deals with his children.'"

Altogether, my "first impression" of Henry Ward Beecher was favourable. He is a fine, manly, generous fellow. If he has faults, they are of the head, not of the heart. He may be unfit for the "regular army" of divines, but he is a chief among spiritual "franctireurs." He is doing a good work, which he can only do in his own eccentric and not always judicious way.

CHAPTER X.

SO much has been written about American hotels that a brief space must suffice to record my own experiences. I went first to the "Metropolitan" in Broadway. It is kept by one of the Lelands, a family having the proprietorship of several of the largest hotels in the States. Like many of the New York hotels, it occupies a long range of lofty buildings, the basements of which are stores. If I give some details which may seem trivial to old travellers, let them remember that I am writing for those to whom the subject is new, and the "Metropolitan" may be taken as a fair specimen of an American hotel. The principal entrance opens into a spacious hall, the centre of which is usually filled with piles of the baggage of arriving or departing travellers. At the end of the hall facing the door is the office counter, with the entry books and messages books, behind which the manager and his assistants have their places. One side is occupied by the cashier's office, and the other by the hotel post-office. The keys of rooms are left, as in Paris, on numbered pegs. Numerous "bell-boys" and messengers are seated near the office. Round the marble-paved hall are comfortable leather-covered lounges, usually filled with newspaper readers and smokers, or chewers. In the evening the hall is filled with a busy crowd, forming a sort of after-hour exchange or mart, the commercial men, by whom the "Metropolitan" is largely frequented, then meeting their customers or friends, while "drummers" or pushing salesmen take the opportunity to ply their business. Newspaper boys, flower girls, and miscellaneous dealers go about amid the throng. The tumult of cries and voices is like that of a little Bourse. The same bustling scene in the evening I saw at the Fifth Avenue and other hotels.

A conspicuous door in the hall opens into the barber's shop, an institution universal in the large hotels. A broad passage on the opposite side of the hall leads to the writing-room, and to the lavatories and other offices. Here also is a stall for the sale of books and papers, a cigar and tobacco stall, a telegraph office, and a booking office for the sale of railway and other travelling tickets. The passage leads to another large hall, connected with the entrance to Niblo's Theatre, a well-known place of entertainment. In this second hall is the bar, and near it the billiard-room. The bar and bar-hall of the " Metropolitan" are also a scene of busy life in the evening. It is a favourite place of concourse for artists, actors, " gentlemen of the press," and loungers of all classes. The profits of the bar, I was told, pay more than the rent and expenses of the hotel; and they well may, for the "drinks" are of extravagant price for the material. A dash of some fiery sort of a spirit gives to a glass of ice-water the flavour of the multiformand many-named American "drinks." For a sherry-cobbler or a glass of B. and S. twenty-five cents is the charge, and indeed a quarter-dollar bill is the average price of a "drink."

While I am writing, I see the following anecdote going the round of the English press, which I quote not only *apropos* of the place and the custom of the country as to bar-drinking, but as a characteristic specimen of the "humour" of American journalism. "A story is told in Washington of a well-known senator who is notorious for taking two cocktails in succession before breakfast. One morning when the senator was practising at the 'Metropolitan Bar,' a friend put to him the pertinent question, 'Senator, why do you take two cocktails as a custom? Won't one tone you?' The senator drew himself up: 'I will tell you why I take two cocktails. When I have taken one, it makes me feel like another man. Well, you see, I'm bound by common courtesy to treat that man, so I take a second.'"

The first floor of the "Metropolitan" is occupied by a range of splendidly furnished drawing-rooms and reception-rooms, nominally open to all, but into which few of the mob of undress bachelors in the house seemed even to penetrate. Here some of the families in the hotel met in the evening for music and conversation, the ladies *en grand toilette.* On the same floor is the newspaper-room, the most comfortable nook in the huge house, but in which, although with windows looking on Broadway, and "smoking allowed," I never saw a dozen men at a time. A handsome corridor leads to the spacious dining-room, where meals are served at stated hours, breakfast from 6 a.m. to 10 a.m., dinner from 2 p.m. till 6 p.m., and tea or supper from 6 p.m. till midnight. The bill of fare contains an immense variety of dishes, served in small portions, more in continental than English style. The variety of vegetables is especially large, and the cookery excellent in all the courses. Iced water is almost the sole drink, and I have seen hundreds at dinner without the pop of a single cork-draw. But for the well-frequented bar, one might suppose the whole people to be water-drinkers. The price of liquors has to do with the habitual abstaining. The cheapest wine is two or three dollars a bottle ; a pint bottle of Bass or Guinness (not an imperial pint) half a dollar, and no draught beer. There are numerous tables, to a place at one of which you are ushered by the pompous coloured head waiter on entering the room, and consigned to one of the table waiters. I often wondered at the cleverness of these fellows (they are all coloured men at the " Metropolitan "); they would take orders from two or three diners, each on an average ordering five or six dishes at once from the *carte*, and they reappeared in five minutes without a mistake. Except at tables where families or friends assembled, silence prevailed, and generally the meal was despatched, and the seats vacated, with swiftness. From soup or fish to the dessert and coffee, a quarter of an hour sufficed for many.

The black waiters I found usually more
active and obliging than the Irish, especially
to any one who spoke civilly to them. I remember being startled by one stooping to my
ear, and asking, " How you get along, sar ; is
it all right?" Sometimes I told darkey that I
did not know all the dishes, and ' wished he
would bring what he thought would be new to
a stranger. In this way I got introduced to
the most thoroughly American dishes.

The Irish soon take the hue of American
independence, and lose the obsequious manner
of the *genus* waiter. The English fee system at
least secures hope of reward as a motive to attention. One fellow I remember, at Cincinnati,
seemed specially grumpy, and took no trouble
in bringing more than what I barely asked.
Having had hard legs of fowl several times, I
said to him, " Pat," says I, " I think the hins
in this country have a great many ligs." He
took the joke in a moment, and whisking off
my plate, brought, then and always after, the
choicest bits of chicken, and cheery attendance
withal. I never met with an American waiter ;
but at some country inns, and dining-stations
on railways, were native damsels, whether
daughters of the landlord or " helps" I do
not know. More likely the former, for American helps are rare, even in private houses.

After a week I grew weary of the constant
bustle and ceaseless change of the " Metropolitan," the great majority of the guests at
which seemed transient visitors. Most of the
time I was the only Britisher in the house, and
would have felt tired sooner but for the busy
work of the days. I was afterwards at the
New York Hotel, on the other side of Broadway, a house frequented by Southerners. In
the entry book I noticed two or three English
and foreign addresses, but scarcely one from
the Northern or Eastern States. It was more
a family than a commercial hotel. Here was no
drummers' mart in the hall, and more quietness in the whole establishment. The dinner,
at 2 p.m. or 6 p.m., was more like the best
tables d'hote of Europe. Being at one fixed
time, and all the guests assembling in their
regular places, there was more conversation
and social enjoyment. Wine was here more
frequently at the table, and the meal was not
hurried over. The bar was a small and less
frequented part of the house. The waiters
were white men, mostly Irish, and for the first
time I saw some English waiters. They were
well disciplined, marching in with each course
at the tinkling of a bell, and on a second signal uncovering some central dishes, while each

waiter then attended to the orders of the guests from the bill of fare.

The daily tariff at this house was five dollars; at the "Metropolitan" four and a half. This was the average rate at the large hotels, up to last autumn. It included board and lodging, with all attendance, no fees being expected for service, except a parting gift to the baggage porter. The routine was the same in most of the hotels where I stayed, from New York to Chicago. In some of the great houses, as at the "Continental" in Philadelphia, there is an "elevator," or vertical railroad, worked by steam, by which one travels to the upper stories, where it was generally my lot to have to go to roost, under mosquito curtains. Only by engaging a room in advance is one likely to have a more accessible apartment. The lower rooms are reserved for families, and for habitual guests. In none of the chief hotels are there now the double-bedded or many-bedded rooms of which we read in former books of travel. The bedrooms are simply but comfortably furnished, and I never was in one with the dingy, stuffy air of the bedrooms too common still in English hotels of the same class. I only slept once in a private house during my stay in America, so I had some experience of hotels, and I never had the slightest discomfort at night except it were from a stray mosquito, the bark of which was worse than its bite.

Some of the hotels, especially in New York, are "on the European plan," without fixed daily charge, except for lodging, the meals being charged as ordered. I doubt if there is economy in this, though convenient to those who may be elsewhere engaged throughout the day. The hotel charges for meals are high, but not more than for the same fare at the private restaurants, which abound in the great thoroughfares, and in connection with some of the hotels. Families residing for some time at hotels make special arrangements for their expenses. There is generally a private entrance "for ladies" and the regular residents in the hotel. Meals are also served in private rooms, at an advanced charge.

The basement floor of some of the great hotels, such as the "Continental" at Philadelphia, is worthy of being inspected. The steam engine which works the elevator is turned to busy use in the laundry, bath, and other domestic departments, and the cookery region is also a scene to be remembered. The laundry is marvellous in the speed and excellence of its work, articles being returned if required within a few hours of being given out, but a high price has to be paid for the accommodation.

The legal enactments about hotels all through the States are good, both for landlords and guests. Extracts from the laws of each State are printed on cards affixed to the doors of every room. A tariff of charges is included in these notices. The landlord is responsible for all property left in his charge, and is required to have a safe for this purpose in the office of the hotel, but is not responsible for any loss of articles from rooms. There is a baggage and coat room, where checks are given for articles deposited, without charge. Among the regulations, I noticed sometimes that "gaming of every description is expressly forbidden in this house."

Some of the great hotels belong to companies, others are owned as well as managed by proprietors. I found these generally men of a superior class, and some of them very wealthy. They have sometimes country houses and farms, the produce of which has helped to the good fare and good fame of their hotels. One landlord showed me a photograph of his country mansion, and pointed with especial pride to the handsome park gate, with pillars bearing "the family arms," which he had no doubt borrowed from some English family of the name. Though of humble origin, there is no knowing but that he may be remotely connected with some armigeral ancestry. The landlord of the smallest hotel I stayed at was a " colonel," but colonel of what I was not curious to inquire, the title being common in America.

There is no real ground for the opinion that the hotel life of America denotes, as in France, a lower estimate of home life than in England. In a country comparatively new, and with distances so vast, and where a large proportion of the wealthy classes is engaged in commercial and money-making pursuits, absence from home is oftener a necessity than in older communities. The difficulty of obtaining suitable servants adds to the trials of domestic life in the States. A few also of the wealthier classes, accustomed to hotel life in travelling, retain the taste on their return. But making due allowance for these things, the Americans are as true to the old love of " hearth and home" as the English.

In American diet I did not observe many peculiarities worth noting. Breakfast is a hearty meal. The wheaten bread is good, and the corn flour and buckwheat cakes excellent. Omelettes with chopped ham were new to me. I saw many men commence with a whole melon, with ice in a hole scooped out, an experiment upon which I did not venture, with the thermometer above 80°. Eggs were generally mashed in a large wine-glass, and eaten with pepper, the waiter making the mess. He seemed surprised when I asked for a hard-boiled egg and an egg-cup,—a convenience not forthcoming in one hotel. The variety of fish at dinner is great, and in strolling through the fish-market I wished I had Mr. Frank Buckland, Inspector of British Salmon Fisheries, at my side. The halibut, bluefish, and lake trout were capital. Beef and mutton were not so good as our own : poultry abundant, and turkey at every table. Game is not scarce ; and at Chicago, prairie chicken, plump as partridges. Of vegetables there was considerable variety : boiled heads of Indian corn, sweet potatoes, egg plant, and others not familiar in England. I never saw a good mealy potato, with all the Irish in the land. They are generally served in butter-fried chips, as in France. The puddings are good, and ices better than ours. The American ladies have the " sweet-tooth ;" little vessels like cream-jugs, filled with syrup, are on every table, to be poured over the hominy cakes or crumpets. The ladies are also great pastry consumers. Hot rolls, and pies, as they call tarts, may partly account for the prevalence of

dyspeptic complexions. A tart in America is
our pie, though it may be as big as the real
Yorkshire or Northumberland pie, covering
half a table. Cheese is rarely seen at dinner,
or if used is mixed with preserves or apple
pie. The manufacture of American cheese is
for the English market, and may it increase and
prosper, for the price has risen forty per cent.
in my recollection.

Of the fame of American oysters I had heard
so much, that I was disappointed in everything
but the size. They tell of Thackeray, that on
his first arrival, a dish of large " saddlebacks"
was set before him. He gazed at them for
some time, and then asked what he was to do
with them. " Why, eat them, of course."
" Oh, eat them," said Thackeray, as if a new
light had dawned upon him ; adding, after a
pause, " Well, here goes ! " When he had performed the feat of swallowing one whole oyster,
seemed stunned by his own courage, till his
friend asked him how he felt. " Feel ! " said
he, " I feel as if I had swallowed a baby !" All
oysters are not of this size, or thus treated.
The methods of cooking them are countless.
But the true " natives," as we get them, or
used to get them, at Pym's, or Lynn's, or Rule's,
sweet fat little Whitstable natives, are as
different from American oysters as a peach

from a pumpkin. Most of them come from rough water, and have muscle and shell strong and coarse proportionally. ' If they were less common they might receive more culture. Still the oystery taste is good, whether *au naturel*, or in soup or other dressing. I found the best form by accident; asking for "fried oysters," in the *carte*, I had as good "scalloped oysters" with bread crumbs as ever I got in Old England. The average price seemed to be not much below our market price as to number, but each fish equal to four of ours for culinary treatment, so far as material goes.

I was disappointed also with the fruit. The peaches and grapes especially were greatly inferior to our own. Melons and apples were up to the mark, but I remember no other fruit worthy of praise compared with our own.

Very little wine is used at table, even in private houses, though always at hand for hospitality's sake to a stranger. Läger beer is the only cheap beverage, retailed at the saloons for five cents a glass. The consumption is immense among the Germans. In the week the news arrived of the capture of the Emperor Napoleon at Sedan, the Inland Revenue issued 200,000 quarter cask stamps beyond the average! The Irish get their own whisky, dear as imported, but often produced in private dis-

tilleries. When I was in New York a raid by
the custom-house officers and police was made
upon the whisky stills in Brooklyn, and large
seizures were effected. The native whisky,
Monongahela or other, is a hard, fiery spirit.
Drinking is very much confined to the bars
and saloons. The number of drunkards is
large, perhaps as large as in England; but
there is a broader line of demarcation between
the temperate and intemperate. The number
of total abstainers far exceeds what it is with
us, and the soaking, boozing habits of British
workmen are rare in America. In every class
the progress of temperance is marked and conspicuous. The head master of a college, a
Scotchman, told me he sometimes longed for a
glass of Scotch ale; but if it was known that
he ordered such a thing, his influence would be
at an end, as the majority of the students were
pledged teetotalers. Another Scotchman, an
official in a Burns Club, told me that when he
first came to America, twenty years ago, "the
nicht wi' Burns" was a night of whisky and
revelry. Now the Burns Club meetings are
often held in the same locality, with nothing on
the table but fruits and iced water. It may not
be so in New York and elsewhere; but the fact
is worth recording, as indicating a change of
manners. As far as I saw, intemperance in

drink is not a national vice in America, although intemperance in eating is still noticeable by a stranger. I have seen Americans order a dozen dishes from the dinner *carte*, and yet drink nothing but iced water.

There was less smoking, and, to my surprise, less chewing than I anticipated. Perhaps the price of cigars has its influence on the former habit. The native tobacco is not palatable, and a good havannah is a costly luxury. The smoking tobacco is sold in little cotton bags, fastened with a government stamp. It is dry, like the bran with which dolls are stuffed. An English smoker will find the American chewing tobacco, moist, in tinfoil, more suited for his pipe, or mixed with the brown bran. I do not think the young Americans chew as much as their fathers. Talking with an old American gentleman in the car going to Niagara, he held a neat silver oval case in his hand: " I thought you were going to offer me a pinch of snuff," I said. He laughed and said, " I would offer you this, but I know you would not accept it," handing for my inspection his tobacco-box. The spittoon will remain ubiquitous for some time longer, in the Senate House as well as in hotels and offices. I saw a curious notice posted in the lobby of a church in Washington : " As the seats are all free, you are requested

not to expectorate on the floor." In another
church, " Dirty boots and tobacco strictly prohibited." Although the use of tobacco is
nationally prevalent, and the offer of a cigar,
like the pinch of snuff in Scotland, or the chi-
bouque in the East, is a sign of readiness for
friendly communication between strangers,
smoking is, on the whole, not so general as
with us. The smoking car on the railroads is
occupied by the roughest of travellers, and in
long journeys I have seen the vast majority
abstaining either from smoking or chewing,
which they could scarcely do if enslaved to the
habit.

What I have said of American diet is only
the result of the experience of a passing traveller in hotels, who saw nothing of private
gastronomic entertainments. Mr. Frank Buckland has lately given in " Land and Water" an
account of an American dinner, chiefly a
" game dinner," to which he was invited by
a New York visitor at the Langham Hotel.
" The dinner," says Mr. Buckland, " consisted
almost entirely of American dainties, sent over
expressly from the other side of the Atlantic
for this occasion. Upon entering the magnificent banqueting room, we found oysters upon
the plates. Some English oysters were served
at the same time: the American oysters had a

decidedly different taste, but they were by no means unpalatable, having somewhat the taste of a very good periwinkle.

" The soups consisted of tomato soup, served with dry sherry, and terrapin soup, served with milk punch. The terrapin (*Malaclemys concentrica*) is a little blackish water tortoise, and varies from three to six inches in length. The flesh is excellent at all times, but in the northern cities it is most esteemed when the animal has been dug out of the mud in its state of hibernation. This terrapin soup is exceedingly good, and I wonder it is not introduced into England in hermetically sealed tins, as lobsters and salmon are sent over. Its taste is not unlike a good turtle soup. Colonel Saunderson, the American manager of the 'Langham,' tells me, however, that in that portion of the United States where terrapin are most esteemed and used, the connoisseur would scorn to eat it save as a stew.

" The *entrées* consisted of

Tournedos of buffalo, sauce Italienne ;
Quail broiled à la maître d'hôtel ;
Salmi of prairie hen, with truffles.

These were served with champagne and bordeaux. The buffalo was exceedingly tender, more so than any rump-steak I ever tasted. Either buffalo-tongue or hump is very good.

8

Among buffaloes proper, are the African buffalo (*Bubalus buffelus*)—'the Cape (*Bubalus caffer*),' whereas the American buffalo is a bison (*Bison Americanus*). The quail I suppose to be the '*Ortyx Virginiana.*' The flesh was exceedingly good, and very white; its feet were unfortunately cut off by the cook. The 'prairie hen' —viz., the *Pinnated grouse* (*Tetrao cupido*)—was exceedingly good. I see these birds are beginning to appear in some of the London poulterers' shops.

> Haunch of elk, with apple sauce ;
> Wild turkey, with cranberry sauce ;
> Sweet potatoes and Lima beans.

"As usual, the dispute as to what was an 'elk' turned up. The animal that we English know as an elk is the moose (*Alces malchis*). The animal called 'elk' by Americans is that magnificent stag the 'Wapiti,' or Canada stag (*Cervus Canadensis*). This is the animal I am so anxious to get introduced into Scotland, to increase the size, weight, and head of the native deer. The wild turkey was exceedingly good—more tender than the English turkey. I had never tasted cranberry sauce before ; it has a nice sharp semi-acid about it, which goes exceedingly well with turkey, and would probably be found to be a great adjunct to roast pheasant.

"At this stage of the dinner an interval took place, and the waiter came round with cigarettes of the most perfect tobacco I ever smoked. After this '*dix minutes d'arrêt*,' as the French railways have it, we began again with

> Roast canvas-back duck ;
> Roast partridge.

"I have often heard that the canvas-back ducks are the finest food that can be placed upon the table ; having now tasted them, I feel convinced that a better dish does not exist. This duck is allied to the English pochard duck; its name is *Fuligula Valesneria.* I am told these ducks derive their name from the appearance of the skin of the back after the feathers are taken off, which resembles very much the canvas as used by ladies for their Berlin-wool work. They are said to derive their flavour from feeding on wild celery, to obtain which they dive to a considerable depth. I do not know what wild celery is : I should much like to have some seeds. A duck called the red-headed duck lives with the canvas-back, and its flesh is almost as good.

"Among the dishes that followed was the marrow-squash, a species of vegetable not unlike our vegetable marrow, only richer. The dinner was followed by some eloquent and witty speeches from various guests. Altogether

CHAPTER XI.

BEFORE saying anything of the quality of American newspapers, I wish to refer to their quantity. In order to appreciate this, let us bear in mind the extent of journalism in Great Britain, which is far in advance of all other European countries.

At the beginning of this year there were 1,450 newspapers in the United Kingdom; of which in London there were published 261; in the provinces, 851; in Wales, 53; in Scotland, 131; in Ireland, 138; in the British Isles, 16.

Of daily newspapers there are 120 in the United Kingdom; of which 88 are in England; 1 in Wales; 11 in Scotland; 19 in Ireland; and 1 in the Channel Islands. Sixty-one are penny, and thirty-four are halfpenny newspapers. In 1866 there were 78, and in 1856 only 35 daily papers.

Now turn to America, with a population

not much greater than our own. There are
at least 5,200 newspapers published in the
United States, of which 550 are daily papers.
It is difficult to give the exact number, because
many spring up and many perish every year,
but these numbers are near the truth. New
York, City and State, has more than 800, with
a population not much greater than that of
Scotland, or at least of Scotland and Wales
together, which have only about 180 papers
between them. New York City alone has 32
dailies. Philadelphia has 16, five more than
all Scotland. Boston, Chicago, Cincinnati, St.
Louis, Baltimore, and several other cities have
each more dailies than any three of our greatest
English towns.

The growth of the press has exceeded even
the rapid increase of population. The first
paper was printed at Boston in 1690. Eighty-
five years after, in 1775, the number was only
34; in 1800 it had risen to 200; and in 1830
to 1,000.

The circulation of many of these papers is
large. Seven of the New York dailies, known
as the " New York Associated Press," print
at least 112,000,000 sheets annually, and the
remaining 25 New York dailies print nearly
the same number of copies. There are about
85 newspapers in the Union, exceeding 20,000

each issue, of which 40 are in New York, 13
in Boston, 10 in Philadelphia, 8 in Chicago,
and 5 in Cincinnati. About 150 have a circulation above 10,000, and 500 have 5,000
each issue. The average of the whole of the
New England papers may be about 1,000 ; of
the New York and Philadelphia, 750 ; of the
papers of the West and South, 500 and 300
copies.

In a recent work on the " Progress of American Journalism," it is stated that " each of
the great daily papers of New York to-day
employs more than a hundred men, in different
departments, and expends half a million of
dollars annually, with less concern to the proprietors than an outlay of one quarter of that
sum would have occasioned in 1840. The editorial corps of the morning papers issued in
New York on the first day of the present year
numbered at least half a score of persons ; the
reporters were in equal force ; sixty compositors
and eight or ten pressmen were employed to
put in type and to print the contents of each
issue of the paper ; twenty carriers conveyed
the printed sheets to its readers, and a dozen
mailing-clerks and book-keepers managed the
business details of each establishment. Editorial salaries now range from twenty-five to
sixty dollars a week ; reporters receive from

twenty to thirty dollars a week; and the gross receipts of a great daily paper for a year often reach the sum of one million of dollars, of which an average of one-third is clear profit. These statistics are applicable to four or five of the daily morning journals of New York."

All this implies a vast circulation of intelligence, and of popular enlightenment and education through the press. In this light the matter is viewed by the United States Government, which franks exchanges through the post. The system of exchanging papers is universal. Every editor gets numerous exchanges for copies of his paper, and so the whole country is kept "posted up" in the news of all parts of the Union.

At the same time there are several great centres of newspaper material and commerce. New York, Boston, Philadelphia, Cincinnati, Chicago, San Francisco, and New Orleans are among the centres of influence, the local papers of the various States and provincial towns distributing the public news from the central newspapers of these great cities. Every town and nearly every village has its newspaper. So that, as to quantity, America is before all the world the land of newspapers; in other words, where there is most free interchange of thought and most influence of public opinion.

But what of the quality of American journalism ? I have no hesitation in affirming that, on the whole, it is as high as our own. They have no daily paper like our *Times*, but they have many as good as any of our best papers excepting the *Times*. The "levelling-up" effected by education and public opinion, which has raised the mass of the American people above that of England, has also raised the press to a higher average standard. It would be easy to contradict this by citing many examples of coarseness, scurrility, and bad taste, culled from 5,000 papers; but the fact remains as to the general high tone, both intellectual and moral, of the American press. I affirm this from personal study of the best journals in the great cities, and comparison of their leading articles with those of our own London and provincial press. I do not deny the too common exhibition of the worst features of journalism, especially in some of the papers which have the largest circulation. The *New York Herald* is probably the most prosperous paper in the Union, but it is so not because of, but in spite of, its bad features. Its success was achieved by the energy and tact of its first founder, who

spared no labour and expense to supply the
earliest and fullest news from all parts of the
world.   To this chief element of success other
less worthy influences were joined.   The tastes
of the lowest classes were pandered to; the
Irish and Popish population and their democratic leaders found here a sympathetic organ ;
and the anti-British prejudices were always
concentrated in the columns of the *Herald.*
But its influence, never proportioned to its
circulation, is less than that of the *Tribune*, the
New York Times, or the *World.*   While acknowledging its business ability, every true American is ashamed of its character; and the
New York Herald, though in some points
the first, is no more to be taken as typical of
American papers than New York is to be taken
as the type and model of American cities.

In no other city than New York could a
paper of so low a moral tone as the *Herald*
attain to such success.   The education and
training, alike of writers and readers, would
not tolerate similar journals in places where
healthy public opinion is not overborne by a
vast foreign and rowdy population as in New
York.   The leading journals of all the great
towns throughout the States, are, with few
exceptions, marked by high moral tone as well
as by intellectual ability.   I am glad to con-

firm this by the testimony of a writer in the *British Quarterly Review*, who says in an article on " The American Press " (Jan., 1871), " There is one aspect of Transatlantic literature which already contrasts favourably with our own, and that is its generally cordial recognition of Evangelical Christianity. With the exception of the German and French newspapers, which chafe under the restraints of a Christian country, and scoff at ' Judaic sabbaths, Pharisaic church-going, and tyrannical priestcraft,' there are no newspapers of any position in the States that are avowedly anti-Christian ; and there is less disposition than formerly on the part of the American press generally to exclude all reference to distinctive Christianity. It was considered a remarkable circumstance at the time of the American revival, that several newspapers, notorious for a thinly disguised infidelity, and for a most undisguised enmity to Evangelical religion, should not only publish the most ample reports of the movement, but commend it in a way that has had no parallel in English journalism, even before the tide of public opinion had turned decisively in its favour. It is the common custom still for American newspapers to print the sermons of popular preachers, and to publish a large amount of religious intelligence.

The press is also intensely Protestant, and has contributed to the growth of that enormous assimilating power by which American Protestantism has absorbed generation after generation of the Roman Catholic emigrants. The statistics of the Propaganda declare that one-half of the whole number has been lost to the Church of Rome; and the explanation is, that they can no more escape from the influence of American ideas than from the effects of the atmosphere and climate."

The recognition and support of Christian truth and influence is here attributed to the ordinary secular press, but besides this the "religious newspaper" has attained a position in America almost unknown in this country. We have various Church papers and Dissenting papers, and organs of various sects and denominations, but of journals professedly Christian rather than Ecclesiastical we can only name two or three. The American papers of the same class, though also representing or arising from special churches, as the *New York Independent* for the Congregationalists, and the *New York Observer* and the *Independent* for the Presbyterians, yet have a vast circulation among all classes, who find them safe and instructive family newspapers, while at the same time supplying sound and profitable religious reading. The "Sunday newspaper" has thus come to be a phrase of very different import from what it has with us, where the chief attraction lies in raking together all the criminal literature of the week.

Having said thus much in praise of American journalism, I have less scruple in noticing some of its defects. The first and most obvious fault is the gross personality in which it indulges. This is partly the result of the violent party spirit kept alive by the political institutions of the republic. Where half the public men of the nation are expecting every four years to unseat their rivals and occupy their places, they are not particular as to the weapons used in the strife. Abuse and slander are freely used against every aspirant to office, and thus public opinion has been habituated to think little of attacks on private life and character. The Americans have not yet attained to high culture in matters of courtesy and good taste ; and hence the press, lacking the restraints of honour and good breeding, is limited in its personalities only by fear of legal penalties.

Another cause of this personality and rancour is the obtrusive position of editors and "gentlemen of the press." In England, the editors who exert most influence are often

utterly unknown to public fame, and the best
newspaper writing is always anonymous.   In
America, as in France, the journalists conduct
their operations under motives not only of
financial gain but of political ambition.   The
names of the editors and contributors are
constantly paraded, and become identified with
the several papers.   Political discussion can
thus hardly avoid becoming personal.   The
whole tone of American journalism affects the
publicity which is characteristic of American
life generally, and which is more akin to French
bustle than English business.   Since seeing
the working of the American press, I am the
more convinced of the advantage of our own
anonymous journalism.

Another obvious fault in American newspapers is the strain of exaggeration, and the
constant striving at "sensational" effects.
Here again the American editors are less like
the English than the French, who care more
for what is wonderful than what is true.   Every
paper aims at having startling and sensational
announcements.   Large capital headings sprawl
down half the column, not on one side of the
paper only, but everywhere except in the
advertisement pages.   For instance, a column
of one of the first papers that came into my
hand was headed in large capitals :

ANOTHER STEAM-BOAT HORROR.

And then followed a succession of announcements :

EXPLOSION OF THE BOILER OF A MISSISSIPPI STEAMER.

THE BOAT BURNT TO THE WATER'S EDGE.

21 KILLED AND A LARGE NUMBER FATALLY INJURED.

PARTIAL LIST OF THE KILLED, WOUNDED, AND SAVED.

Another column of the same paper was
devoted to

THE NATHAN MURDER.

OBSEQUIES OF BENJAMIN NATHAN.

SOLEMN SERVICES, GREAT CROWDS, AND UNIVERSAL
SYMPATHY.

IGNIFICANT CHARGE OF JUDGE BEDFORD TO THE GRAND
JURY.

TRACES OF THE MURDERER.

A STARTLING STATEMENT.

This style of announcement is but an exaggeration of what is common in our own papers
on exceptional occasions, but in America it
seems the constant habit of the press.

A more peculiar feature in the American
newspapers is the use of small-capital inter-
polations in the middle of articles, in this
style :

"One of the speakers" (referring to a meeting in Canada)
" made

A HIT WORTHY OF BARNUM

by lugging out of his coat-tail pocket the rope with which the hands of Scott were tied when Rial executed him. We doubt whether the feeling would have

CULMINATED IN BLOODSHED,

for fortunately cooler counsels prevailed. The meeting was organised by the Montreal annexation party.   Thus we see that the   .

FLAMES HAVE BURST OUT."

And so on.*

What has been said relates to the native American press. Outside of this there is a vast domain of journalism for the foreign population. The Irish have their own papers in all the great cities, and a more miserable and mischievous set of journals could not be imagined. Most of those which make the support of Popery their chief aim are conducted by perverts from Protestantism, who are as

---

* Two amusing sentences from the same number of the *New York Herald* we quote, the first of which shows the way in which English style is habitually corrupted. The summary of the news by the last European mail thus begins :— "The *exhibits* published in our columns to-day will be useful for future reference on questions regarding the motives and *animus* of great *contestants*, as well as the relative positions of the neutral powers and *peoples*." Another paragraph seriously recommends to the Holy Father "the advantages of a permanent removal to the United States, where he would be secure against all European intrigues, complications, coalitions, and chances of war ; and where his infallibility as the head of the Church would excite no dangerous jealousies, and could do no harm."

usual the most bigoted in their new creed, and most extreme in support of Ultramontane views. The impudence of some of these American papists, exceeding even such European writers as Veuillot of the *Universe*, is such as sorely tries the freedom of the press. Mr. Brownson, the most conspicuous of this class of writers, boldly asserts the right of the Church of Rome to adopt repressive measures whenever it has the power, and defends the punishing of heretics even by death. In the European war these journals from the first violently took the side of the French, as being the Roman Catholic power. The vast majority of the American press sided with Prussia, till the French Republic was proclaimed. The mere name "republic" carried them away. They have not the sagacity of Louis Napoleon, who said to an American "interviewer" at Wilhelmshöhe, that a republic in France meant something very different from a republic in America.

Other Irish papers are more national than religious, and generally take an extreme anti-British tone, prospering on the credulity of the Fenian sympathisers in the States. These papers are also mischievous in their way, retarding the education of the Irish emigrants, and hindering them from becoming assimi-

9

lated with the institutions of their adopted country.

The German press in America is not distinguished by much ability, but is less troublesome to the country. Their papers are numerous, New York alone having five or six German daily papers. There are about 260 German newspapers throughout the States, Pennsylvania having the largest number. Other nationalities have their organs. The Scandinavians have about a dozen. The Spaniards have eight or ten, the Italians four, the Welsh three, and at San Francisco there is one in Chinese and English. In wandering in the newspaper region of New York, near Nassau Street, I came upon the office of the *Scottish American.* The Scotch do not generally interfere in local politics, but they, as well as their kinsfolk, the Ulster Presbyterians (who are rather to be reckoned as Scotch than Irish), are among the most prosperous and valued members of the American commonwealth.

I must add a very few words about periodicals other than newspapers proper. Of what are called " religious newspapers," combining politics and religion, I have already spoken. There are about 275 religious periodicals, associated with various religious sects and denominations. Their total circulation may be about 65,000,000.

Not above a dozen of them have a circulation over 20,000. The Jews have many journals, and the Spiritualists, Swedenborgians, and other bodies have their own organs. There are not more than two or three avowedly infidel publications, but the number of obscene or criminal illustrated papers, as well as of sensational serials, is unhappily on the increase. On some of the railway lines the directors do not allow these polluting periodicals to be sold. The attention of magistrates and the local governments may well be given to this growing evil, which is undermining much of the good influence of popular education. Though the best way of meeting pernicious literature is to provide cheap periodicals of a wholesome kind, the power of law may be fairly exercised in repressing publications obviously inciting to vice and crime.

Class periodicals abound in the States. Every profession, trade, and occupation has its organs. There are nearly 160 journals devoted to special subjects. Of commercial journals there are many. Of musical journals there are more than twenty. The printers have six, and the booksellers five periodicals. The Freemasons have about twenty papers, the Odd Fellows half as many, and the Temperance cause, which here means total abstinence, about forty.

Of sporting papers and periodicals there are
ten. The "Woman's Rights" movement has
five or six representatives in the press, one of
them with the portentous name of "The Revolution." The agricultural interest is the most
strongly represented of any, having above
a hundred papers or journals. Educational
journals are also numerous, some of which are
aided by grants from the legislature.

The scientific journals are many of them of
a high order, which may also be said of the
medical and legal publications. The literary
periodicals are not of the same excellence, five
or six magazines at most being worthy of
notice. For periodicals, as for books, the
Americans are still largely dependent on the
old country. The *North American Review* has
a good reputation, but the *Edinburgh* and the
Quarterly, and several other British reviews
and periodicals, are regularly reprinted in the
States. This tacit acknowledgment of defi
ciency does not, however, apply to theological
works. There is the *Bibliotheca Sacra* of An-
dover, well known to scholars; and the *Princeton Review*, long edited by Dr. Hodge, the
oldest quarterly in America, is still the best, and
in general articles on history and philosophy,
as well as theology, is second to none.

As to the general book trade, there were

published in the States in 1870 about 2,000 work $\cdot$, including new editions. Of these 1,250 were original or compiled in America, 585 reprints of English works, and the remainder were reprints or translations of foreign books.

CHAPTER XII.

IT is scarcely forty years since the first railway in the United States was opened.   Ten
years after, in 1840, 2,000 miles of line had
been laid; in 1850, nearly 9,000 miles; in 1860,
31,000; and in 1870, above 50,000.   The rapid
progress is stated in other forms, as when we
are told that in 1851 the railways of the States
did not exceed 5,000,000 tons, and the total
earnings from freight and passengers did not
exceed 20,000,000 dollars.   In 1869 the tonnage
of all the lines exceeded 100,000,000 tons, and
the earnings from freight and passengers had
risen to 300,000,000 dollars.   In that period,
while the increase of tonnage was twentyfold,
the increase of earnings was only fifteenfold,
showing that, though there has been a general
rise in all values, there has been a decrease in
the cost of railway transportation.   The new
lines planned, or in course of formation, exceed

in extent those of any other country, except it
may be Russia or British India.

" Appleton's Guide," the " Bradshaw " of
America, gives a wonderful idea of the vastness
of the railway system of the States. There are
about four hundred distinct lines or companies,
and above five hundred and fifty including
branch lines. The number of stations in the
index is above 4,300. Besides the general
railway map of the whole country, Appleton
gives about seventy distinct maps of various
lines. There is an ingenious method of econo-
mising space in the time-tables, the names of
places being printed only once, in the centre of
each page, for what we call the Up and the
Down trains, thus :—

a.m.	p.m.	miles.			miles.	p.m.	p.m.
			Leave	Arrive			
8.30	12.3	0	NEW YORK		228	4.10	10.20
9.	1.	9	Newark		218	3.20	9.45
11.50	4.10	90	Philadelphia		138	12.40	6.49
3.35	8.15	189	Baltimore		39	9.	2.40
5.15	10.10	228	Washington		0	7.25	12.45
			Arrive	Leave		a.m.	p.m.

The American railway cars differ from the
English carriages in internal arrangement as
well as in size and make. They are long, holding fifty or sixty passengers, instead of ten or
twelve as with us. Some of our second and
third-class carriages hold as many, when there

are open partitions, and seats on which some sitters are with their faces, others their backs, to the engine, or, in some cases, with benches running sideways. In the American cars all the seats face the engine, and are arranged in rows of two seats on each side, like an arm-chair of double width, with a passage in the middle. In some cars the backs of the seats are reversible, so that a party of four can make a compartment for themselves face to face. There is no locking of doors, but free ingress or egress, with passage from one car to another, from end to end of the train, a bridged iron platform with handrail being over the coupling of the cars.

The average speed on the American lines is about twenty miles an hour. The express trains rarely exceed thirty miles. On the old lines there is as much security, as well as regularity, as on any English railroad. Communication with the guard and the engine-driver is effected by a cord passing inside the roof of the cars.

Nominally, there is but one class of passengers, and one scale of fares. Every traveller takes his place where he has a fancy, except that a car is reserved for ladies and for gentlemen accompanying ladies. But, though in theory all are equal, there are practically various classes of passengers. On the main lines there are cheap trains for emigrants. There are attached to most of the trains " drawing-room cars," " reclining-chair cars," and " sleeping-cars," or night-cars, for which additional charge is made. Some of these select cars belong to speculating builders or companies, who purchase the privilege of attaching them to the trains, and make their profit by the extra charges. The most notable of these speculations are the Pullman " Palace Hotel cars." In one of these I travelled from Niagara to Chicago, leaving in the forenoon and arriving on the morning of the next day. Two of us chartered a compartment, like the cabin of a ship, with a comfortable sofa, above which a board was fixed at night, so as to form a second sleeping-berth. The beds were regularly made, boots put outside the door for cleaning, and hot water brought in the morning by an active black boy. Meals were served on a table carried into the cabin. The bill of fare contained more variety than in many English hotels, and at moderate charges. For lamb chop or mutton chop and tomato sauce the price was seventy-five cents; fresh mackerel, fifty cents; omelet, with ham, forty; a spring chicken, a dollar. There was ample choice of vegetables, fruits, and relishes, with five or

six kinds of wine, in the *carte*. A cup of
French coffee, tea, or chocolate was fifteen
cents.   The kitchen, clean and commodious,
had every appliance for cooking, and the
dressing compartment was equally convenient.
In trains not having these luxurious append-
ages, the meals are provided at regular stations,
as used to be the case in the old coaching
days.   Some of the drawing-room cars are as
luxurious as those of royal or imperial carriages on European lines, with mirrors, lounges,
chandeliers, piano, and bookcases.   A novelty
in some of the cars on the Pacific line is an
outside balcony, from which the scenery can
be surveyed.

   The whole system of the American railways
in regard to passengers' luggage (or " baggage," as it is called,) is admirable, both for
safety and convenience.   In England, luggage
is a constant encumbrance and cause of anxiety,
except for the few who have a valet or courier
to take it in charge.   There is trouble in seeing
it ticketed ; trouble in looking after it ; trouble
in finding it when the journey is over.   In the
scramble of the crowd on arrival, mistakes
are numerous, and frauds frequent.   Gangs
of thieves live by stealing luggage at the
stations.   A few years ago, in a street near the
Edgware Road there was a house purporting

to have apartments to let, and at which piles of luggage seemed to be arriving at all hours of the day and night. For months this went on to the growing surprise of the neighbours, who were also annoyed by the noisy and disorderly conduct of the lodgers or tenants of the house. A friend living next door described to me the peals of laughter and loud revelry overheard after new arrivals of baggage. The robbers were overhauling the contents of the trunks and portmanteaus which had been seized by members of the gang, female and male, at the arrival of a train, and transported to this receiving house. Suspicions were at last aroused, and, on the police being set to watch, the gang dispersed. There is nothing, however, to prevent similar depredations being carried on ; and they are still carried on, though on a smaller scale, on all our railroads. In America, nothing of this kind is possible. On arriving at a railway depôt the passenger goes straight to the baggage office, where a metal badge, stamped with the place of destination, is attached to each article of luggage. Duplicate numbered checks are given to the passenger, who is then relieved from all care of *impedimenta*. The articles are deposited in the baggage cars under custody of the guard. It is not even necessary on arriving at his destination to claim the baggage in person. Before reaching the end of the journey, an agent of one of the Baggage Express companies goes through the cars, and undertakes to transport the baggage to any address for a fixed fee. He gives a printed receipt on the checks being handed to him, and the baggage will be found at the hotel or house, sometimes before the passenger's arrival. Why should not a similar plan be adopted on English railways?

Another nuisance in English railway travelling could be easily remedied by following the American example. At our stations, especially in London and the great towns, there is often a dangerous and disagreeable scramble for tickets. The window is not open till a few minutes before the train starts, while the clerks are often heard chatting and laughing behind the screen. In America the tickets can be purchased at any time, at offices in hotels and throughout the towns.

The American tickets are not, as with us, only available for the day of issue, but are good for a long period. For distant places they are divided into coupons, with leave for the passenger to break the journey. They are also transferable, so that the remainder of a ticket can be sold or bought at any agent's office. Everything, in short, is done in America for the convenience of travellers, while everything in England seems contrived to multiply restriction and annoyance. Our directors, with their free passes, have not personal experience of the troubles of travelling, or they could scarcely persist in the stupid and harassing bye-laws of their passenger traffic.

The arrangements in England are equally ingenious for the discomfort of travellers on the journey. In cold weather there is no provision for heating the carriages, and in hot weather no sun-blinds, except in the first-class carriages. The second-class and third-class carriages are made as uncomfortable as possible, with the stolid idea of inducing larger numbers to pay the higher fare. Increase of comfort would tempt greater numbers to travel, and so more surely increase the revenue of a line. Except in the occasional excursion trains during the summer season, hardly any one thinks of travelling by rail for pleasure in England. In America, the ingenuity of the directors seems to be exerted for the comfort of the poorest classes, instead of for their discomfort, as with us. The carriages are large and well ventilated, with stoves for wintry weather, and Venetian blinds and sun-shades at every window in summer. The seats are roomy and well cushioned. For parcels or

small baggage there are plenty of pegs and
wire racks.   There is a barrel of filtered water,
iced in summer, at one end of the car, and
lavatories and closets at the other.   The conductor traverses the train at intervals, and sees
that all is right.   Whatever is within the power
of official management is done for the convenience and safety of the passengers.

Notwithstanding all this, there is room for
discussion as to whether railway travelling on
the whole is better in America.   The jumping
and jolting on many of the lines is terrible.
The rails are laid upon big wooden sleepers,
which seem often of needless irregularity in
level.   Great is the dust and glare in hot
weather, and the draught in cold weather.
The unwholesome air of the stove neutralises
the advantage of the heat.   When the car is
crowded, each seat being double, you may be
paired for a long period in too close proximity
to an ineligible neighbour.   In one journey
I sat beside a big Irishman, who, when the
heat became oppressive, pulled off his coat
and sat in his shirt-sleeves.   The shirt was
clean, however, and the coat better, I'll be
bound, than the last he wore in " ould Ireland."
There are other discomforts in American cars
to which one may be exposed, but my remark
is not the less true, that the official manage

ment is in general far better than our own, where the discomfort of the poorer classes of travellers seems a first principle with directors and boards.

Except in the larger towns and at the hotel stations, the depôts are generally very plain wooden structures, with few "fixings," and at night cheerless and ill-lighted. The scarcity, or apparent absence, of attendants strikes an Englishman used to our civil station-masters and active porters. No distinguishing dress is worn by the *employés* in America, except the conductor, and even if you discover an official he is too independent to attend to passengers. The grumpiness or rudeness, however, disappears if they are addressed in tones of equality, and not as "servants of the company," and is only part of the repulsive as-good-as-you manner bred by democratic insti tutions.

A novelty in the American cars to the English traveller is the trafficking "on board" by the newsboys and other dealers. For the privilege of trading, a sum is paid by speculators, whose agents find profitable sales for newspapers, periodicals, fruit, sweetmeats, and miscellaneous goods. The stock is deposited in the baggage van, from which the dealer emerges at intervals with a load of articles for sale.

The newsboy passes through the cars, handing
to every passenger a copy of a paper or maga-
zine, and having made his journey he quickly
returns to collect the deposited copies or the
price from purchasers.   Then the same process
is gone through with eatables, or bonbons, or
other articles for sale.   A favourite stock,
from which large profits must be made, is
pasteboard boxes of sweets, every one of which
is declared to contain an article of jewellery,
or a gold or silver coin.   The price of these
boxes is half a dollar or a dollar.   It is, in
fact, a sort of lottery.   The coins are rare,
and the jewellery consists of Brummagem trinkets, leaving broad profit to the fox, and narrow benefit to the geese who invest.   This
trading, except in the newspapers, becomes a
nuisance to most travellers.

My first railway ride in America has left an
indelible impression, so full was it of novelty
and interest.   It was from New York to Boston,
by the "Shore line," by way of New Haven,
New London, and Providence.   I started about
noon of one of the sultry days in the August of
1870.   Depressed and fatigued by the enforced
activity of sightseeing in the great city, it was
a relief to get on board the cars, and to be
passively borne towards fresh fields of observation.   At this season the mass of travellers

were attracted to the boats which reach Boston by the Long Island Sound. There were few passengers by the train, and the roomy car allowed me to move about from seat to seat, and from window to window, as new objects presented themselves to view. Having reached the depôt on the hotel coach, taken my ticket at the hotel office, and got rid of my baggage in return for checks, I could give myself to free enjoyment of the journey.

The construction and arrangements of the railway cars I have already described. Among other things different from our own trains, I noted the comfortable sheltered box for the engine-drivers, and wondered why our drivers should not have similar protection. The fuel is wood, stacks of which are in reserve at stations on the line. The railway whistle is not shrill, as with us, but deep-toned like a trumpet. Above the engine is suspended a bell as a signal for passengers, which rings on nearing crossings or depôts. Its sound always reminded me of the line in Milton's "Il Penseroso," describing the far-off curfew—

" Swinging slow with sullen roar."

At the crossings there was seldom any fence or swing gate, but merely a notice, conspicuously fixed, " Look out for the engine," the

10

approach of which is signalled by the deep-
toned bell.

After passing the straggling, unfinished
northern region of New York, with its new
streets laid out up to the 150th, and suburban
factory settlements, one of which is that of the
sewing machines of Elias Howe, the first in-
ventor, we got speedily into scenery " truly
rural," among farms and orchards, and trees
and fields.   Stacks and " shocks " of maize
or green corn formed the most novel feature
in the agricultural prospect.   There are no
hedges, but wood rail fences, and here and
there loose " stone dykes," as in the northern
counties of England or the Scottish lowlands.

As we traverse New England the connection
of the geology and physical geography with
the character of the people is apparent.   Poor,
shallow soil, with the rock cropping out in the
fields, is not the place for indolent husbandmen.
The first settlers on such a coast had to work
for their living, and so have their descendants.
The physical firmness of the race was thus
secured, and the moral elements of character
are seen in the churches and schools in the
villages as we pass.   There must be much of
old primitive agricultural life still in the New
England States.   I saw oxen at the plough, and
oxen in carts with heavy wooden wheels.   Yet

the smart speculating enterprise of American
city life is ever near. Along the line, the
railing and rocky boulders, and all conspicuous objects, are painted over with advertisements. This I saw everywhere throughout
the States. Advertising agents have penetrated every corner of the land, with their
paint pots and brushes. As we got farther
north, the line often ran close to the sea,
creeks of which we crossed by bridges, or the
whole train was shipped over by a ferry boat.
In winter it must often be a stern coast, stormy
and rockbound, but now the sea curled to a
pleasant breeze, and the blue waves were
dotted with the white (cotton) sails of coasting
ships and pleasure yachts. The cars became
fuller as we neared Boston. At New London
groups came on board from a great camp
meeting at Mystic, which had broken up that
day. This was about 106 miles from Boston,
and at Providence, 44 miles, the new comers
filled every seat in the cars. The whole
distance from New York is 230 miles, the
train, starting at 12.15, arriving at Boston
about 9.30. From the competition of the
boats, the fare is low—only six dollars, or
less than three cents a mile.

My last day in America was devoted to a
trip up the Hudson to West Point by river,

and back by rail. A brief recollection of this sail will suffice for what is most worth noting about American steamers. In general construction they are much alike, whether on the rivers or lakes. They have two and sometimes three decks, the upper deck surmounted by a canopy, not of canvas, but of sheet iron, for protection from the showers of sparks and dust of the wood used as fuel. On the fore main deck the baggage is stowed, and here are the bureaux of the cashier and other officials of the boat, always including a well-stocked book and newspaper store. On the upper deck the main feature is the great saloon, generally furnished in the most splendid drawing-room style, with mirrors, painted panelling, richest carpets, and every luxurious fitting. "Floating palaces" these American boats are often called, and those which travel long distances are also "floating hotels." Every comfort and luxury can be obtained on board, and it is common in summer for families to live for days or weeks on these steamboats. Bookcases, pianos, work tables, and all conveniences, as in the best hotels, give the aspect of a luxurious home, with the enjoyment of cheerful company, and first-rate living. On some of the boats there are regular concerts and other entertainments given during the voyage. Corridors lead from the saloons to the state rooms, also splendidly decorated, especially the " bridal state rooms," for newly-married couples.

The latter, by the way, seem to abound in America beyond older countries, or the majority of them love to display themselves in a most ostentatious way in their new relationship. I noticed this so often that I note it as a trait of national character. At Niagara I was amused by seeing a string of carriages, in each of which a newly-married couple was posed for being photographed, with the Falls for a distant background. At the hotel I was told that there were often twenty "newly-married couples" sitting in the public room at dinner.

But to return to our Hudson River steamboat. Sitting on the open, airy, but shaded upper deck, I enjoyed the magnificent scenery of " the Rhine of America." It was a lovely day, in early October, when the woods are gorgeous with colour, gold and scarlet and crimson foliage, contrasted with which the hue of our richest autumnal tints would seem but sober russet. From the commencement of the Palisades, the long range of lofty cliffs on the western shore, up to West Point, fifty miles above New York, every spot on either bank is interesting, either from natural beauty or historic association. Fort Lee and Fort Washington,

Yonkers, Dobbs' Ferry, Verplank's Point, Stony
Point, and many places besides, recall the days
of Washington and the Revolutionary War. At
Tarrytown, where Major André was arrested, we
are reminded also of more pleasing associations,
amidst scenes of poetry and legend—Sunny-
side and Sleepy Hollow, Irving and Ichabod
Crane. But older ghosts than these haunt the
river. It was in 1607 that Hendrick Hudson,
in his good Dutch barque the " Half Moon,"
first sailed up these waters, to the amazement
of the Indian natives. Exactly two centuries
after, in 1807, the first steamboat, the " Cler-
mont," carried Robert Fulton in the wake of
Hendrick Hudson. What a revolution has
been wrought in these two centuries ! And
with what accelerated speed has been the progress since Fulton's time ! Yet there are places
within a few hours of New York as wildly primitive as in Hudson's days, amidst which the
summer tourist may forget the busy turmoil of
American life. There are many secluded spots
and Sleepy Hollows yet, even among the High-
lands and the Catskills. And when we get
farther away, among the Vermont lakes, or the
New Hampshire mountains, the scenery is of
the grandest character. In New York State
itself, the region of the Adirondack mountains,
and the Saranac lakes, west and south of Lake

Champlain, is still a primitive forest, where the wild deer have never been startled by railway whistle, and where, amidst the mountain ravines, the tourist almost expects to find aboriginal Indians resenting the intrusion of "the pale faces." The Adirondacks, and other native tribes, however, have long since disappeared, and the lofty ranges and deep forests are only visited by tourists and sportsmen. Several of the mountain peaks in the district are above 5,000 feet high, and the monarch of the range, Mount Marcy (or Tehawus, "the cloud-splitter," in Indian language), is 5,470 feet high. Game is abundant in all the districts, and the lakes and brooks afford capital sport to the lovers of the gentle craft.

Speaking of game and sporting, I saw an advertisement of a book on the "Game Laws." Having an idea that there were no game laws in America, I was curious to see this work, and found that in this, as in many matters, legislation is in advance of our own. No code of game laws could be framed more comprehensive and concise, at once humane, and having regard to public convenience, than is in force in the State of New York. It is a brief act, divided into thirty-three sections, of which the following are the most important :—

"Deer of every description to be hunted,

killed, or exposed for sale, in August, September, October, November, December only.

"Not to kill fawns whilst in their spotted coat.

"Rabbits to be killed only in November and December.

"No wild pigeon to be killed or disturbed by gun or otherwise in nesting season.

"No wild ducks to be killed between 1st February and 15th August. All punt guns, etc., except shoulder guns, prohibited. No wild fowl to be disturbed or killed while resting at night.

"Penalties for the above misdemeanours— maximum fine, 50 dols.

"No wild birds' nests to be robbed—5 dols. penalty.

"No wild birds to be killed excepting in August, September, October, November, December. Exemption in favour of naturalists and persons preserving fruit from depredation.

"Grouse to be killed only on owner's ground —penalty, 10 dols. .

"Woodcocks between January 1st and July 4th; quail, January 12th and October 20th; partridge, January 1st and September 1st; prairie chicken, February 1st and July 1st, not to be killed .or exposed for sale—penalty, 10 dols. Quail and partridge not to be snared at any time—penalty, 5 dols.

" On Sunday, no hunting, shooting, or trapping—penalty, 5 to 25 dols. ; 5 days' to 25 days' gaol.

" In special districts—wild fowl of any description not to be killed after sunset, nor the use of engines permitted to take fowl—penalty, 50 dols.

" Trespass on land in pursuit of game or fish after a notice as below—penalty, maximum, 25 dols., and loss of game taken on trespasser.

" The notice requires advertisement in local paper three weeks in April or May in each year ; two sign-boards, 1 foot square, to be placed in conspicuous places on the lands."

The above is an epitome of the whole of the game and trespass law of the State of New York, where field sports may be said to stand higher in public estimation than in any other part of the Union. The protection that is afforded to every description of bird during the nesting season is a wise piece of legislation, and accords with the feeling of all humanity, that a mother and her young are sacred. As an article of food, as well as a protection against insects, winged or creeping, birds are thus placed in the position assigned them by nature. If in a country whose waste lands represent ten to one of its cultivated, such strenuous laws are passed for the preservation of feathered life,

much more ought a country like England, con-
sisting chiefly of cultivated grounds, to be
amply protected. Wild fowl are specially
cared for, and that pernicious evil, the punt
gun, is prohibited. Moreover, legislation goes
so far as to protect them from disturbance
during the night. The question of trespass is
as simple as it is effective. The remainder of
the act refers to fishing, net and rod, and ob-
structions to the passage of fish. Sunday sport
is prohibited.

Compare this brief and effective code with
the complicated machinery and the numerous
special acts of our English legislature on the
subject, and it confirms what I have stated as
to the excellence of American law in matters of
social welfare.

I have said nearly as much as my space per-
mits about travelling. In the densely populated
and most civilised parts of the United States
there is little to reward the traveller who may
be in search of the picturesque. Scenery is
another name for physical geography, and of
that the main element is geological structure.
The vast proportion of the surface in the old
States is Tertiary or other recent formation.
Here and there older rocks appear, and the
scenery rises into grandeur. Get among the
White Mountains of New Hampshire, or the

Blue Mountains and the Alleghanies of Virginia, and there is grand and imposing scenery. But vast tracts of country are of the tamest and most monotonous aspect. Art has done little to cloak the natural features of the soil. There are no picturesque villages, and few ornamental plantations. Plain wooden rail fences divide the fields, where cultivation has encroached on the forest or waste land. Few of the great cities have the advantage of commanding or beautiful situations. Vastness is the dominant impression on the mind of the traveller as he passes through the country. The site of Boston is striking, from its seaboard and many islands. No other city struck me, so far as relates to external scenery. But it was the people, not the country, I went to see, and so I was not disappointed. For exploring the scenery of a continent, more than two or three short months are required; but briefer time suffices to see the connection of geology and physical geography and climate with the character and pursuits of the people. I saw enough to understand how the New England States, by physical as well as moral constitution, rule the Union, and will determine its destiny. The rapid growth of the West may somewhat shift the centre of political weight; but, come what may, the brain of the giant nation will remain up in the north-east corner. There is a familiar proverb at election time, " As Maine goes, so goes the Union." Take in the other Northern States, to Massachusetts and Connecticut, and down, through New Jersey, to Philadelphia, and an Englishman understands the saying in a broader sense—foreseeing that this hardy and well-trained people will determine the future of the great republic.

But I have got off the " travelling line." If I have said anything expressing disappointment at American scenery in its ordinary aspects, I conclude with the admission that never in any part of the world have I enjoyed a sail on a river so beautiful as the Hudson, nor a railroad ride so romantic as among the Blue Ridge hills and ravines in Western Virginia, between Marietta and Harper's Ferry.

CHAPTER XIII.

BOSTON—"THE HUB"—HISTORICAL SCENES AND
ASSOCIATIONS—RELIGIOUS STATISTICS—BOS-
TON AND EDINBURGH COMPARED—COMMON
SCHOOLS—CIVIC GOVERNMENT—CHARITABLE
SOCIETIES—THE LADIES OF BOSTON.

I SAW Boston with surprise, left it with regret, and remember it with admiration. I
was surprised at the size and beauty of the
city, the culture of its people, and the excellence of its government. I was surprised at
the number of its churches, schools, libraries,
newspapers, book-stores; its places of amusement as well as instruction ; and, above all, its
charitable and philanthropic institutions. To
an old traveller who had seen many cities, and
had settled down into the *nil admirari* spirit, it
was a new sensation to be roused into admiring
enthusiasm as I was at Boston. Far inferior to
Edinburgh in picturesque site, to Venice or
Rome or Grenada in romantic association, to

many a city of the Old World in historical fame,
I yet felt deeper interest in Boston than in any
place I had visited in days of younger and
more susceptible emotion.   I know not why,
except it be that here Christian civilisation has
attained the highest reach I had hitherto witnessed, not perhaps in individual advancement,
but in the general elevation and well-being of
the community. I do not wonder at an Englishman like Mr. T. Hughes saying that if he
were obliged to leave his own country he would
choose Boston as his residence. I thought so
too till I had been at Philadelphia, which may
contest with Boston among modern cities the
capability of securing "the greatest possible
well-being of the greatest possible numbers."
Both cities are in advance of the best cities of
the Old World, in whatever can be effected by
free institutions, and educational culture, and
Christian civilisation, to ameliorate and elevate
the masses. Much remains yet to be accomplished, and many evils mar the pleasant picture, but I saw here realised more than I had
elsewhere seen of the ideal which Dr. Chalmers
propounded in his " Civic Economy of Great
Towns." As a citizen of the old country, I felt
no humiliation, but rather pride, in the progress
of the Anglo-Saxon stock, and of what a traveller has happily designated "Greater Britain."

I do not ascribe the advance to political institutions, and think it would have been greater
with less of democratic license ; but I ascribe
it to the transplantation to fresh soil of the best
social and domestic life of the old country,
and to the leavening influence of the Bible,
the true source at once of individual happiness,
and of the " righteousness which exalteth a
nation."

In bearing this strong testimony I am fully
aware of the dark side of Boston life. Nowhere
is intellectual pride more arrogant, learned
vanity more conceited,* free thought and free
living more daring, vice and immorality more
unblushing. The law and police records, the
prisons and asylums, show this. But the two
statements are quite consistent. Extreme forms
of folly and notable cases of crime often appear
in the best communities, and the co-existence
of great good and great evil seems a common
law of social life. What I affirm is, the general
elevation of the masses of the people to a
higher level than has been elsewhere attained,
and the small proportion compared with other

* The dome of the State House, resembling the centre of a
huge waggon-wheel, is nicknamed " the Hub," and the word is
in playful metaphor applied by other American cities to Boston
itself, the assumed centre of intellect and learning, " the Hub
of the Union," or, as Carlyle would say, " the Hub of the Universe ! "

cities, say Glasgow and Edinburgh, or Liverpool and London, of a degraded and almost
heathen substratum of society.   I have gone
about for days in Boston without hearing the
gross and profane language which habitually
vexes the ear in our streets, or witnessing by
day or night the scenes of repulsive vice so
common in our thoroughfares.   There is little
to be seen also of the squalid, abject poverty of
the English courts and alleys, and of the Scottish closes and wynds.   The result is partly
due, I suppose, to better municipal and sanitary regulations ; but the moral effects must be
fairly ascribed to the influence of education and
Christian training.   Philanthropy has not to
deal with the hopeless chaos which intemperance and pauperism have produced in our
great towns. And still more would be achieved
in Boston but for the jealousy of interfering
with popular liberty, which thus is allowed to
run into license.   Hence the growing influence
of " the liquor traffic interest," and the circulation of criminal literature, and other agencies
counteracting the good work of education.
The magistrates and respectable citizens of
Boston had better check this license with
stronger hand, or their city will not continue to
hold its claim to admiration for the social and
moral character of its people.

I have little to say about those things in Boston which authors have most enlarged upon in their books of travel. At the time of my visit, the literary notables were all absent, and the season of lectures and meetings had not commenced.

Boston is rich in scenes and associations belonging both to English and American history. The name was given in honour of the Rev. John Cotton, who came from Boston in the old country. The first European inhabitant of the peninsula now covered with Boston city was another minister, the Rev. John Blackstone. Here he lived alone till joined by a party of emigrants, headed by John Winthorp, afterwards the first governor of Massachusetts. In 1635 Mr. Blackstone sold his claim to the whole peninsula for £30! The island on which East Boston is built was the homestead of another solitary settler, Samuel Maverick. Much of the earlier history is ecclesiastical rather than political. The first emigrants carried with them the forms and traditions of Puritan England, and laid a solid foundation of Anglo-Saxon institutions. The first American newspaper, the *Boston News Letter*, was commenced in 1704. In 1760 the population was only 18,000 ; during the revolutionary war it receded to 12,000, and only reached 18,000 again in 1789, the year that Washington was elected first President of the United States. In the fiftieth year of Independence, in 1826, the population was 50,000 ; in 1860, 190,000 ; and at the last census had risen to 250,000. Being one of the oldest cities of the Union, its streets are not laid out in neat, dull parallelograms, but have grown with the growth of the population, in an irregular fashion, according to the requirements of site, space, and other circumstances. There are two great lines, Tremont Street, skirting the Common, and Washington Street, roughly parallel to Tremont Street, with Court Street running across the northern extremity of both lines. Beyond Court Street, going north-east towards the Harbour, I more than once lost myself among networks of intricate crooked little streets, with names dating from British times, though the old inn signs of which we read in early Boston annals have long vanished —" King's Arms," and " Queen's Arms," and " St. Georges," and " Red Lions." It is curious to read about one of these ancient hostelries, that " at the ' Ship,' Sir Richard Carr, carousing on Saturday night, was arrested by John Mason, constable, who said he would have arrested the king himself if breaking *the Sabbath eve.*" The Puritan spirit in its strictness has vanished with the old inn signs. The observ-

ance of the Lord's day is still honourably maintained in Boston, and the churches are well
attended, but the large foreign population
and the freer customs of modern times have
modified the ancient laws and usages as to the
Sabbath.

My first day in Boston seemed like a long
pleasure stroll through a historical gallery or
museum. Turning to the right on leaving
Tremont House, I passed under a row of fine
elm trees, in front of a railed graveyard. These
trees, I was told, were just a century old, being
planted in 1770 by a loyal Englishman, Colonel
Paddock, who left, on the Declaration of Independence, for Nova Scotia, where his descendants remain. The churchyard, now closed,
contains, among other notable tombs, that of
the parents of Benjamin Franklin. A few paces
farther on I found one of the entrances to the
Common. Here the chief visible relic of historic
times is a venerable elm, familiarly known as
" Liberty Tree," the centre of many a patriotic
gathering. The Bostonians are justly proud
of their Common, with its shady walks and
healthy slopes, and its fresh lake, which is
jestingly nicknamed " the frog pond " by other
Americans.

I saw the people of Boston gathered on two
or three nights in the Common for music. A

powerful and well-trained band occupied a raised
orchestra, and a vast multitude sat on the slopes
or stood around. The concert did not begin
till eight, and the great mass seemed to consist
of the working classes. There must have been
above 100,000 present, and I was astonished at
the order and good conduct of the vast assemblage. When the programme was ended, and
the lights of the orchestra extinguished, the
crowd quietly and quickly dispersed. In less
than half an hour the Common was almost
empty. Except a policeman at the gates to
prevent crushing, there was nothing to enforce
the orderly conduct of the crowd. I could not
help contrasting the scene with the assemblage
such an entertainment would attract in our parks.
Where are " the roughs " ? one might well ask
in Boston. There are plenty of them, no doubt,
in the second seaport town of America, yet
they form but an insignificant proportion to the
well-educated and well-governed population.
I saw other signs of the general orderliness and
elevation of " the lower orders." There were
two theatres not far from the hotel, places
which here as elsewhere attract the loosest sections of the people, but not many minutes after
the hour of closing the street was clear, and
nothing to be seen or heard of the vice and
revelry which disturb and disgrace some of our

London thoroughfares at night. There is in Boston as in New York much immorality and drunkenness, but a stranger to see this must go to the haunts of vice. No impartial witness will deny that in the outward aspect of a well-ordered and well-conducted community, Boston is ahead of British towns of the same population—far ahead of Edinburgh, for instance, to which in other respects it bears most resemblance.

At one corner of the Common, at the top of Beacon Hill, occupying a most imposing site, is the State House of Massachusetts. From the dome a·magnificent view is obtained of the city and surrounding region of sea and land. Joined to the mainland and Roxbury suburb by a narrow isthmus, called the Neck, the city proper is united to Charlestown, South Boston, and other suburbs, by numerous bridges and broad causeways crossing the salt-water lagoons, and giving a Venice-like appearance to the site. The old Cambridge bridge, across Charles River, to the Cambridge and Harvard Road, is about 2,760 feet in length, with a causeway of 3,422 feet. Another causeway a mile and a half long extends from the foot of Beacon Street across the bay to Sewell's Point in Brookline. From the dome of the State House may also be seen the many quays and

docks, the channels and islands, and distant
landscapes of wonderful beauty, not forgetting
Bunker's Hill, with its monumental obelisk, and
the green heights of Mount Auburn Cemetery.
The building itself contains many monuments
and memorials of the Revolution, especially a
sculptured record bearing the dates of the
most remarkable events of the War of Independence, ending with this patriotic appeal,
referring to the Beacon Hill on which it was
originally placed: "Americans! while from
this eminence scenes of luxuriant fertility, of
flourishing commerce, and the abodes of social
happiness meet your view, forget· not those
who by their exertions have secured to you
these blessings."

Descending from the State House, I visited
the Old State House; the original building
remaining, but now occupied by commercial
offices. Thence I went to Faneuil Hall, " the
cradle of liberty," as it is popularly called,
having been the scene of many a council and
assembly in the days of the fathers of the
Revolution, who are presented in pictures and
statues. Then I went to the City Hall, and
many other public buildings notable in Boston
annals of earlier or later date. But I have
no space to spare for describing places,
only referring to them in connection with

my general impressions of the city and its
people.

The Americans have a saying which hits off
the characteristics of their three great eastern
cities. " At New York the question is what a
man has, at Philadelphia who a man is, but at
Boston what does a man know." In spite of
proverbial Yankee * smartness, dollars do not
take precedence of books in Boston society.
This Athens of the New World is justly proud
of her poets, historians, and men of letters.
This last conventional phrase sounds ungallant
in such a connection, for we might as well say
" women of letters." Half the ladies in Boston
would be considered " Blue " in many other
towns. Even young ladies in their teens are
often well versed in science as well as literature,
and talk with amazing fluency and self-posses-
sion. Sidney Smith's bantering description of
the young ladies of another " modern Athens "
came to my thought, when he says he overheard
the neighbouring couple in a quadrille discussing philosophy and " love in the aibstract."
The Boston dialect even in best circles somewhat grates on English ears, but it is as musical

* Yankee is a term applied to the people of all the six north-
eastern states, collectively forming New England, Maine, Massachusetts, Vermont, New Hampshire, Connecticut, and Rhode
Island ; but in Massachusetts and its capital, Boston, Yankee
'cuteness is developed *par excellence*.

as the twang of the Lothian ladies. Both by
contrast and resemblance I was frequently—
sometimes amusingly, sometimes painfully—reminded of Edinburgh, as I knew it of old in
my college days. I was amused at the general
rage for learned and philosophical lectures; at
the enthusiastic talk about favourite preachers;
at the official deference paid to professors
and other titular representatives of learning; at the exclusiveness and self-importance
of the little coteries of *literati.* Some of these
traits I only gathered from conversation, my
visit being at a season of the year when all the
lights were out and the benches empty in the
Boston Walhalla. Even at Harvard there were
but two or three dons, unknown to fame, keeping
guard: Longfellow and Lowell, and Holmes,
and every notable man, Harvard official or
resident at Cambridge, being scattered for the
season.

I went on Sunday morning to the " Old
South Church," a place of many historical associations. Here Franklin was baptized, his
birthplace being near. Here George Whitfield
preached. Inscribed in the church records, or
on the gravestones of the churchyard, are memorials of Cotton, Winslows, Eliots, and other
well-known New England names. The building is plain, but the lofty spire, fine bell, and

conspicuous clock are familiar to all Bostonians, and arrest the notice of strangers as they pass down Washington Street. An inscription tells us when the first church was erected, and when it was rebuilt, and how it was desecrated by the British in the revolutionary war. The pulpit and pews were broken up for fuel, and many books from the library burned. The body of the church was made into a cavalry riding school, hundreds of cartloads of gravel being brought in to raise the level. The galleries used to be filled with spectators, and resounded with the cries of getting liquor and refreshments. When Independence came, the "Old South" was all the more "a sanctuary of freedom." Many a "sermon for the times" has been heard here, and many an "election" sermon, in other sense of the word from that understood by the old Puritan pastors. The present minister is the sixteenth in succession from the first pastor of the church before the middle of the seventeenth century. There is a venerable air even now about the interior, with its heavy pews and lofty pulpit of the "tub" kind, covered by a large old-fashioned sounding-board. In almost all modern churches of the Congregationalists, the broad platform with railing in front takes the place of a pulpit. I went, not knowing to what denomination the "Old South" belonged,

but found it a genuine descendant of the early
New England Independent Churches. The
service was much the same as in similar congregations in England. There was a brief
extempore invocation prayer; a hymn (performed by the organist and choir, most of the
people sitting); then notices read; another
prayer and hymn; then the sermon. It was a
plain ordinary discourse, not by the regular
minister. A short prayer followed, and a hymn,
the congregation standing this time, so that
probably there is no fixed usage. It was Communion Sabbath, and strangers were invited to
remain. The elements were distributed to the
members in their pews, after the usual prayer
and address from the minister. The company
of venerable deacons, ranged in twos in front
of the Communion table, looked exactly like
the "douce" solemn elders seen in Scottish
churches on such occasions. A coloured
female sat near me, and one or two others were
in the church, proving that in this community
at least there is oneness of Christian fellowship
for all complexions, as well as all social grades.
The concluding address had some novelty to
me, being a special exhortation to prepare for
"the yearly campaign of Christian work."
"From the Fall (autumn) to the beginning of
May," the minister reminded his hearers, " is

the season for activity in all good and beneficent undertakings," referring, as I afterwards
learned, to the general migration of the richer
classes to the country or the seaside throughout the summer months. I was told that there
is still a valuable library, including many
curious pamphlets and manuscripts, belonging
to the church. The present edifice was erected
in 1730. The last service in the old church
was in March, 1729; and so decayed was the
timber found to be, that it was thought the
crowded congregation had a " gracious preservation." The first minister of the church was
Thomas Thatcher, from Salisbury, England, a
doctor of medicine, as well as in holy orders.
The fourth in succession from him was " good
Dr. Sewell," pastor for fifty years, who, when
so feeble as to be carried up to the pulpit, still
preached the Gospel with earnest animation.

When and how the New England States
lapsed from the old Puritan standard of orthodoxy is not recorded. The declension was probably gradual, as in the old country, where a
similar spiritual blight seems to have settled
down on the churches both in England and
Scotland. The early part of the eighteenth
century was the time of this decay. In England the Presbyterian churches slowly merged
into Socinianism, retaining the old name, so

honourable in the previous century, only when
necessary for the sake of holding endowments
and property.   The standards of the Church of
England secured a greater extent of nominal
adherence to orthodoxy, but it was often but
the lifeless form of the creed of the Reformers.
Infidelity prevailed throughout the nation, so
that when Bishop Butler published his " Ana-
logy," he wrote these memorable historical
words :—" It is come, I know not how, to be
taken for granted, by many persons, that
Christianity is not so much a subject of inquiry;
but that it is now, at length, discovered to be
fictitious.   And accordingly they treat it as if,
in the present age, this were an agreed point
among all people of discernment ; and nothing
remained but to set it up as a principal subject
of mirth and ridicule, as it were by way of
reprisals for its having so long interrupted the
pleasures of the world."   Bishop Butler's book
led the way in the learned and able Christian
apologetical literature of the country, but it
was only in the "revival" caused by the
preaching of Wesley and Whitfield and their
followers that the eclipse of faith passed from
the face of England.   In Scotland, the revival
from the dark days of "moderatism" came
later, but was more energetic and thorough,
even as had been the work of reformation in

earlier times. When Chalmers was in the zenith of his fame, the scepticism of the previous century had utterly disappeared as a national feature, and there are at present in all Scotland not more than two or three congregations of professed Unitarians.

Strange to say, this obscuration of Gospel light lasted down to a far later period in New England; and especially in Boston, where Unitarianism is nominally one of the most numerous and influential of the denominations. They call themselves Christians, for the number is small of those who avow themselves Deists, or even Socinians. But with a large proportion, the Unitarian profession is only a tribute paid to social position. To deny Christianity would in these times in America be regarded as implying want of character, if not of intellect, and the Unitarian churches admit of Christian profession with least disturbance of personal freedom of thought and action. But the thing is fast degenerating into a hollow sham. Nominally, there are still more Unitarian than any other kind of churches in Boston. They count 25 churches out of about 145 in all; the denominations next in number being Congregational Trinitarian, 20; Baptist, 17; Methodist Episcopal, 17; Roman Catholic, 15; Episcopal, 15. The Presbyterians, who predominate in

other parts of the Eastern States, have only six
churches.   But while the Unitarians count
twenty-five churches, their relative position has
greatly altered within the last twenty years.
It is not now as in the time of Channing and
his associates.   A large section has drifted,
under preachers like Parker, into wilder regions
of free thought in religion, while other churches
have drawn very near to evangelical truth.   In
fact, the cold cheerless system is fast breaking
up.   It still stands clear and erect, but it is
like an iceberg which has floated into warmer
latitudes, and the base being eaten away, it
will soon topple over and be dispersed.   It is
impossible that, amidst the new warmth and
life of the churches, in this age of Bible circulation and missions, and active works of Christian beneficence, the creed of Unitarianism
can long hold its sway in such a city as Boston.
It will probably survive longest in the little
cliques of literary people, and in the class-rooms
of Harvard University, but even there its days
are numbered.   Let us hope this spiritual cloud
that overhangs the grand city of Boston may
soon be dispersed, and the old civic motto,
in the fulness of its signification, again shine
forth, " SICUT PATRIBUS SIT DEUS NOBIS."

I received an interesting report of a visit
paid to Boston the year before by Dr. M'Cosh,

the distinguished President of Princeton College, New Jersey, the worthy successor of America's greatest metaphysician, Jonathan Edwards. He was invited to give a series of lectures on the Christian evidences. This was a subject not likely to be attractive in the programmes of lectures to which the *literati* of Boston flock. The place of meeting was, therefore, one of the Methodist Episcopal churches, and the addresses were ostensibly given as a course of instruction to theological students. The high reputation of the lecturer attracted increasing numbers, till at last the place was crowded to the door, and all the intellectual aristocracy of Boston were among the audience. In one of the lectures the President bore high testimony to the eloquence and uprightness of Channing, and to his noble efforts in the cause of freedom. After reading passages from his works, he contrasted his opinions with those of Parker and others who now profess to be the leaders of Unitarianism, showing that it was impossible to remain in the position at present occupied. There must be either a rapid downward course to infidelity, or the steps of honest inquirers must be retraced toward the solid standing ground of revealed Christian truth.

The impression produced by the lectures was great; and Dr. M'Cosh was invited to preach before the University of Harvard—a very handsome and liberal thing, considering his well-known and outspoken views. In the academic chapel he was listened to with marked attention, and was thanked by the officials for his discourse.

I afterwards at Princeton asked Dr. M'Cosh about his visit to Boston, and, though averse to narrating his own proceedings, he spoke in warm terms of the kindness and courtesy with which he had been received, especially at Harvard University. He said that he there preached a plain gospel sermon, such as he would have addressed to any village congregation. It was this, no doubt, which struck his audience more than if he had delivered a more formal oration. Probably many of those present had never before heard an evangelical sermon. Dr. M'Cosh seemed much gratified by his visit, and said that the Boston Unitarians only wanted a man of power to rise up among themselves, as Chalmers had in Scotland, to lead them to a higher and nobler platform of thought and feeling.

I have extended my remarks on the outward religious aspect of Boston, because it really was one of the things which had puzzled me, and which made most impression in America; which at a distance seemed most strange, and was only made clear by close inspection. It seemed strange that Unitarianism could prevail, to the extent that it was said to do, in the centre of American thought and life. But I found the adherence to it now chiefly traditional. It has not increased with increase of population, nor in the ratio of other religious denominations. In another generation I have no doubt that Boston, as it is the head of intellectual, so will be the head of moral and evangelical influence in the Union.

I was at Boston about two months after the death of Charles Dickens, and everywhere saw marks of the public mourning which the news had caused. His portrait, draped with black or wreathed with immortelles, was in many booksellers' windows, with pressing announcements of new editions of his works. In the Boston Free Library a department has been formed for collecting every scrap of literature bearing upon the name of Dickens. I was told that on his second visit, so intense was the *furore* for hearing his readings, that *queues* were formed overnight to find places, where these had not been secured by fabulous payments. I was taken to see a window in a publisher's shop opposite the Common, at which groups were reverentially staring, and was told that at this window Dickens used to sit surveying the passing

I 2

crowds. So far as it goes, this tribute to Dickens is very honourable to Boston, all the more after the freedom of his criticisms, in his own style of exaggerated caricature, in the "American Notes," and in "Martin Chuzzle-wit." But the intensity of the admiration of his works was somewhat amusing. One Boston editor said to me seriously that he ranked Shakspeare and Dickens nearly on a level as to humour and the delineation of character. Now, without intruding any remarks of my own, I take leave to transcribe, for the benefit of Boston readers, and as a small contribution to the Dickens literary museum, the following striking passage from a writer too little known, I fear, in America —Hugh Miller.

Hugh Miller was shown the Visitors' Album at Shakspeare's House in Stratford-on-Avon, by the woman in charge. The first name she turned up was that of Sir Walter Scott; the second that of Charles Dickens. "That will do," he said, "now shut up the book."

" It was a curious coincidence. Shakspeare, Scott, Dickens! The scale is a descending one ; so is the scale from the lion to the leopard, and from the leopard to the tiger cat; but cat, leopard, and lion belong to one great family ; and these three poets belong unequivocally to

one great family also. They are generally one ;
masters, each in his own sphere, not simply of
the art of exhibiting character in the truth of
nature—for that a Hume or a Tacitus may
possess—but of the rarer and more difficult
dramatic art of making characters exhibit themselves. It is not uninstructive to remark how
the peculiar ability of portraying character in
this form is so exactly proportioned to the
general intellectual power of the writer who
possesses it. No dramatist, whatever he may
attempt, ever draws taller men than himself:
as water in a bent tube rises to exactly the
same height in the two limbs, so intellect in
the character produced rises to but the level of
the intellect of the producer. Viewed with reference to this simple rule, the higher characters
of Scott, Dickens, and Shakspeare curiously
indicate the intellectual stature of the men
who produced them. Scott's higher characters
possess massive good sense, great shrewdness,
much intelligence : they are always very superior if not always great men ; and by a careful
arrangement of drapery, and much study of
position and attitude, they play their parts
wonderfully well. The higher characters of
Dickens do not stand by any means so high ;
the fluid in the original tube rests at a lower
level ; and no one seems better aware of

the fact than Dickens himself. He knows
his proper walk; and, content with expati-
ating in a comparatively humble province of
human life and character, rarely stands on
tiptoe in the vain attempt to portray an intellect
taller than his own. The intellectual stature
of Shakspeare rises, on the other hand, to the
highest level of man. There was no human
greatness which he could not adequately con-
ceive and portray. His range includes the
loftiest and lowest characters, and takes in all
between."

Many other things I noted in the civic or
social life of Boston on which I might enlarge,
but I have more than filled my space. I must
only gather up a few miscellaneous recollections.

To the efficiency of the Public School System
I have already referred. It is estimated that
the number of children in the city between the
ages of five and sixteen is 35,000, of which only
one-tenth attend no school, one-tenth are in
private schools, and eight-tenths are in the
public schools. Half this number are in the
primary schools, and half in the grammar and
higher schools. There are twenty grammar
schools, and thirty primary schools, with about
1,100 male and 500 female teachers. The
"Public Schools Committee" consists of the

Mayor and the President of Common Council, with six members elected for each of the sixteen city wards. There is a superintendent, with a salary of 4,000 dols. ; a secretary, 1,800 dols. The salaries of the teachers range from 400 dols. to 800 dols., the head masters of the Latin and English High Schools, the Girls' High School, and Normal Schools having the largest salaries. Among other highly-paid teachers I found that the drawing-masters in the high and grammar schools had 2,500 dols., and the assistants 2,000 dols., and that the professor of " vocal and physical culture " had 3,000 dols., and the assistant 2,500 dols., showing the value put upon these special branches of training. Some of the higher schools are of old foundation, the City Latin School having been founded in 1635, and the Roxbury Latin School in 1645.

The people of Boston take enlightened interest in the management of the schools, and indeed in the affairs of the city generally, not holding aloof, as in New York, from public life, and so leaving a set of mismanagers and plunderers to grasp the government. Committees of the Common Council have superintendence of finance, health, markets, bridges and ferries, lighting and paving, charities, and other departments. The arrangements for fire alarms are of the most complete kind. The whole of

the city and suburbs is divided into upwards of
250 numbered sections, each with a fire-alarm
box, communicating by electric wires with the
central alarm station in the City Hall. The
keys of the boxes are with the police. On an
alarm being given for any district, its locality
is at once indicated by the corresponding number being sounded by the alarm clock. Thus,
if the fire is in section 213, the alarm strikes 2
blows, with a pause, then 1 blow, pause, and
3 blows—for 213. The fire watch is on duty in
the City Hall dome day and night. The same
system of combined signals I afterwards found
in use at Chicago and other great towns. It is
the only point in which the American fire brigade system has advantage over our own.

In the population of Boston, the proportion
of natives to foreign-born citizens is a little
more than double. The number of coloured
people is less than I expected, being under
3,000. The number of voters is about 50,000.
Of the sexes, the proportion before the last census was about 90,000 males to 103,000 females.
The last return I have not seen. The average
number of persons to a family was 5·06; to a
house 9·31 ; of families to a house 1·84. These
statistics are useful for comparison with other
cities in estimating social or sanitary conditions.
Water is plentiful, and the rates fixed by the

City Council. At present the water-rate for
private dwellings is 6 dols. a year for a house
of 1,000 dols. rated valuation. Hotels are
charged 3 dols. extra for each bed, and shops
and stores at various rates, according to schedules. The same careful administration extends
to other matters under municipal control. But
beyond these public departments there is a wide
field for the labours of charitable and benevolent administration. A vast number of societies take up every form of human suffering
and want. In regard to spiritual destitution,
the labours are almost wholly supported by
voluntary contributions, the work of the churches
being supplemented, as with us, by City Mission,
Young Men's Christian Association, and other
agencies. Nor is the religious activity confined
to home operations. Bible and Tract Societies
are well supported, and the Mission House in
Pemberton Square includes the office of the
American Board of Foreign Missions, an
agency of great influence in various parts of
the world, especially in the East.

The organisation of benevolent work·· and
charitable relief is somewhat defective, though
abundant in resources. There are between
sixty and seventy charitable institutions in the
city, besides the private charities of the several
churches, and those of Freemasons, benefit

societies, and the like. Upwards of forty of
the charitable societies are for the relief of the
poor, the sick, and the unfortunate ; of these,
twelve or fifteen are for the relief of the poor at
large, in addition to the city charity, supported
by rates, which expends as much as all the other
societies. In so large a number of distinct organisations there must be great waste of resources in working expenses, besides the risk
of being imposed upon by professional beggars,
when there is little communication between the
various offices of relief. To meet this, an attempt has been made to organise a central
relief bureau, the office of which is under the
same roof as the City Bureau of Charity, so
that the cases of claimants can be readily sifted.
This charitable " clearing house " has already
been found to work well, and the idea is worth
being carried out by our multiform charitable
societies in London and other great towns. All
denominations, and Roman Catholics as well
as Protestants, work harmoniously in Boston,
so far as the relief of the poor is concerned.
One of the most active managers of the Boston
Provident Association told me that but for the
constant immigration of new Irish poor, the
pauperism of the city could be kept thoroughly
under control, a great achievement with a
population of 250,000.

In looking over this long chapter, I notice I
have said not a word about the ladies of Boston,
except figuratively as to the colour of their
stockings. I must set this down as the last but
not least of my impressions—that in brightness
and elegance Boston beauty is far above the
average ; I never saw fewer plain faces, even in
the middle and lower classes. And as to dress,
the intermingling of all classes in the schools
has led to a general tidiness and taste that
must be noticed by every stranger. Education
also gives intelligence and expression, which
are visible on the countenance. I speak of the
masses of the people, not of the upper classes,
whose refined style of features has often been
celebrated. Ill-natured people say that the
beauty is only of the face, is often accompanied
with chicken-breasted shape and delicate health,
and generally soon passes off. It may be so
among girls in New England fashionable life ;
but I can only say that in average looks the
women are equal to those of any European town
of the size ; and as to the beauty being short-
lived, I never have seen so many nice-looking
old ladies as in Boston.

CHAPTER XIV.

NIAGARA.

WERE you disappointed with Niagara? The question was so frequently asked that I began to think some feeling of disappointment was almost expected. Well, I was disappointed, and I was not disappointed. The first sight of the Falls was something quite different from what imagination had ideally forecast; but the actual impression remaining far surpasses even the vastest anticipation of what was to be seen.

My first sight of Niagara was at a distance of three or four miles, from the railway-car on approaching the suspension bridge by the Grand Trunk line. I was unprepared, and on looking out from the window, suddenly saw the whole range of the Falls, with the overhanging cloud of mist, lighted up by the clear sunshine. The view was only for a few short minutes, being soon hidden again, but this first sight remains as a picture rather of beauty than of sublimity.

Again, from the bridge there was a nearer view, but still it seemed like a beautiful picture, in which the Falls formed only part of the broad sweep of landscape, set in a bright blue sky. The country for many miles before approaching Niagara is tame and flat, the line passing between rail-fenced fields, dotted with stunted and often charred trees, and with patches of forest at intervals. Nothing else breaks the monotony of the prospect. Looking in the direction of Niagara, there is no lofty range visible, and no scenery that might indicate or give expectation of the grand spectacle to which we are hastening. The noise of the train also conceals the roar of the " thundering water," as Niagara means in Indian language. In the stillness of night the sound is said to be audible at more than thirty miles distance, but this element of grandeur was also absent from the first introduction to the Falls.

I went to the International Hotel, one of the two great houses on the American side. The other, the Cataract Hotel, is higher up, on the brink of the Rapids. The International is nearer the Ferry House, and the Grove, one part of which, View Point, is always crowded with wondering gazers and sketchers. This is certainly the place for obtaining the finest near view of the Falls. The eye looks across the whole breadth of the nearer division of the river, at the end of the Rapids, just as the water is about to sweep over in the long line of the American Fall. The breadth of this division is here about 800 feet. On the other side is Goat Island, densely covered with trees, and beyond is seen the Canadian or Horseshoe Fall, about 1,800 feet in width. From the Great Fall there constantly rises a column of spray, spreading like a cloud before the wind, and in sunshine sparkling or iridescent.

Gazing on the scene from this spot, the grandeur of Niagara "grows upon you." From the first near view every feeling of disappointment has vanished. Long hours I stayed at this spot, fascinated by the scene.

Looking from the Falls to the river below, I was struck with the strange stillness of the water. It seemed hardly to be in motion. Long streaks of foam floated here and there, in fantastic shapes, and with scarce perceptible progress. A little ferry boat was passing to and fro, rowed leisurely by a single oarsman, within pistol-shot of the descending cataract. There used to be a small steamer, the " Maid of the Mist," which took passengers up amidst the spray of the Horseshoe Fall, so little disturbed is the surface of the water after the great plunge. I suppose the motion is intenser at

greater depth, for the river less than a mile
farther down shows tumultuous agitation.
Some miles lower there are rapids again.
When the erection of the suspension bridge
rendered the trade of the steamer less profitable, she was sold to a Montreal speculator,
and in a wonderful way escaped being dashed
to pieces in passing this point of the river, and
in a shattered condition at length reached her
destination.

The strange stillness of the water below the
Falls is more striking on returning from a ramble along the margin of the Rapids, where the
water is seen wildly careering towards the great
plunge. There is a footpath close to the stream,
behind the International and Cataract Hotels.
Many will think the Rapids a more impressive
sight than the Falls. Certainly there is more
sense of active power in the swift, resistless
course of the hastening torrent, before it comes
to its passive, mechanical descent at the Fall.
I met an old man who was one of the party
actively engaged in the attempt to rescue a
poor fellow who had been carried down from a
boat which had upset. He clung to some timber which got fixed in a little islet in the midst
of the Rapids. Twice a boat was launched, but
the rope of one got entangled in the rocks, and
the other was rolled over by the torrent. A

raft was formed, and floated towards him. All efforts were useless, and he was at last hurried away by the surging torrent into the abyss. Many tragic narratives and legends of this sort are told at Niagara.

A light bridge across the. Rapids leads to Goat Island, with its wonderful sights, the " Cave of the Winds," " Biddle's Stairs," the " Terrapin Tower," and other often-described scenes. There is rather too much of the artificial in Goat Island, but the sight of the Great Fall surpasses in sublimity all that has been anticipated. At the " Horseshoe" centre of the Fall, the colour is bright green in sunshine and dark green in shade, the volume of water being estimated here at about twenty feet in thickness. At shallower parts of the Fall the water is broken into white foam as it curls over to its plunge. The vastness of the volume of water can now be realised, and we better understand the estimate that " every hour ninety millions of tons are poured over the precipice, or twenty-five millions of cubic feet every minute!" The total area of the great lakes, Superior, Michigan, Huron, St. Clair, and Erie, is said to exceed 80,000 square miles, and all the surplus water of these vast inland seas has to pass by this small outlet towards the ocean.

" What a waste of water power!" was the

exclamation of a practical American after surveying the Falls. In a small way the power
is utilised, the stream of the Rapids being used
for a paper mill on Goat Island, and other
minor factories; but all such utilities tend to
disturb the grandeur of the natural scenery.

The same disturbance of enjoyment is effected
by the obtrusive guides, and touters, and sellers of relics and curiosities who infest Niagara.
The little town which has grown up beside the
Falls is a busy bazaar during the season.
Rows of " curiosity shops" attract the visitors,
some with real and others with sham Indians,
engaged in manufacturing the objects for sale.
Excepting the articles cut out of the limestone
rock of the place, and the photographic views,
none of these objects have any special connection with Niagara. The bazaars are filled with
trinkets and fans and ornaments, sold by smart
shop-girls, as in the Broadway or in our Bur-
lington Arcade. In winter the shops are shut
up, and the sellers go back to the cities, leaving but a small resident population. The
hotels are also shut up for the winter. I was
told by one of the residents, whose house was
among those nearest to the Falls, that the
grandeur of the scene in winter is indescrib-
able. Huge masses of ice borne down the
Rapids add to the wild tumult of the cataract.

He told me that, before a tempest, either of rain or snow, the noise of the Fall is intensified, and the ground is shaken so that the lamps and movables in the house vibrate with the motion. For some months the country round is covered with deep snow.

Crossing by the suspension bridge to the Canadian side, I saw the magnificent view from the Clifton House Hotel, which commands the whole range of both Falls. A little above the hotel is a small inn, with a museum, the proprietor of which reaps a rich harvest during the season. On one day during my stay a monster excursion train of Freemasons came down ·to Niagara, with band and banners. Five or six hundred half-dollars paid as entry money to the museum, besides the purchase-money for curiosities, must have been a good haul for the sagacious showman who exhibits his Indians, and moose deer, and other animate and inanimate wonders.

I enjoyed most the early morning and late night strolls, when the place was free from crowds of visitors. It was the full moon of September on one of the nights when I was there, and I witnessed the beautiful scene of a lunar rainbow on the American Fall. The roar of the cataract could be best heard at some distance. In the Grove near the Ferry

House, the sound was overpowered by the croaking of bull-frogs, and the ceaseless chirping of the Katidid crickets. I never heard, even amid Italian marshes, such a riotous uproar of batrachian and insect voices.

I have written more than I intended of my own impressions of Niagara, but will make up for the triteness of the remarks by presenting to my readers a most interesting extract from the " Travels of Father Hennepin," the first European who ever saw, at least the first who ever described, the Falls. I found a copy of his book in the library of the Historical Society of Boston. He was a Franciscan missionary in Canada in the last part of the seventeenth century, and made a journey towards the region of the Great Lakes.* Here is the passage in which he describes Niagara :—

" Betwixt the Lake Ontario and Erie there is a vast and prodigious cadence of water which falls down after a surprising and astonishing manner, insomuch that the universe does not afford its parallel. 'Tis true Italy and Sweedland boast of some such things ; but we may well

---

* His book was first published in France in 1678, and was translated into English. An abstract of it is given in the first volume of the " Transactions of the American Archæological Society." The French edition is very rare. There is a copy of the English translation in the British Museum.

13

say they are but sorry patterns, when compared to this of which we now speak. At the foot of this horrible precipice, we meet with the river Niagara, which is not above half a quarter of a league broad, but it is wonderfully deep in some places. It is so rapid above the descent, that it violently hurries down the wild beasts while endeavouring to pass it to feed on the other side, they not being able to withstand the force of its current, which inevitably casts them down headlong, above 600 feet.

"This wonderful downfall is compounded of two great cross-streams of water, and two Falls, with an isle sloping along the middle of it. The waters which fall from this vast height do foam and boil after the most hideous manner imaginable, making an outrageous noise, more terrible than that of thunder; for when the wind blows from off the south, their dismal roaring may be heard above fifteen leagues off.

"The river Niagara having thrown itself down this incredible precipice, continues its impetuous course for two leagues together to the great rock above mentioned, with an inexpressible rapidity; but having passed that, its impetuosity relents, gliding along more gently for two leagues, till it arrives at the Lake Ontario or Frontenac.

"Any barque or great vessel may pass from

the fort to the foot of this huge rock above
mentioned. This rock lies to the westward,
and is cut off from the land by the river
Niagara, about two leagues farther down than
the Great Fall; for which two leagues the
people are obliged to carry their goods over-
land, but the way is very good, and the trees
are but few, and they chiefly firs and oaks.

" From the Great Fall unto this rock, which
is to the west of the river, the two brinks of it
are so prodigious high that it would make one
tremble to look steadily upon the water, roll-
ing along with a rapidity not to be imagined.
Were it not for this vast cataract, which inter-
rupts navigation, they might sail with barques
or greater vessels above four hundred and fifty
leagues farther, cross the lake of Huron, and
up to the farther end of the Lake Illinois ;
which two lakes we may well say are little seas
of fresh water."

Then he tells how Sieur de la Salle intended
to build a fort, to keep in check the Iroquese
and other savage nations, and to form a commerce in skins of elks, beavers, and other
beasts for the English and Dutch in New
York.

The title-page of the book is worth tran-
scribing :—

" A new discovery of a vast country in

America, extending about four thousand miles between New France and New Mexico ; with a description of the great lakes, cataracts, rivers, plants, and animals : also the manners, customs, and languages of the several native Indians, and the advantages of commerce with those different nations ; with a continuation giving an account of the attempts of Sieur de la Salle upon the mines of St. Barbe, etc. The taking of Quebec by the English ; with the advantages of a shorter cut to China and Japan. Both parts illustrated with maps and figures, and dedicated to His Majesty King William. By Lewis Hennepin, now resident in Holland. To which are added several new discoveries in North America, not published in the French edition. London : Printed for M. Bentley, J. Tonson, H. Borwick, O. Goodwin, and S. Manship, 1698.''

The frontispiece of Father Hennepin's book is a view of the Falls as he and his companions saw them. It is to be observed that the line of the Great Fall is straight, not curved as now into the form which has given it the name of the " Horseshoe Fall.'' The form of the cataract is slowly but constantly changing. The reason is to be found in the geological formation—the rocks being partly shale and partly limestone. The shale is more readily worn by the water and the frosts, and moulders away more rapidly than the harder limestone. The rate of recession has been calculated, and the time must come sooner or later when the cataract will approach the upper lakes and the length of the Rapids diminish. As it is, there are from time to time huge avalanches of falling rock, which already accumulate at the base of the Falls, especially on the American side. At some places the *débris* rises nearly a third of the height of the water, reducing greatly the apparent size of the Fall. Father Hennepin exaggerated the height when he guessed it at six hundred feet. It scarcely exceeds a fourth of this height. The Victoria Falls, on the Zambesi river in Africa, and the recently discovered Falls in British Guiana, exceed Niagara in depth of fall; but the vast volume of water, and the beauty as well as grandeur of the scene, still keep Niagara at an immeasurable distance as the greatest of waterfalls.

CHAPTER XV.

CHICAGO was the place of all others in
America I was most curious to see, and
which has left the deepest impression. It was
certainly to me *the* wonder of the New World.
Here is a city scarcely forty years old, with
300,000 inhabitants, enjoying all the advantages
of the oldest and most civilized communities.
In trade, commerce, and wealth, as well as
population, it is already one of the first cities
of the Union. It is the centre of the greatest
railway traffic in the world. The average
number of trains arriving at and leaving the
depôts of the twelve main lines is estimated at
two hundred and fifty daily through the year.
In 1850 was laid the first railroad, with forty

miles of track; now there are more than forty different railroads having direct connection with the city. Nor is Chicago wonderful only or chiefly for material progress. Its schools equal in number and efficiency those of the oldest States. It has a flourishing university, possessing the most unique library and the most powerful telescope in America. There are five seminaries of different religious denominations, ahead of any similar institutions in the country. There are nearly two hundred churches. Sunday-schools and the multiform agencies of Christian usefulness assist in the religious training and spiritual oversight of the people of all ages and nationalities. The newspaper press is second to none in the Union for enterprise and ability. In a city so vast and so new, only crystallising, as it were, into shape and order, and into which immigrants are constantly pouring, there will be found many rough and troublesome elements : but the power of good government and of Christian influence prevails, and will secure a high and healthy standard of public opinion. To those who feel that "the proper study of mankind is man," there is deeper interest in witnessing so remarkable an instance of human progress, than in beholding the grandest natural scenery or the most venerable monuments of

antiquity. It is worth crossing the Atlantic to
see Niagara. It is more worth crossing the
Atlantic to see Chicago.

Forty years ago the name of Chicago did
not appear on the best maps of America. It is
not in the Atlas of the Society for the Diffusion
of Useful Knowledge, published in 1831. In
some maps there is a small creek marked Chi-
caque, which a French exploring party from
Canada (in the days of Louis XIV.) entered
when coasting the shore of Lake Michigan.
This is the first record of the name said to be
given by the natives to the river and creek.
Hennepin and La Salle afterwards visited the
same district. We hear nothing more till, in a
treaty between the United States Government
and the Indian tribes near Lake Michigan,
mention is made of " a tract of land six miles
square at the mouth of the Chicago river."
The object of obtaining this and other localities
in the West was for the establishment of trading
stations and forts for the protection of the
traders. In 1804 Fort Dearborn was erected,
a rough block-house, round which a few fur-
traders, Indians and half-breeds, squatted. The
first white man who settled on the site was John
Kenzie, who came across the Lake from De-
troit or St. Joseph. In August, 1812, when war
with Great Britain broke out, the fort was

abandoned. The provisions and clothing were distributed among the Indians, but the " fire-water" and gunpowder were thrown into the lake. This exasperated the Indians, and led to the fearful massacre of the retreating garrison and settlers, which forms a dark page in the early annals of Chicago. In 1816, at the close of the war, the fort was rebuilt, and garrisoned until 1832, when it served as a refuge for above 700 persons during an inroad of hostile Indians upon the settlers in Northern Illinois. The Indians being routed, and their chief, Black Hawk, taken prisoner, the whites remained in undisputed possession of the territory. The Indians were removed beyond the Missouri river, farther west, in 1835; and in 1837 the fort was finally abandoned, as no longer necessary.

During these times successive detachments of traders had settled in the district, all of them engaged in the fur trade with the Indians. A more permanent purpose of colonization origi-nated in the plan of connecting the great chain of lakes with the Mississippi. As early as 1814 the Illinois and Michigan Canal was pro-jected; but it was not till 1829 that an official surveyor, James Thompson, proceeded to form the canal and to lay out a town near Fort Dearborn. The only white residents then were

John Kenzie, his son-in-law, Dr. Woolcott,
Indian agent, and a few traders living in log
cabins west of the river.   The first map, from
Mr. Thompson's official survey, bears date
August 3rd, 1830.   The first religious services
on record were held during the following winter
in the fort, conducted by Mark Noble, of the
Methodist Episcopal Church.   The first tax list
and first treasurer's report date in the year
1832 ; the first street being also then laid out,
and the first Sunday-school begun, attended
by thirteen children.   The first postmaster was
appointed in 1833, and on November 26 of the
same year the first newspaper was started,
" The Democrat," edited by John Calhoun.
Already in August of the same year, the great
event occurred of the incorporation of Chicago
as a town, with a board of trustees.   Not till
March, 1837, was a formal City Charter
granted, when the first municipal election was
held, and W. B. Ogden chosen mayor.   The
first State Census, taken on July 1st of that
year, showed 3,989 whites, of whom 518 were
under five years of age ; 77 coloured ; and 104
sailors belonging to vessels owned in the port,
making a total of 4,170.

Since that time the growth of the city has
been continuously progressive, though checked
in rapidity by various calamities, especially by

a severe visitation of cholera. In 1830 the population was 170, many of whom were Indians and half-breeds; in 1840, 4,853 ; in 1845, 12,088; in 1850, 29,963; in 1860, 110,973; in 1865, 178,900; and in 1870, 299,227.

The reader will be amused by the following account of the " chief towns in Illinois," given in a large work in two quarto volumes, " The History and Topography of the United States, edited by J. Howard Hinton, M.A., assisted by eminent men in America and England. London, 1832."

" Illinois was admitted into the Union in 1818, and contained that year 35,220 inhabit- ants.* Kaskaskia, lately the seat of govern- ment, is on the right bank of the Kaskaskia river, eleven miles from its mouth. It contains a land office, a printing office, and about a hundred and sixty houses scattered over an ex- tensive plain. The town was settled upwards of one hundred years ago by emigrants from Lower Canada, and about one-half of the in- habitants are French. The surrounding country is under good cultivation. Cahokia is a French settlement on the Mississippi, fifty-two miles

---

* The decennial census of Illinois State gives the following numbers :—1810, 12,280 ; 1820, 55,162 ; 1830, 157,445 ; 1840, 476,183; 1850, 851,470 ; 1860, 1,711,951 ; 1870, 2,537,910.

north-north-west of Kaskaskia, and about five miles below St. Louis. Shawneetown is on the north bank of the Ohio, twelve miles from the mouth of the Wabash, and twelve miles east of the salt-works belonging to the State, or Saline Creek. The inhabitants are supported principally by the profits of the salt trade. Edwardsville is a flourishing town on the Cahokia river, twenty-two miles north-east of St. Louis. Vandalia, fifty miles north-east of Edwardsville, is now the seat of government."

Chicago is not even mentioned in this summary!

From the last annual "Report of the Trade and Commerce of Chicago " (the 13th Report, 1871),* I take a few extracts, showing the commercial growth and prosperity of the city.

The receipts of wheat for the year 1870 were 17,394,409 bushels, being 500,000 bushels in excess of 1869, and the largest quantity received in any year. Of corn or maize, the receipts were 20,189,775 bushels; of oats,

---

† I am indebted to a fellow-passenger in the "Scotia" Colonel John Mason Loomis, merchant, formerly of the 26th Illinois Regiment, for sending the last statistical reports of Public Works, Board of Health, Trade and Commerce, Schools and Education. If Colonel Loomis reads this note he will forgive the apparent incredulity with which some of his statements were received before the writer had visited the Queen City of the West.

10,472,000 bushels ; of rye, 1,093,500 ; of bar-
ley, 3,335,653 bushels. Most of the Indian
corn was for home consumption, a considerable
quantity being also used for distilling.

Of hogs, the number received, live or
dressed, was 1,953,372. The receipts of cattle
were 532,964 head. The latter branch of the
provision trade is diminishing, many cattle
being now slaughtered by the packers at
Kansas city, and other places nearer the
pasturage grounds.

Produce of the forest, in form of timber or of
shingles, wool and hides, and spirit known by
the trade name of "highwines," form a large
portion of the commerce of Chicago. The
production of highwines was above seven
millions of gallons, very little of which is ex-
ported.

Of these various industries the most notable
is that of pork-packing. In fact, this is one of
the chief sources of wealth in the whole of the
Mississippi valley, the States of Illinois, Ohio,
Missouri, Indiana, Kentucky, Wisconsin, and
Iowa all presenting large returns in the trade.
But Chicago has far outstripped the older
centres. Cincinnati was long the chief provision mart—Porkopolis *par excellence*; but in
1870 the number of hogs dressed in Chicago
was 688,140, against 337,330 in Cincinnati.

St. Louis, in Missouri, ranks next, with 241,316; Louisville, in Kentucky, 182,000; Milwaukie, in Wisconsin, 172,626; St. Joseph, in Missouri, 61,300; Keokuk, in Iowa, 47,400. The whole amount of hogs used in pork-packing in the Mississippi valley during 1870 was above two millions and a half. Chicago has become the metropolis of this trade, rising by rapid advance from 22,036, the number packed in 1850, to 271,805 in 1860, and 688,141 in 1870. The increase of wheat and corn having been in like ratio, there is no fear of lack of food for any number of mouths that the increase of population may bring, either by births or immigration. Malthus and the political economists are not wanted for some generations in the far west, so far as questions of food and population are concerned.

The same astonishing progress appears in regard to railway and canal traffic, ships and steamers on the lake, and all matters depending on commercial enterprise and manufacturing industry.

There would be little satisfaction in recording material progress alone. But the development has not been less remarkable in mental and moral statistics. The churches in Chicago I have stated to be nearly two hundred. This number I give on the authority of a letter lately received. Some of these " churches," I suspect, must be only " stations," or small congregations. At the time of my visit the number was under 170. The denominations most largely represented were—Methodist 23, Presbyterian 22, Episcopal 21, Baptist 20, Roman Catholic 19, Congregational 13. Among the other places of worship were five Jewish synagogues, two African Methodist Episcopal, and a Scotch Presbyterian church.

The educational progress is not less notable, the common schools and the Sunday-schools being proportionally numerous and efficient. Nor is this activity confined to primary education. I knew there was a university at Chicago, for a friend in London had a degree of LL.D. lately sent to him. The reception of a degree from this remote city of the west, chiefly known to Londoners as a " pig-sticking and pork-curing emporium," had been the cause of much banter, characteristic of English ignorance of America. I thought I would visit the university, in order to convey to my friend a report of his *alma mater*, little expecting to find anything worth seeing, apart from this private motive. I was rewarded by one of the greatest of many surprises experienced in my travels, and by here spending one of the pleasantest of my days in America.

In the morning daily papers I saw the following advertisement :—

UNIVERSITY OF CHICAGO.

Year opens Sept. 10, 1870.

I. LAW DEPARTMENT.—Dean, Judge Henry Booth.

II. COLLEGE WITH THREE COURSES.—1, Classical. 2, Scientific. 3, Special; including the option of Chemistry, Astronomy, Civil Engineering, or any studies of the college course.

III. ACADEMY.—Boys above twelve years admitted to prepare for any college, or to acquire a good business education.

The buildings and situation, on the shores of Lake Michigan, are unsurpassed in beauty, convenience, and healthfulness.

Apparatus includes the great Clarke Telescope, the largest refractor in the country; Chemical, Philosophical, and Engineering Instruments, Cabinets, etc.

Libraries, 25,000 volumes.

Expenses.—Board, 2.50 dols. to 4.00 dols. per week. Tuition, 50 dols. a year. Total necessary expenses, 200 dols. to 250 dols. Money is loaned or given to young men who lack means to pursue their studies.

Address, J. C. BURROUGHS, President.

I was directed to take " Cottage Grove cars," a line of tramway or horse railroad. The route was along the shore of the lake for four miles —houses, and shops, and villas reaching the whole of the way. The university buildings stand in a fine piece of ground, " donated," I was told, by the late Senator S. A. Douglas, to whose memory a monument is erected on a commanding site overlooking the lake. The university was founded in 1855, and the buildings commenced in 1858. The main central building was completed in 1868, at a cost of 110,000 dols. Attached to the university is an observatory, the cost of building which was 30,000 dols. The chief feature is a massive octagonal tower, the "Dearborn tower," founded on solid stonework, containing among other valuable instruments the Clarke telescope. This instrument had been ordered by a Louisianian college, but not being taken, on account of the war, was secured for Chicago. It is a magnificent instrument, the focal length of object-glass being twenty-three feet, and the aperture of object-glass eighteen inches and a half; diameter of declination circle thirty inches, of hour-circle twenty-two inches. The circles are read by two microscopes each, the hour circle to seconds of time, and the declination circle to ten seconds of space. The possession of the refracting telescope, under the charge of Professor T. H. Safford, has obtained for Chicago the honour of taking part in the new survey of the heavens and catalogue of the stars, the formation of which is divided among four or five of the chief observatories in the world. There are other instruments, the value of which would be appreciated by scientific visitors, especially a meridian circle of the first class, with ingenious arrangement for illuminating the field and the wires, and for record-

14

ing declination, invented by the makers, Messrs. Repsold and Sons, of Hamburg.

From these scientific sights I passed to the literary departments, where I had even greater surprise. My courteous conductor, Mr. Howe, the head of the classical department, took me to a part of the main building, and introduced me to Mr. Everts, the curator of the " Hengstenberg Library." Mr. W. W. Everts, son of the minister of the first Baptist church in Chicago, was a student in Berlin in 1869, when Hengstenberg, the learned scholar and theologian, died. His library, rich especially in Patristic and Ecclesiastical works, and Rabbinical and Oriental literature, was to be sold. It was proposed to be purchased for the University Library of Berlin, but the Minister of Instruction refused the funds required to complete the purchase. Other movements were made to secure so valuable and unique a collection for Germany. Meanwhile young Everts wrote to Chicago an account of the prize that was within reach. His public spirit was rewarded by the return of a telegraphic message to secure the library. Before the end of the year the books were packed in forty-one huge boxes, and shipped off to the new world for the University of Chicago. Of this library Mr. Everts has been appointed the secretary. I found him busy among the unpacked but yet half-arranged literary treasures. At a recent counting there were found 10,000 bound volumes, with several thousand paper-covered books and pamphlets still strewn on the floor. The larger divisions number 2,400 for theology, dogmatic and practical; 1,700 for Old Testament Hebraistic literature; 1,400 for Church history. Under classics are ranged about 800 volumes, histories 400, commentaries on New Testament 750, Oriental books 500, Church Fathers 320, including a complete set of the folio Benedictine edition. The cases including philosophy, geography, general literature, books of travel, and miscellaneous, contain about 1,500 volumes. Most of these are German books, but there are between 200 and 300 standard English works. Of the early writings and editions of the Reformers there is a large collection, including some rare volumes, such as the first editions of " Melancthon's Loci Communes." I was shown many ancient curiosities and rarities, and some modern treasures, such as Neander's own copy of his Church History, presented by the author " to his dear colleague, Dr. Hengstenberg." It was a place to spend days instead of hours. I parted from the librarian admiring his intelligent enthusiasm, and grateful for his patient courtesy.

It was curious to come unexpectedly upon this bit of the Old World transplanted to the New, and the contrast was the greater in such a bustling place as Chicago. The possession of this library is an honour to the city, as well as to all concerned in its purchase. Besides his various gatherings of rare and valuable volumes as a book collector for forty years, it was Hengstenberg's custom to purchase every book which he had occasion to consult as Professor of Theology, Commentator on the Scriptures, or Editor of the " Evangelical Gazette." His ample means admitted of this expenditure, and he rarely availed himself of the abundant resources of the Royal Library or other Berlin collections. Hence his library will prove a treasury for scholars engaged in studying or illustrating the Holy Scriptures. It is a library of reference which Boston, or Philadelphia, or Princeton might covet. Dr. Koner, of the Royal University Library, Berlin, in a report he was requested to make, with view to purchase, said : " It offers, in a rich assortment of exegetical commentaries, means for the study of the text, and explanation of the contents of the books of the Bible, as proposed by the learned of all times ; in a costly treasure of works on church history, dogmatics, symbolics, ethics, and philosophy, it presents all-sufficient instruction upon the principles and systems of doctors of the Church. In short, it satisfies all demands that are now made upon a thorough knowledge of theology."

Such is the collection which forms the nucleus of the Free Theological Library, attached to the University of Chicago, but available for students of the various theological seminaries of the State of Illinois,* and for scholars from all parts of the Union. I have dwelt at some length on this University and its library, because it illustrates the public spirit of the American people in the highest matters of culture. It is one of many proofs that the energy of the West is not all expended on the pursuit of wealth and of material progress, as is too commonly believed.

To the majority of travellers, however, the chief impression conveyed at Chicago is that of bustling commercial and trading activity. The scene at noon on 'Change in the great hall of the Board of Trade is one which will not readily be forgotten. The sides of the hall are lined with tables, with samples of wheat and other produce, and the floor is crowded with noisy traders and speculators. As the clock

* I have since heard that the Methodist College, theological seminary at Chicago, has obtained the library of Schultz, another well-known book-lover of Berlin. Well done, Chicago!

strikes twelve, the rap of the president's hammer commands silence, when the latest prices of produce and of stocks at New York, London, and other places, as conveyed by telegraph, are announced.   I have already mentioned the strange effect produced by hearing the closing prices at Mark Lane proclaimed at Chicago at noon of the same day.   The grain, of which samples are shown, is stored in immense granaries called elevators.   Seventeen of these warehouses receive from various railroads and canals, and have capacity of storage for above $11,000,000\frac{1}{2}$ bushels of grain.   One of them stores 1,600,000 bushels, and the storing capacity of three others is 1,250,000 bushels each.   The Board of Trade has stringent rules for the inspection, weighing, and transfer of grain ; but it is not to be supposed that a purchaser obtains in bulk the exact produce of which he has seen the sample.   Produce of nearly the same value from many different sources is stored in the same elevator, just as in the warehouses of our London docks wines from many vineyards are mixed in vast reservoirs, in rough approximation of strength and quality, to be drawn therefrom for retail wine merchants.

One of the worst features of commercial life in Chicago I observed in the grain-trade speculation. The storing of the grain is entirely under the control of the inspectors, who allot the consignments to the various classes of grain in the elevators, where it is stored for twenty days, giving to the storers certificates of quality. There is often unfairness in the classification; but, supposing this to be all right, these certificates become the objects of unlimited speculation by the " operators " in the grain market. Millions of dollars are gambled for every day on 'Change with these paper certificates, without the transfer of a single bushel of actual produce. The effect of this gambling is most demoralising, and the grain operators include as worthless adventurers as the worst bears and bulls of our own Stock Exchange. It is a rotten system, and it is difficult to see how the honest farmers who grow the grain, and honest purchasers, can again be brought into communication, without the intervention of the gamblers in grain certificates.

Provisions, especially pork, cured in various forms for the markets of the world, form the other chief trading feature at Chicago. There are nearly fifty firms engaged in the pork-packing business, receiving for this purpose not far from two millions of hogs annually. The live-stock yards, as well as the curing and packing establishments, are worthy of inspection. The Great Union Stock Yards cover a space of 345 acres, with accommodation for nearly 120,000 animals—cattle, hogs, and sheep. There are said to be in these yards thirty-one miles of drainage, seven miles of streets and alleys, three miles of water troughs, ten miles of food troughs, 2,300 gates, 1,500 open pens, and 800 covered pens. In the construction 22,000,000 feet of timber were used, at a cost of 1,675,000 dols. The water is supplied by an artesian well 1,100 feet in depth.

The vast animal as well as human population of Chicago renders the good drainage of the city the more important. The accomplishment of this is one of the perplexities of the place. The site is low; in fact, the ground was a mere swamp where now stand buildings of solidity and architectural taste unsurpassed in the older cities of the Union. Still, there is necessity for securing efficient drainage, and plans are made for artificial currents by canals and steam machinery to aid the natural sewerage towards the lake. The flatness of the site and the nature of the soil enhance our admiration of the engineering skill displayed in rendering the city habitable for so vast a population. The same engineering skill has solved the problem of water-supply. The impurity of the lake water near the shore forbade its use as the population increased. A tunnel has accordingly been bored under the stiff blue clay bed of the lake, two miles long, of solid brick masonry, having a clear width of five feet, and a height of five feet two inches. A gigantic wooden structure, called the Crib, marks the end of the tunnel, with a lighthouse, serving the double purpose of a guide to the harbour entrance and a protection to the Crib. By powerful pumping engines the water is raised in a lofty iron column overtopping the highest house in the city. The supply is at present about 20,000,000 gallons daily, for about 25,000 houses. The city engineer, E. S. Chesborough, the projector of the Lake Tunnel, deserves honourable mention for the great work.

Some parts of the city are still, however, ill supplied with water, and entirely undrained. I examined some statistical returns of the Board of Health, showing in a striking manner the influence of sanitary conditions on the health and death rate of different localities. Even with these disadvantages, the total rate of mortality was far below that of our great towns.

The main streets, on some of which there is prodigious traffic, such as Clark Street, are paved with wooden blocks, Nicholson's patent, which has been adopted in many other American cities. It is found more serviceable and durable than stone blocks or macadamised roads, provided the filling and pressing of the subsoil is carefully done. The side walks of the main streets are stone, but the largest part of the city has still only plank side walks. Probably not more than thirty miles out of above six hundred of side walk or foot pavement are stone. Fifteen years ago, there were only about 150 miles of side walk, all plank. The whole of the city, and for miles out, is traversed by horse railways, of which about fifty miles are laid, with about 150 cars, employing 550 men and 900 horses. This convenience of locomotion marks the streets of all the great American cities, and might put to shame our backwardness in this respect, the extension of tramways even in London being retarded by the stupidity of English vestries and the apathy of the public.

I was at Chicago soon after a great fire, which will long be remembered, the whole of the magnificent block of buildings on Wabash Avenue, corner of Washington Street, known as Drake's Block, being demolished. The fire broke out on Sunday afternoon, September 4th, in a paper store. I saw the ruins still smoking, and the water playing on the hot *débris*. There was a lamentable loss of life, and property was destroyed to the value of three million of dollars, only about half of which was insured. Every exertion was made, but the materials in the stores were of a kind which could not be saved. Laflin's paper store contained 250,000 dollars of stock, Farwell's dry goods store 180,000 dollars, and Smith and Nixon's piano and music store 150,000 dollars. A boot and shoe store lost 250,000 dollars. These amounts show the magnitude of retail business in the city.

The arrangements for fire signals resemble those which I have already described at Boston. The telegraph wires from the various districts centre in the signal room in the lofty tower of the Town Hall.

Wandering about the city, I found some districts to be occupied almost wholly by emigrants and inhabitants of separate nationalities. Thus on the northern side I saw a large colony of Norwegians and other Scandinavian settlers. Near one of the bridges almost every name on the stores and houses was German. Southwest from the City Hall I reached a quarter entirely occupied by coloured people, who, in most of the cities in what used to be Free States, are led, by practical experience of social inferiority, though possessing political equality, to congregate together. The Irish also tend to dwell apart, and I am sorry to add that this segregation is encouraged by the Romish Church, which establishes separate schools from those of the community. The poor Irish are thus losing the best of the advantages which they used to derive from emigration to America. Their children at the common schools had some chance of acquiring independence of character as well as useful learning. Now they are trained, like their fathers before them, in degraded submission to popery and the priesthood. The zeal and energy of the Romish Church ought to stir emulation in the Protestant Churches to look more carefully after the emigrants professing the faith of the Reformation.

The completion of a ship canal from Lake Michigan to the Mississippi, the tapping of the Indian coal-fields by opening a line of railway, and the formation of a canal between the lake and the north river to secure constant sanitary current, seem the works most promising for the aggrandisement and convenience of the city. By the residents it is often called the "Garden City," apparently on the *lucus a non lucendo* principle, for gardens and parks are as yet in a rudimentary condition. It is more worthy of the titles, also claimed for it, of "Queen City of the Lakes," or "Queen City of the West."

I should like to have said much more about Chicago—its monster stores and hotels, its avenues and public parks, its docks and shipping, its trades and manufactures, its banks and insurance offices, its hospitals and charitable institutions. The insurance business seems to flourish, and I was told that the law of the State of Illinois requires every company to deposit a large sum for security, and to publish annually its list of members and detailed statement of accounts for examination by official auditors. I should like also to have spoken of the newspapers, some of which are admirably conducted, and exert wide influence. But further details would only serve to illustrate the one point of the wonderful growth and prosperity of the place. The inhabitants themselves have no hesitation in boasting that Chicago is destined to outstrip every city in the New World, and that it ought to be made the capital of the Union. It is possible that it may yet double its size and population and commerce.

So marvellous has been the progress within a brief time, that future historians may say of Chicago that it " rose like an exhalation." Some already say that it resembles Pandemonium in other respects than in the rapidity of its growth. I often heard it spoken of as a fearfully wicked city. That many rough and

lawless characters are among its immigrants
may well be expected ; but that stronger influences are busy on the side of order and law, of
education and religion, is attested by the good
municipal government, and by the number of
schools, churches, and charitable institutions.
The vast and rapidly increasing population and
wealth might cause feelings of depression rather
than exultation if viewed alone ; but with this
growth and activity there is also greater growth
and greater activity in all good and beneficent
works.   Some travellers may like to parade
statistics of crime, or to quote the large number of divorces in the State of Illinois, but more
generous visitors will prefer to note what gives
promise of a happy and well-ordered commonwealth.   In this spirit I would conclude my
recollections of Chicago, by referring to one
scene which left a deep impression.

From the busy tumult of the Chamber of
Commerce, one day soon after noon, I was
taken by my kind guide, Mr. Glen Wood, to
a public building in a side street, not far
off.   I was not told what I was going to see or
hear ; but found myself in a large hall crowded
to the door, the vast majority being men.   It
was a religious assembly, "the noonday prayer-
meeting " it was called, an institution which
has been known for some years in most of

the large American cities. I had attended a
similar meeting in Boston, but it was a formal
affair compared with the hearty and animated
meeting at Chicago. An address was being
delivered when I entered by an earnest and
energetic evangelist, D. L. Moody. Other
brief addresses and prayers followed, one
stranger from the old country, the Rev. Henry
Allon, of Islington, expressing the great pleasure he had in assisting on such an occasion.
The singing was the heartiest I heard in
America, as lively as in any Methodist meeting. The fact of such a service being kept up
in the centre of the city, at the busiest time of
the day, was a striking proof of spiritual life
being active in the midst of an atmosphere
of worldly influence. It is true that religion
shows itself in the common duties and daily
occupations of life; but the best men feel
refreshed and strengthened by a brief midday
season of prayer and Christian communion.
It used to be so in the city of London in the
time of good old Mr. Watts Wilkinson, when
St. Margaret's, Lothbury, every day at noon,
was crowded with bankers and brokers and
merchants; and in some degree similar scenes
have been witnessed in more recent years. To
witness such a scene in Chicago was a pleasant
surprise, even after hearing of the number of

places of Sabbath-day worship. The aggressive agency of these "revival" meetings reaches many who do not attend regular services at church, while the most respectable church-goers are none the worse for the quickening sometimes obtained in hours of devotion such as are experienced at the Noon Prayer Meeting.

Feverish hurry is the most disagreeable feature of public and commercial life in Chicago. New York is slow in comparison. The people walk faster, eat faster, talk faster, live faster in the western city. Business is all carried on at express speed. I was sorry to find also that the newspapers are published on Sundays as on week-days. Even on the lower grounds of health and political economy, the benefit would be found of a better observance of the beneficent "day of rest."

I think I have given a fair sketch of the condition of Chicago, both in its material and moral aspects. The general impression left on my mind was of the most favourable kind. Admitting all the worst that can be said of the place, the influence of good over evil is marked and progressive, and I end as I began by describing this great western city as the pride and wonder of the New World.

CHAPTER XVI.

COMMON SCHOOLS IN CHICAGO.

THE common school system of education in Chicago is so admirable that we give a special account of it, prepared for this work by a London clergyman, the Rev. R. Demaus, well versed in educational questions. It is earnestly commended to the attention of members of school-boards, and all who are interested in educational movements in England.

We have before us the last "Annual Report of the Board of Education for the City of Chicago," and we propose to select from it what may enable the reader to appreciate the grand and comprehensive spirit in which the subject of education has been treated in this "Capital of the Lakes," and also what may serve at the present time as topics not unworthy of being considered by all to whom the proceedings of school-boards are matters of interest. Chicago, it may be premised, is precisely one of those places where the ques-

tion was surrounded by special difficulties.
The city is only forty years old, and its
growth, as we have already shown, is without
parallel in the world. Twenty years ago it
was a town of the size of Dover, and the
reader will probably look in vain for it in
most English atlases published before 1860;
but its population has increased with a rapidity
which will probably outstrip Manchester or
Liverpool before the completion of another
decade. In such a place the education question presented most formidable difficulties; the
population was not only multiplying at a ratio
which seemed to defy any adequate educational provision, but it was of a most hetero-
geneous description, including almost every
creed and nationality under the sun. The
inhabitants, however, who thought nothing
of lifting huge piles of buildings into the air
and raising their level, were just the men to
relish the difficulty of providing education for
the swarms of children in their streets. They
set to work, therefore, to devise a scheme of
education, acting upon the principles which
are expressed in the opening sentences of the
Report. ·

" The common school system of education,
supported and liberally endowed by the State,
free from sectarian and other pernicious in-

fluences, is the best system ever devised by man.

" The instruction of the children in the public schools, such as is furnished in the primary, grammar, and high schools, constitutes the bulwark of American civilisation and independence.

" The foundation of our institutions, and of political, civil, and religious liberty, rests and depends upon the education and intelligence of the people.'

" It is the duty of the State to educate its children, and any State which neglects the performance of that duty, inflicts upon itself an irreparable injury. Chicago is performing her part of that duty faithfully and well."

In pursuance of these principles, it was enacted that "all children living within the limits of the city who are upwards of six years of age shall be entitled to attend the public schools of the city;" and efforts were forthwith made to provide at the public expense the necessary school buildings and teachers. Suitable sites were procured, and school buildings were erected in a substantial manner, the provision being annually extended so as to meet the growing dimensions of the juvenile population. The number of public schools has doubled within six years, and amounted in

1870 to thirty-six; and these, it must be remembered, like everything else in the States,
are on a scale of grandeur to which in
England we are utter strangers. Some of
them have nearly *thirteen hundred children* in
daily attendance; and the whole number of
pupils enrolled in the year 1870 amounted to
very nearly *forty thousand*, or one-eighth of
the entire population. This, it must be noted,
is independent of a very considerable number
of private schools, and seminaries of various
kinds, which are in no way interfered with by
the public schools. The value of the school
buildings erected since the commencement of
the scheme is estimated at considerably upwards of a million of dollars, or nearly a quarter
of a million sterling; and the annual educational expenditure during the last year for
teachers' salaries, cost of superintendence, fuel,
furniture, and repairs, was 607,396 dollars, or
a hundred and twenty thousand pounds sterling. There has been no "cheeseparing" in
providing what was recognised as a great
public advantage; nor, on the other hand, has
there been any lavish expenditure on merely
ornamental adjuncts.

"School buildings," says the President of
the Board, "in which our children are educated
should be convenient, comfortable, pleasant,

and attractive. *Schools which are unsuitable for the education of the children of the wealthiest citizens are equally unsuitable for the education of the children of the poorest.*" With this republican equality there has been conjoined admirable republican simplicity. The school buildings, while excellently adapted for their purpose, are all "perfectly plain in design," built of brick with " stone window caps and sills."

The teachers are dealt with on the same sensible principles. " There is no economy," says the ·president, " in employing poor or ordinary teachers ; any price, however small, is too large for a poor or indifferent teacher." The teachers are accordingly remunerated on a scale which might almost tempt our national teachers to emigrate in a body ; the head masters are paid *two thousand two hundred dollars*, or upwards of *four hundred pounds* a year, and no assistant receives less than *a hundred and twenty pounds.* In return, however, all the teachers are kept strictly to their work by a most efficient system of superintendence ; and they are absolutely debarred from any petty system of levying illegitimate profits from their scholars by the sale of books and school stationery. It is not unimportant, as illustrating the peculiar character of the educational difficulties that existed in Chicago, to observe that, except the

head masters, all the teachers are females.   In
a country where there is boundless scope for
energetic men of education, it is found impossible to procure masters in sufficient numbers,
and mistresses are therefore employed ; the same
expedient has been suggested by some of the
ablest English Inspectors, but has never been
adopted here.

The necessary funds for meeting this expenditure are provided partly from the rents of
property given for this purpose from the city
estates, but chiefly by an educational rate, which
amounted in 1870 to 454,902 dols., or £90,000,
being at the rate of six shillings a head on the
entire population of the city.   In this country
it has been calculated that the average cost of
the elementary education of the lower classes
amounts to nearly *thirty shillings* per scholar ;
in Chicago the expenditure is on a vastly larger
scale, and reaches *twenty-five* dollars, or a *hundred* shillings, for each child in average attendance, being more than three times the cost of
similar education in England.   Of course there
are many circumstances which must be taken
into consideration in comparing the cost in the
two countries ; but after allowing due weight
to them all, it seems impossible to doubt that
in Chicago the cost is actually as well as rela-
tively greater than with us.

The *religious difficulty*, of which we have heard so much lately, has been settled in Chicago by two provisions : (1) it is absolutely prohibited to make any appropriation, "or to pay from public funds anything to help, support, or sustain any school controlled by any religious denomination whatever," so that there are no denominational schools assisted with public money; and (2) it is enacted that "the morning exercises of each department of the several schools *shall* commence with reading the Scriptures, without note or comment, and this exercise *may* be followed by repeating the Lord's Prayer and by appropriate singing."*

The education is entirely *gratuitous ;* the children pay no fees whatever; they are, however, compelled to provide themselves with books. *No compulsion is resorted to :* all children *may* attend and enjoy what the State provides ; *none are compelled to be present.* Such a system, it is often asserted, is sure to lead to irregular attendance on the part of the pupils; in Chicago, however, the average attendance is far better than has ever been realised in this country.

There are various points in the Report which seem worthy of consideration in England at

* Similar rules are found in the educational codes of all the States. In some of the New York schools alone, under Irish and Popish influence, is the reading of the Bible omitted.

present, and to which we shall briefly direct attention.

1. The small proportion of the expenditure which is allocated to *official* purposes is well worthy of note. The whole sum expended on inspection and what may be called office expenses scarcely amounts to *one-twentieth* of the total expenditure; and the salaries of the officials, inspector, and clerks, instead of being as with us five or six times as large as those of the teachers, are never in any case twice as large. The " Clerk of the Board of Education of Chicago," instead of being paid, as in London, six times the salary of a teacher, is actually paid £40 a year *less* than any head master employed by the Board. Some such economy is urgently required in this country, where the probable cost of administration is certain to prove a formidable obstacle to any attempt at a truly national educational system.

2. The Chicago system of education, like that established in Scotland three centuries ago, is complete, and for all classes: in England we have never aimed at anything more than a rudimentary education for the poorer classes alone. In Chicago, as in Scotland, the rich and poor "are received and taught on terms of perfect equality;" they are not only treated alike, they are educated alike. The

primary schools provide for all alike a sound elementary education somewhat more advanced than that of our national schools; and the pupils pass from them, by examination, into the *high school* (also maintained at the public expense), where they are taught the classics, mathematics, and modern languages. In short, that system which has for centuries contributed so wonderfully to the success of Scotchmen, by throwing the avenues to knowledge freely open to all classes, has been adopted in Chicago, doubtless with equally good results, though these, of course, remain as yet to be manifested in the future. It was, it will be admitted, a noble ambition on the part of these bustling citizens of the far West thus to provide a system by which the poorest child might have the way open to the university. We should like to see English boards of education following their example, and not expending their whole energies in devising a scheme of education that is " good enough for the working classes."

3. In Chicago, instead of trusting to the annual visit of an inspector, and a mechanical system of "payment by results," as checks against carelessness on the part of teachers, a system of constant and efficient superintendence has been adopted which ensures the reward of all who are diligent. The process of

"payment by results" which we have devised
has such a specious air of practical good sense
that it will probably take a whole generation
to convince the English people that it is ex-
tremely unfriendly to the real interests of education; but the Scotch have all along known
better, and the Yankees were too 'cute to be
deceived by it. The direct tendency of "payment by results," as practised in England, is
to lower and retard all education; it sacrifices the clever in a school for the sake of
the dunces; and its results are sufficiently
important to deserve a brief explanation of the
merits of the two rival systems.

The object of all parents, and especially of
all poor parents, in sending their children to
school, is that they may as quickly as possible
acquire such education as is wanted, whatever
the amount of it may be, or for whatever purpose it is required. This object the system
adopted in Chicago exactly meets. A child on
entering school is placed in the "grade" for
which its attainments adapt it; and according
to its ability it is promoted after examination
from grade to grade, till it passes from the
primary to the *grammar* department, and from
the latter to the *high* school, where, if an apt
scholar, it may be prepared for the universities, or for any educated profession. A clever

boy is promoted rapidly, sometimes passing through a grade in a couple of months; while a stupid boy lumbers on slowly, and perhaps requires fourteen months to secure a single step in advance. The English system of " payment by results " works in a very different way; it compels all pupils to move through the school at a uniform rate, and as the pace must of course be accommodated to the slow locomotion of the dunces, those whose abilities are above the average are necessarily sacrificed, and are, in fact, not properly taught. This naturally operates very unfavourably in retarding the progress of education in England ; and in an age like the present this is a matter deserving of the most serious consideration. It is quite certain that English children at the age of thirteen are, not from any want of sharpness, but from a faulty system of education, two years behind children of the same age educated on the more natural system adopted elsewhere ; and this conclusion is confirmed by the examination papers contained in the Report of the Chicago School Board. The question, which of these systems possesses the greatest advantage on the whole, is one of far greater importance than most of the educational questions which have been discussed at such length amongst us. As yet, the English public has

paid little heed to it, but thoughtful men have
not overlooked it; and when English education
has risen above the sphere of political and
sectarian polemics, this matter will doubtless
receive due attention.

Did space permit, there are many other
points in the Report to which we should gladly
direct attention.   It contains an admirable code
of rules and regulations for teachers and pupils,
characterised by excellent sense and an evident
desire to secure that everything shall be done
in the most thorough and yet most economical
manner.   England has now fairly awakened to
the necessity of devising some national educational system, and all over the country school
boards are discussing schemes for carrying
into execution the work that has been so long
neglected ; but if all this is not to end in the
mere promulgation of impracticable theories,
and the perpetration of a gigantic and expen-
sive failure, it will be necessary to depart a
little from our own narrow routine, and to consult the experience of other nations who have
successfully solved the difficulties of this great
problem.   We should be exceedingly sanguine
of good results here, if we were told that the
members and officials of our school boards are
in the habit of carefully reading and digesting
such invaluable records of experience as the

Annual Reports of the Department of Public Instruction of the City of Chicago.

THE GREAT FIRE AT CHICAGO.

To the recollections of Chicago in its prosperity a painful interest is added by the disaster of this year. On Monday, Oct. 11, the startling news reached London by telegraph that Chicago was almost utterly destroyed by fire ! General Sheridan, telegraphing to the Secretary of War at Washington, on the 9th October, said : " The fire last night and to-day has destroyed almost all that was very valuable in this city. There is not a business-house, bank, or hotel left. Most of the best part of the city is in ruins. I think not less than 100,000 people are houseless, and those who had the most wealth are now poor. It seems to me such a terrible misfortune that it may with propriety be considered a national calamity." The fire began on Sunday evening, about eight o'clock ; and a strong south wind blowing, by midnight raged beyond control. By three o'clock it reached the heart of the city, and the next day sun set on three square miles of smoking ruins. The fire exceeded in devastation the great fire of London. These ruins, from the Tower to

the Temple, did not cover more than 440 acres.
About the same number of houses, 12,000 to
13,000, were destroyed, and as many families
made homeless as in the London fire.   Three-
fourths of the city being built of wood, the roofs
generally being of asphalted wood, sixty out of
six hundred miles of sideway being plank-ways,
all this rendered the efforts to check the flames
hopeless.   The blazing fuel was swept by the
wind through the air to great distances, over-
leaping the gaps which the firemen made by
gunpowder in the attempt to circumscribe the
limit of the conflagration. The loss of property
is incalculable, and of lives deplorable.   The
generous and practical help sent from all parts
of America, from England, and other lands,
served to relieve the immediate desolation.
As to Chicago itself, its prosperity has only
received a temporary check.   If there was any
drawback to the admiration which every stranger
felt in visiting the wonderful city, it was the
pride of the inhabitants, too much in the vaunt-
ing spirit of the old king,—"Is not this great
Babylon which I have built by the might of my
power, and for the honour of my majesty?"
Chicago will rise from this desolation humbled
and chastened, and therefore nobler and greater
than before. On the day after the fire, an
article in one of the journals expressed the

prevailing feeling of all classes of the community : " In the midst of a calamity without
parallel in the world's history, looking upon the
ashes of thirty years' accumulation, the people
of this once beautiful city have resolved that
Chicago shall rise again. . . . The losses we
have suffered must be borne ; but the place, the
time, and the men are here, to commence at the
bottom and work up again ; not at the bottom
either, for we have credit in every land, and the
experience of our rebuilding of Chicago to help ,
us. Let us all cheer up, save what is left, and
and we shall come out all right. The worst is
already over. In a few days all the dangers
will be past, and we can resume the battle of
life with Christian faith and Western grit. Let
us all cheer up." Such was the universal spirit
which animated the people, and with this spirit
there is no fear as to the future of Chicago.

CHAPTER XVII.

CINCINNATI—ITS HISTORY AND STATISTICS—A
PUBLIC MEETING—AMERICAN NATIONAL AND
PARTY POLITICS.

TO a traveller going westward, Cincinnati
may appear a half-grown, half-settled,
recent city, but coming back upon it as I did
from Chicago, it has a staid, compact, and
almost venerable look. Smoke has helped to
impart this aspect of premature antiquity. It
is one of the smokiest and " Auld Reekie "-like
cities in America. The brick-built streets have
a sombre appearance in the older districts.
The main part of the city is in a hollow, surrounded by a cordon of heights, except on the
side of the Ohio. The river is crossed by a
splendid bridge,* connecting the city with
Covington and Newport in Kentucky. Above
the steep incline of the river channel stretches
a flat plateau, which gradually rises to a second

* The architect, John Roebling, was also the engineer of the
Niagara Suspension Bridge.

plateau, or older river bank, beyond which the ascent is rapid towards Mount Auburn, Mount Adams, Spring Grove, and other ridges, crowned with beautiful suburban houses and villas. From these heights we look down upon the densely-occupied and smoke-enveloped streets of the business part of the town.

Cincinnati was long the great commercial emporium of the West—next to New Orleans the largest city beyond the Alleghanies. Forty years ago, when Chicago was beginning its existence, Cincinnati had its court-house, gaol, college, medical school, museum, public library, five classical schools, forty-seven common schools, and twenty-five churches, and was a place of great trade and extensive manufactures. It was about that time Mrs. Trollope gave her amusing account of the city in her book on the "Domestic Manners of the Americans."

The town was first laid out in 1789, on the site of Fort Washington, a frontier outpost occupied for defence against the Indians, just as Fort Dearborn had been on the site of the great Illinois city. The first church was built in 1792, the first newspaper published in 1793. The population was only 500 in 1795, besides the troops in garrison. In 1819 it was first made a city, the census of the next year showing nearly 10,000 inhabitants. In 1830 it had risen

16

to near 25,000; in 1840, 46,000; in 1850,
115,000; and in 1870, the number was 218,900.
It now stands eighth on the list of cities in
number of people.   There would not be the
same interest to a reader in seeing detailed
statistics of Cincinnati as in the newer city of
Chicago.   It will suffice for comparison with
the 25-churched city of 1831 to say that there
are now about 120 churches, the Roman Catholics alone having 25 churches or stations.   The
other denominations most largely represented
are Methodist Episcopal, 20; Presbyterian, 18,
including two United Presbyterian and three
Presbyterian Reformed; Baptist, 10; Congregational, or Independent, 4; German Evangelical and Reformed, 7; Lutheran, 3; German
Episcopal Methodist, 3.   The Moravians, or
United Brethren, have 3 churches; the Friends,
2 meeting-houses; the Jews, 5 synagogues;
while the Unitarians, Universalists, and various
sects of divers names and opinions have about
a dozen places of worship among them.

The number of newspapers and periodicals
is also a fair test of an American city, and there
are in Cincinnati 8 daily papers, 40 weekly, 2
semi-monthly, and 18 monthly publications.
The *Cincinnati Commercial*, the *Cincinnati
Gazette*, the *Cincinnati Inquirer*, and *Cincinnati
Times*, have all large circulations, and most

of the journals are conducted with ability and respectability.

The schools and educational institutions of Cincinnati have long been noted. There are many charitable and benevolent societies, and the people may be justly proud of their new infirmary, which in its whole arrangements and management is equal to the best and newest of European hospitals. But I must not stay to describe places, passing on to communicate my own first impressions.

I consider Cincinnati at the present time one of the most "representative" and fairly average of the great cities of the States. It is equally removed from the condition of the older cities of the East and the South, and of the newer cities of the West, such as Chicago or San Francisco. Boston and Philadelphia, Charleston and New Orleans, date from old British times, and, with republican institutions, retain the continuity of social life and historical tradition from before the War of Independence. Cincinnati has sprung up since American nationality began, but has existed long enough to acquire all the distinctive features of American life and character, both social and political. The foreign or immigrant element, both Irish and Continental, in its population is large, and influences the affairs of the city in the same

ways, and much in the same proportion, as
throughout the Union.   The difficulties which
American   statesmen   have   to   encounter,   in
political and social life, from diversities of nationality and of religion, here present themselves
in a marked manner.   Observing this, I saw
that in Cincinnati I could study the present
position and future prospects of the American
republic better than in most other cities, and
therefore prolonged my stay beyond the proportion of time required for mere sight-seeing ;
in which, indeed, there is not much to attract
the traveller.

I found the city in political excitement, the
electioneering campaign having begun.   The
Republican party prevails in Ohio ; but various
causes had conduced to secure the Democrats
a majority in some districts.   A meeting was
advertised to be held in Mozart Hall to hear
addresses from the Hon. Job Stevenson and
Aaron F. Perry, Republican candidates for Congress, a meeting of the opposite party having
been held in the same hall a few evenings before.
Eight o'clock was the time.   For about an
hour previously a splendid band occupied an
outside balcony, discoursing lively music to the
vast crowd assembled in the street.   On approaching, I was not a little astonished to hear
the familiar, and, to British ears, spirit-stirring

strains of "God save the Queen." But be-- fore I had time to speculate on the cause of this loyal outburst, the notes were gradually growing feebler, while the confused undertone of another melody struck in, growing in clear- ness and strength, till "Yankee Doodle" triumphed over the National Anthem. Pre- sently the revolutionary strains in their turn died away, and, with a prelude of irregular notes like gun-shots, the strains of "Rule Britannia" swelled forth. But again the grand old melody died away before the increasing sound of "Hail Columbia," which closed the piece, amidst tumultuous cheering and clapping of hands. Similar musical effects used to be heard in M. Jullien's monster concerts; but this was an interesting illustration of American national feeling.

Shortly before the hour of meeting the band took its place in the orchestra, and entertained the audience, which by this time filled the hall. Exactly as the clock struck, a secretary came alone on the stage, paper in hand, and read a brief programme of the proceedings, asking if the meeting approved of the same. With a shout of " agreed " and applause, approval was signified, and the secretary, retiring, ushered in the chairman and the speakers, attended by their committee. This orderly commencement

of the meeting was characteristic of the proceedings throughout. The body of the hall
was densely crowded, and many foreigners and
coloured men were among the audience. There
were no reserved seats—working men, store-
keepers, and aristocrats sitting together. There
were a few women among the spectators in the
amphitheatre stalls, or gallery.

The chairman, the Hon. Benjamin Eggleston,
spoke only a few sentences, acknowledging the
honour of being called to preside, and giving
pithy reasons for belonging to the Republican
party, "the party of freedom and the party of
progress." He then introduced Job E. Stevenson as one "who was going to whip Sam Cary
(the Democrat candidate) out of his boots."

Amid cheers and rounds of applause, Mr.
Stevenson advanced. A brief notice of some
points of his speech will exhibit the existing
state of American politics, and the chief subjects
which divide public opinion, since the conquest
of the South by the North and the suppression
of the slaveholders' influence.

The first part of the speech referred in tones
of congratulation to the fact that " Reconstruction " was finished, and that the amendments
of the Constitution, especially the giving
equality of political rights to every citizen, were
accepted by patriotic men of all parties, in the

South as well as the North. If only lawless and violent men would cease from the spilling of Union blood (referring to the Ku-Klux assassinations), a general amnesty might be proclaimed, and the whole republic would be not only united and free, but happy in all its borders.

Although no attempt to interfere with " Reconstruction " arrangements would succeed, it is to be expected that much discontent and ill-feeling will remain for a time in the South. It will not be easy for the planters to meet coloured men on a footing of political equality, far less to submit with patience to the domination of their former slaves. But this humiliation they have brought upon themselves.

Next came the subject of Finance. The desire to diminish the national debt led to pressure of taxation, but it was only temporary, and the object was worth the inconvenience and self-denial.

The most difficult part of the speech was in touching on the " high Tariff." The speaker was cautious in avoiding advocacy of " protection " to native industry, though that has certainly been an incidental result of the policy of the Government since the war. In the great agricultural districts of the West it is a hard thing that the produce of the soil cannot be

exchanged for British imports, but that the
farmers have to pay immense prices for the
inferior manufactures of New England and the
Eastern States. The Democrats are gaining
largely in influence by this feeling of antagonism to the Government in their high-tariff
system. In fact, this is the greatest danger to
be feared by the Republican party in coming
years, a division of interest between East and
West, as before between North and South. For
a liberal party to oppose free trade and advocate
protection would be strange, and therefore it
was put to the electors of Cincinnati as a question of patriotism, the reduction of the national
debt being the point aimed at. "I myself,"
said Mr. Stevenson, "would have preferred
some other arrangements, but you have to take
things sometimes as you can get them, and if
you get enough you should be satisfied. So we
have made this reduction, and that is the state
of finance—the receipts increasing, the debts
decreasing, the expenses decreasing, the account running well both ways. Taxation reduced, people ought to be satisfied. Hereafter
it will be our task to remodel laws laying taxes
on the people, and so to reform them as, so far
as possible, to equalise the burdens of taxation
between different localities and different classes ;
and, if it so be that we cannot equalise, then let

the heavier burdens fall on those better able to
bear them, remembering this, that the Republican party never has, never will, and never can,
knowingly, either establish, foster, or maintain
any monopoly, either domestic or foreign. In
seventeen months since Ulysses S. Grant 'the
Silent' sat down in the Presidential chair, his
administration has paid of the public debt one
hundred and seventy-five millions. And at
this rate, which is over one hundred millions a
year, the debt would be paid, according to my
calculations, abating the interest as you pay, in
about fifteen years. The interest alone upon
what has been already paid, now amounts to
ten millions a year in gold saved perpetually
until the debt is obliterated. We are all anxious to see the debt paid, and I hope to live
to see it, and I know my young Democratic
friends, many of them, will live to see it. If
you let the present taxes alone, they would pay
it in fifteen years. You may ask me why then
we reducee thes taxes ; why do we not let them
alone. I say that we have preserved this
Union at countless cost of blood and treasure,
not only for ourselves, but for our children and
our children's children's children's children to
the last generation of time, and we do not propose to bear all the burden. We propose to
fund the greater part of the debt, and let it go

over for twenty or thirty years, and let the rich
and prosperous and glorious republic of that
day pay it and not feel it.   In thirty years the
people of this republic will probably number
one hundred millions.   Cannot they afford to
pay a part of that debt?   It seems so to me,
for when there are one hundred millions of
people, they will have one hundred billions of
money.   Therefore, we have reduced the taxes,
and I, for one, humble as I am, would not
willingly release the part I have taken in that
work.   We have reduced the burden of the
people's taxes eighty millions per annum, and
yet we shall have a surplus, and we can pay
twenty or thirty millions per year, and support
the Government."

After discussing the question of land grants
and subsidies to railroads, for the abuses of
which both parties, Democrat and Republic,
had equally the responsibility, and the Homestead Law, which required amelioration, Mr.
Stevenson spoke in defence of President Grant,
especially in regard to his foreign policy.

" It is very fashionable to denounce Grant
as a failure because he does not say anything.
We are such a talking people that when we
approach a public man, if he does not get up
and spout at us, we think he is a failure.   The
silent men win these days.   How was it across

the water? They say Grant talks ' horse,' and
that sort of talk. Well, I am told that the
Chief of Staff of Prussia (Moltke) is silent.
They say that he is silent in seven languages,
but he speaks loudly in the language of gunpowder. When the campaign was about opening, after that theatrical exhibition at Saar-
brucken where the French Prince was baptized
in fire, as Moltke was walking the town with
brow depressed, considering, no doubt, that
grand strategy which has struck the world
with amazement, a busybody—perhaps, some
Yankee—approached him, determined to have
something out of him anyhow, and so he said,
' How are matters coming on, General?
' Well,' said the General, ' my cabbages are
doing very well, but my potatoes want rain.'
No doubt that man thought he was a failure ;
didn't know anything because he wouldn't tell
it. Now, that is something like General Grant's
manner. But if you want to know whether
there is a man in his clothes, go to him and try
to do something he does not want you to do—
try to keep an office he is determined to put
you out of; try to get an office when he is
determined you shan't; try to turn him from
his conscience and his judgment, and you will
find there is a man in his clothes who is enough
for you, whoever you are.

" Now what is his foreign policy ? What is
it ? It is just no policy at all, and that is just
what we want in foreign affairs. Almighty
God when He made the world and set apart
America for this free people, put the oceans
round her to keep the world away. And it
never was wise for us to entangle our destinies
in the web of foreign affairs. Let it alone, and
let them let us alone. We will affect them ;
we will govern them very much without their
will—and, it may be, without their knowledge ;
but it will be by our example, and by the attractions of our matchless institutions and our
unexampled prosperity.

" We govern them now more than they know
of. As the sun governs the snow on the mountain millions of miles away, so the light and glow
of our free institutions governs and melts the
crowns and thrones and imperial dynasties of
the Old World.

" So let us govern them. I know some hun-
ger and thirst after Cuba—and Cuba will be
ours some day : but then if we get her, we
must not first dabble her with blood or stain
her with wrong. She will come to us finally
by force of attraction, and when she comes she
will come freely, and we will receive her
righteously ; and if we would be blessed in
Cuba, or have Cuba blessed in us, we should

righteously make the union between us. Wrong cannot prosper."

The Alabama claims having been referred to, the speaker gave his opinion regarding the sympathy for France, which led at that time many to desire interference in her behalf.

" But what now shall we do ? Rush in to save the shattered armies of France ? Suppose we did, is not Prussia there ? And how shall we meet that power ?

" But does anybody want us to help Prussia ? Prussia does not need our assistance just now, I think, and there is no need for us to entangle our affairs with theirs. Let us not, in our sympathy for nominal republican institutions, or for real republican institutions anywhere, forget first principles, and one first principle is, that when a war is righteously commenced, it may be righteously prosecuted to a righteous peace, and a righteous peace may well include ' indemnity for the past and security for the future.' And if the victor on the fields of Europe was right in defending his country against invasion, he is right in fighting on until he gets just terms of peace. But they tell us he recognises his God as the source of his power, and, therefore, we should have him put down. I am not so sure. I do most heartily deny that any ruler rules by any right except that given by the

people ; and yet I had much rather see a man
who believes himself such by the grace of God,
than see one on the throne who believes and
knows himself to rule by the machinations of
the devil.   So much for foreign affairs.   They
are foreign. Thank God they are not ours, and
let us keep out of them.''

Other points of public policy being discussed,
the speech closed with reference to local or non-
partisan questions : '' I want to present to the
people of Cincinnati some material considera-
tions for them to reflect upon. Cincinnati is pe-
culiarly situated as to communication. Some
wonder why she does not grow more rapidly.
Let such go down to the wharf at the foot of
Main Street, and look out to the front and to
the right and to the left, and reflect on the condition of that country, and they will understand.
What does Cincinnati want ?   She wants a free
river from Pittsburgh to the Gulf.   What else
does she want ?   She wants a broad high railway leading down from Cincinnati to Chatta-
nooga. And what else does she want ? She
wants an outlet by water to Norfolk.   Give her
these three lines, and she will plume her wings
anew and soar into regions of prosperity far
beyond her rivals. With them she wants a per-
fected system of port of entry, by which her
goods may come from foreign countries without

delay in New York or elsewhere. Now the country is safe, and the Democratic party is safe too ; one safe on the road to prosperity and glory, unexampled in the past, unrivalled in the history of the world, and the other is on the broad downward road."

Mr. Aaron Perry's address also went over the various points dividing the two parties, with a peroration appealing to the patriotic feeling of the audience, who were proud of Ohio and its great city : " Let us advance ! Casting our eyes to the surrounding hills, we find them, from hill to hill throughout the entire circle, adorned with institutions of learning, like jewels in the diadem of our valley queen. They speak of the future. Tracing the rich valleys which concentrate here, we see them obviously des- tined to become the seat of a vast population. They speak of the future. Looking abroad upon our noble State, to its history, its influence, its capacity, they suggest a future of incompar- able happiness. Yet among all there is nothing so bright and glorious as the untroubled peace, the rooted liberty, which fill our whole twenty degrees of latitude and extend from sea to sea."

At the close of Mr. Perry's speech the " meeting adjourned, with three cheers and a tiger for the ticket," the tiger being a strange compound of shout and howl.

I have given some space to my recollection of this meeting, both because it gives opportunity of referring to some of the chief questions of American political controversy, and because of the impression made by the meeting itself. The same orderly and intelligent conduct marks political life throughout the Northern States, out of New York. There may be strong hostility and even violent antagonism; but the opponents speak and act from personal conviction, and as influenced by appeals to their reason and interest through the platform or the press. There is nothing of the hired ruffianism of our English electioneering mob, when besotted and ignorant " lambs " fight for the mere colours of the candidate whose agent has hired them. In nothing is the superiority of the American over the English " lower orders " more evident than in the conduct of their political elections.

Since the settlement of the slavery question, and the reconstruction of the Union, there is no national problem more important than the management of the vast and increasing foreign population. If the emigrants were fewer, or if they all came from Protestant lands, there would be no difficulty. In earlier times all foreigners, even the Irish papists, were absorbed and assimilated, their children going to the common schools, and growing up intelligent and orderly members of the community. But latterly the number of these emigrants has so increased, that not in New York alone, but in all the larger cities, they are forming separate organisations, both under political and religious leaders, and causing much trouble and anxiety. The German element is also large and well organised, but its influence is to be considered more in relation to party questions than to those which affect the general welfare and progress of the commonwealth. Before many years another element of disturbance may be expected in the increase of Chinese emigration, interfering with wages and labour, and other social arrangements. But the most important and pressing difficulty is in connection with the system of common schools and education. In the States of New York and of Ohio this question has already vexed and disturbed the community. Although attracting less notice than the party controversies which divide Americans, this is really of deeper importance, as threatening to interfere with arrangements affecting the national welfare. All patriotic Americans, whether Republicans or Democrats, are interested in maintaining their institutions against this element of disturbance.

17

CHAPTER XVIII.

A N important case, as to the exclusion of the Bible from the common schools of Cincinnati, was decided in the Superior Court of that city a few months before I was there. A brief report of this case will clearly explain the difficulty to which I before referred, the difficulty of uniting various creeds and nationalities under American institutions. In one of the Articles of the Constitution of Ohio State, after declaring religious equality and the rights of conscience, it is added, "Religious morality and knowledge, however, being essential to good government, it shall be the duty of the General Assembly to pass suitable laws, to protect every religious denomination in the peaceable enjoyment of its own mode of worship, and to encourage schools, and the means of instruction."—(Art. VII. of Bill of Rights.) Under a law of 1829 the common schools of Cincinnati were first organised, and for forty years it was the usage to read the Holy Scriptures, without note or comment, in the schools, a portion being read either by the teachers or scholars as an opening exercise.

In the year 1842, at a meeting of the trustees, it being suggested, among other things, that the Catholic children were required to read the Protestant Testament and Bible, it was resolved that " no pupil of the common schools shall be required to read the Testament or Bible, if its parents or guardian desire that it may be excused from that exercise."

This resolution was afterwards discussed by the trustees and visitors of the school then composing the Board of Education, in 1852, when it was again determined that " the opening exercises in every department shall commence by reading a portion of the Bible, by or under the direction of the teachers, and appropriate singing by the pupils ; the pupils of the common schools may read such versions of the Scriptures as their parents and guardians may prefer ; provided that such preference of any version, except the one now in use, be communicated by the parents and guardians to the principal teachers, and that no notes or marginal readings be allowed in the schools, or comments made by the teachers on the text or any version that is or may be introduced."

This was the rule, to which no exception seems to have been taken until November, 1869, when a majority of the Board of Education passed these resolutions : First, "that religious instruction and the reading of religious books, including the Holy Bible, are prohibited in the common schools of Cincinnati, it being the true object and intent of this rule to allow the children of the parents of all sects and opinion in matters of faith and worship to enjoy alike the benefits of the common school fund." Second, "that so much of the regulations in the course of study and text-books in the intermediate and district schools as reads as follows : The opening exercises in every department shall commence by reading a portion of the Bible, by or under the direction of the teachers, and appropriate singing by the pupils—be repealed."

These resolutions of the majority of the School Board were passed by a combination of infidels with Jews and Roman Catholics, strengthened so far by the declared opinion of some good men, that religious instruction could best be given apart from secular teaching. There is no doubt, however, that the resolutions were in the main the result of hostility to revealed truth, and to Christian influence in education. The minority of the Board filed a petition for an injunction against the promulgation, enforcement, or putting in operation of the resolutions. The argument of the case before the full bench of the Superior Court lasted five days, and the decision of the majority of the Court, delivered by Judge Bellamy Storer, was to the effect that the resolutions were opposed to the constitution of the State of Ohio, and were therefore invalid. The use of the Bible was restored, the parents disapproving of the use of the Bible still having the liberty of restraining their children from attendance during the time the Scripture was read. This liberty exists everywhere throughout the Union, but is hardly ever taken advantage of except in circumstances of public agitation, as in Cincinnati. The children of all creeds and nationalities join in the opening exercises, just as we find in India little objection made by parents to the use of the Bible in mission schools, unless when it is put into their heads to murmur by mischievous people, under pretext of guarding against proselytising.

The published opinion of Judge Storer, in giving his decision, was a lucid and masterly statement both of law and principle. He showed

how the Legislature of the State in a variety of
instances recognised the Bible as the foundation
of religion :—

" We find in the class of exemptions of personal property from execution, the family Bible
is especially named, and this, too, before the
homestead and the present privilege of the
debtor were secured by law. So, in the Apprentice law, one of the conditions in the
indenture binding on the master is that he
shall give to the apprentice, at the close of his
term, a new Bible ; and in the statute regulat-
ing county jails, each prisoner is to be supplied
with a copy of the Bible. By the 19th section
of the Penitentiary law, it is made the duty of
the warden to furnish each criminal with a
Bible—who shall permit, as often as he may
think proper, regular ministers of the gospel
to preach to such convicts ; and we are assured
the same rule is adopted in the government of
all our benevolent institutions, including the
House of Refuge and Reform School. Now
it must be recollected that all these institutions
are sustained at the public expense, the property of every person in the State being taxed
to furnish the necessary means. And yet,
while .the Scriptures are made indispensable
for every penal, reformatory, and benevolent
institution, it is claimed they cannot be intro-

duced into the common schools, and if found there, either used or read, shall thereafter be prohibited.

" Nay, more, while that volume is found in every court of justice, and the two houses of the General Assembly, upon which we, the Judges of this Court, have been sworn to administer justice and uphold the constitution and laws, it is expelled from our common schools, thus making it the only exception to its recognition as an exponent of religion and morality. There is, then, no prohibition of the Bible, by law, as a book to be read or used in the education of our youth, nor do we think that it can be implied from the letter or the spirit of our organic law.

*   *   *   *   *

" But it is said by one of the counsel who has so ably argued for the defendants, ' that when the constitution says religion and morality and knowledge are essential to good government, it simply means that the intuitive sense of right and wrong shall be brought out by exercise and developed ; the only religion that it considers vital to the preservation of the State is that which is written upon human nature.' This is a bold proposition, and one that is, it seems to us, most difficult to sustain upon any other

ground than that which would justify the devo-
tee to be crushed beneath the car of Juggernaut,
the Hindoostan widow to cast herself upon the
funeral pile of her husband, or the revolting
cannibalism that once prevailed in the islands
of the South Sea.   Nay, further, on this hypo-
thesis we may vindicate the orgies of the heathen temples in the most enlightened ages of
the past, when the Roman could utter the exclamation, ' *O dii, immortales,*' and yet sacrifice
to Venus, to Bacchus, and to Mars.

"To our apprehension it does not appear
probable that our law-makers would have sanc-
tioned such a rule, if it had ever been proposed ;
and their silence as to such a suggestion is ra-
tionally conclusive that they never could have
seriously entertained it.   Without the teachings
of the Holy Scriptures there is, we believe, no
unvarying standard of moral duty, no code of
ethics which inculcates willing obedience to law,
and establishes human governments upon the
broad foundation of the will of God.   Hence, it
was the great purpose of the clause in the Bill
of Rights, to which we have already referred, to
announce the deep conviction—we might say,
the authoritative opinion—that religion was
necessary to good government, not the sha-
dowy view of man's duty which lets in upon the
vision a faint ray of light to make the surround-

ing darkness more visible, but the recognition of an Almighty power, demonstrable, it is true, by what meets our vision, but alone subjectively taught by His revealed will.

" Yet, it is said, the natural conscience is to be taught, the instinctive sense of right and wrong is to be brought out by exercise and developed ; but we are not told what is to be the exercise, or how the development is to be effected. What is to be the process by which the minds of the young are to be cast into the crucible and refined from any innate or acquired impurity ? What high and holy motive is to be addressed to the pupil, when his origin, the purpose of his probation on earth, and all knowledge of a hereafter, are not only to be withheld, but the volume which discloses them is ostracised as one not only unfit to be read, but as conflicting with the conscience that has never yet, perhaps, been enlightened by its truth ?

" It cannot be claimed that good government can exist where there is no religion which embodies the idea of obedience to God ; but, on the contrary, the will of every man may be the true arbiter of his conduct and the measure of his responsibility ; for if such a dogma should be allowed, all restraint upon human passion, every check upon the oppression of the few by the despotism of the many, would cease, every individual being a law unto himself, defending his conduct by the assumption that he conscientiously believed he had the right to do so. In such a war of conflicting elements the strife of opinion would be uncontrolled, and the moral power of our republic be made to depend upon individual caprice, precipitating, at no distant day, the now freest and happiest government on earth into remediless ruin."

These are weighty words, and if space allowed I would gladly quote more of the learned judge's opinion, as applicable to discussions arising in our own School Boards. It is possible that the agitation in America will continue, and modifications may be made in the organisation of schools in some places; but every well-wisher of America will rejoice in the defeat of these attempts to separate religion from education.

Judge Storer clearly laid down the distinction between "religion" and "religious denominations;" the latter including all shades of theoretic as well as practical belief, but the former being essential as the foundation of morality and order in a Christian commonwealth.

Failing to exclude the Bible and religious teaching from the schools, an attempt has been made in New York and elsewhere to divide the school rate, and apportion it to schools of various creeds and principles. This also has been successfully resisted, and the Roman Catholics and other malcontents have to provide funds for their own separate schools. It is to be hoped that all true Americans will keep united and firm in maintaining the Common School System,* which is the greatest strength and glory of their commonwealth.

It may be well to mention what is the "use of the Bible," about which so much ado has been made. This is what I saw in the Ninth District School of Cincinnati, one of the largest and best-ordered schools of the city, except that there is no playground or space of any kind for amusements. And I may remark, in passing, that there is too commonly a deficiency in physical training in the schools. Much work and little play is the rule, and the health of the children suffers from over-study and "competition." But to proceed. The school meets at nine, and commences with what are

---

* It may be necessary to inform some readers that there is no national system of education in America—that is, under the Central Government. Every State has its own educational laws and usages, varying in many respects, but agreeing as yet, in using the Bible. In the Southern States, before the war, Common Schools were almost unknown ; but they have been since established, and are rapidly multiplying.

called the "opening exercises." There are
numerous rooms, in pairs, for boys and girls
of various ages, from five or six to fourteen
years, and various stages of advancement. In
the girls' schoolroom, when I was present, the
German master took his place at a piano, and
folding or sliding doors being opened, the boys
from the adjoining room marched in to the
notes of a cheery strain, accompanied by their
teachers. A hymn was then sung, and capi-
tally sung, too; then the senior master read a
portion of the New Testament, without comment. This was followed by another hymn,
after which the boys marched back in the same
orderly way to their own class-room. There
was nothing in this to touch the prejudices or
susceptibilities of the most bigoted parent or
proselytiser. The uniting in familiar words of
praise and thanksgiving, and the reverential
use of God's revealed word, cannot but have a
good influence on the feelings and habits of the
young; and the formal exclusion of the Bible
thus used can only be sought by those who are
opposed to all acknowledgment of Divine power
and goodness. A blessing is sought, and may
be expected from the official recognition of
religion in the "opening exercises." But in
reality the controversy about the detention or
the removal of the Bible can have little influ-

ence in a practical way. A godly teacher could instil principles of piety and virtue if the use of the Bible were interdicted, while an ungodly teacher could injure the minds of his pupils, even if creeds as well as the word of God were required to be taught. In America, as well as with us in England, the vital point is to have teachers of the right stamp, both of head and heart. It would be a disgrace to the State of Ohio, and the School Board of Cincinnati, if the Bible were expelled; but if the training schools for teachers do their duty, all will be well. It is the schoolmaster that makes the school.

At Cincinnati I found a good many Scotch residents, more in proportion than in other cities. A firm of brewers, three brothers from Edinburgh, were said to brew the best beer in these regions, and Cincinnati is famous for its beer. The Germans are numerous, and are great consumers of malt liquors. The chief bookseller in the place, Robert Clarke, is a Scotchman. From another Scotchman, Mr. James Macgregor, who had known the city for forty years, I obtained much interesting information about its history and progress, and feel grateful for his generous and unwearied attention. At Mount Auburn I went to visit a veteran of the British army, Colonel Lachlan, infirm in health, but with mind clear and active. He was a native of Edinburgh, and I remember him coming back there with his regiment, the 17th, after serving in India and Burmah. On retiring from the army he had emigrated to America, first residing in Canada and afterwards at Cincinnati. It was pleasant to have a talk about Edinburgh scenes and people in his retreat at Mount Auburn. I have since heard of his death, in his ninetieth year.

I went one day with my aged friend to the funeral of the daughter of a neighbour on Mount Auburn. The parents being much respected, and the girl much beloved, a great company had assembled, friends of the family, and members of the church, in the Sunday-school of which she had been a teacher. The two large rooms on a ground-floor were densely filled, and numbers also sat in the hall and on the steps of the staircase. The coffin, with glass top, stood on trestles in the room in which the service was conducted by the officiating minister. The service resembled that in use in Scotland—prayer, reading the Scripture, and an address. The latter was as long as a sermon, but the minister may have thought more than usual was expected from him, as he had been invited all the way from New England, being an old friend of the family. The

most unreal part of the service was the singing
of a set anthem by a quartette choir, brought
for the purpose and seated in the hall. These
quartette choirs were already too familiar to
me as performing by proxy the service of song
in the churches, but their intrusion at a funeral
startled me. After the service, the whole of
the guests passed round the coffin to take a
last view of the deceased. The coffin was carried to the ornamental hearse outside by eight
or ten young ladies, fellow-teachers at the
Sunday-school. This custom, I suppose, has
been introduced by the Germans. The body
was richly attired, the coffin strewed with
myrtle wreaths, and the bearers dressed in
white. I have already described the ornamental hearses used in America, and the absence of general mourning, whether in dress or
in the appearance of the coaches. Of these
there was a large number, as upwards of a hundred people went to the place of burial in
Spring Grove Cemetery, three or four miles
distant. I find it is the custom to have imposing funerals, a custom often entailing need-
lessly heavy expense. But at such seasons bereaved families are as helplessly at the mercy
of " funeral fashion " as in our own country.
There appears also to be an immense amount of
ostentation and emulation in the monuments

of the cemeteries. I noticed this elsewhere, but had more time at Cincinnati to make observations and inquiries. There are many monuments at Spring Grove Cemetery which cost thousands of dollars each. I saw several of Peterhead granite, which had been brought across the Atlantic to New Orleans, and thence up the Mississippi and the Ohio to Cincinnati. Some of these polished granite monuments must have cost at least 5,000 dollars. Marble pyramids or columns surmounted by an angel seemed a favourite design. By far the most striking monument in the cemetery is that over the bodies of soldiers who fell in the war of the rebellion,—the bronze figure of a sentinel, armed as on duty, watching the burial-place,—a monument grand in design and in execution.

CHAPTER XIX.

COLUMBIA DISTRICT — WASHINGTON CITY — THE
CAPITOL — THE TREATY OF WASHINGTON —
YOUNG MEN'S CHRISTIAN ASSOCIATION — THE
FREEDMEN'S BUREAU.

THE "District of Columbia" is a tract of
country with an area of sixty square miles,
set apart as the seat of the Federal Government.
It is neither State nor Territory, but a neutral
soil appropriated to the Commonwealth. The
land was ceded by Maryland State, which
bounds it on three sides, the fourth side being
bounded by the Potomac, which separates it
from Virginia. Originally, the District occupied one hundred square miles; but forty,
ceded by Virginia, were restored to that State
in 1846. Columbia District is under the direct
government of Congress, its inhabitants having
no representatives, and no voice in the Federal
elections.

The object in setting apart this District was
to secure a site free from the influence of any

18

particular State. Proposals have been made
to transfer the seat of government to one of
the larger cities. Washington, it is said, is
situated in a *cul-de-sac*, "in the foot of a stocking," as one of its people described it to me,
off the great highways of travel, and "leading
nowhere particular." So much the better for
Washington and for the Federal Government.
If Congress were held in New York, or any
great city either of the North or South, or in
St. Louis or Chicago, the latest claimants for
metropolitan dignity, the advantages of seclu-
sion and independence would be lost. The
choice of the founders of the Republic was
prudent and far-seeing, and it is well that both
the supreme legislative and judicial courts sit in
the serene atmosphere of Columbia District.

It was Washington himself who chose the
site, and who laid the corner-stone of the Capitol, and approved the plan of the metropolitan
city. This was in 1793, seven years before the
removal of the seat of government from Philadelphia.* Though intended to be free from
the influence of any of the State capitals, the
hope was cherished of the metropolis of the

* In 1814, the Capitol, with the President's house and other
buildings, was burnt by the British. It was repaired in 1818;
and not till 1851 was the foundation-stone laid, by President
Fillmore, of the new buildings, by which the original design was
enlarged to more than double its size.

Union becoming itself a great city. The ground was laid out, and the avenues and streets planned, on a vast scale. Only a small part of the design has yet been completed, and · hence the sarcastic epithet of "the city of magnificent distances." It is a city of magnificent edifices, at all events. Besides the Capitol, the grandeur of which surpasses expectation, the Patent Office, the Post Office, and above all the Treasury, are worthy of the great Republic. The President's mansion, or the White House, the Smithsonian Institute, and several of the hotels, are also imposing buildings.

The city has certainly an unfinished aspect, and is a place of prospective rather than present grandeur, like the huge truncated structure—looking now like a gigantic milestone—intended to be "the Washington Monument." But I did not find Washington so desolate a place as I had been led to expect from the exaggerated statements of travellers. Some of the streets were alive with traffic and business, and the splendid Pennsylvania Avenue always cheery and animated. I was there in September, the dullest season of the year, when few carriages or equipages are to be seen, but the omnibuses and cars were well filled. Few cities present greater contrast at different seasons. During the session of Congress, the population is largely increased.   But even without this accession there is an air of healthy progress about the place.   The census of 1850 gave the population about 40,000; in 1860 it had reached 61,000, and in 1870 the number was 109,388. Chicago and St. Louis alone of all the great cities showed a larger ratio of increase in the last decennial period.

I stayed at Ebbitt House, near the Treasury, one of the most comfortable of the many great hotels with which Washington abounds.   It is a house frequented by government officials and others who have to pass much time in the city, and I have pleasant recollections of the courtesy and companionship of men I met there. It was an agreeable change and quiet resting-place from the *caravanserais*, with their ever-shifting multitudes, in the great commercial towns.   Street cars from the railway depôt pass the door, and Pennsylvania Avenue is only a few paces distant.   I see that the Avenue, one of the grandest thoroughfares in the world, a mile long and over a hundred feet broad, has been lately paved with wood, an improvement much needed and long spoken of.   The citizens had a regular "carnival" on the occasion, with music and all sorts of sports, including burlesque masquerades, parades, and processions, in which public personages were cleverly "taken off."

One of the groups was " the first female President of the United States," with a cabinet of ladies, and a body-guard of female voters, a ludicrous illustration of the contempt in which the advocacy of "woman's rights" is held in the American capital.

At the same time, the Government sets a good example in providing legitimate occupation for females, by largely employing them in the public offices. These close early in the afternoon, and several times when at the door of Ebbitt House I saw squads of " the Treasury regiment" pass, on their way home from work, and smart, cheerful, independent-looking girls they were. All over the union, in post offices, telegraph offices, and other public institutions, female *employées* are found, to far larger extent than with us in England.

Georgetown, the only other town in Columbia District, is a place of some interest. Dating from old British times, there is an air of antiquity about it, compared with the modern capital. The surrounding heights are covered with fine mansions and villas, and Oak Hill cemetery is a beautiful spot. From the Capitol to Georgetown there is a tramway, and the three or four miles of road seemed always busy with traffic.

On seeing the historical fresco paintings on

the walls of the Rotunda in the Capitol, I recognised scenes already familiar to me from
their being engraved on the dollar bills and
paper currency of a higher value. The American bank notes have always been famous for
the excellence of their pictorial work. The
drawing and engraving being the best that the
country can yield, attempts at forgery are easily
detected. The artistic skill necessary for producing these pictures is rarer than the mechanical skill by which frauds in paper marks, or
in printing, could be executed. Imitations of
unpictured notes of smaller value are more
frequent.

Of the eight pictures, the early scenes, such
as that of Columbus in sight of the New World,
and De Soto discovering the Mississippi, represent historical events in which all spectators
have a common interest. The later scenes,
such as the surrender of the British troops to
General Washington, are not flattering to British visitors, some of whom describe the humiliation and vexation with which they view them.
I confess I had nothing of this feeling, but
rather regarded them with as much pride and
pleasure as any native American. Washington
and the other founders of the Republic were
true Englishmen, British colonists of the right
stamp; and the victories they won were victo-

ries of freedom and right over tyranny and wrong. They maintained on the soil of the New World the same principles which the people of England held in opposition to the Court. They were the successors of Pym and Hampden, of the puritan heroes and pilgrim fathers of the seventeenth century. Every liberal Englishman now condemns, as much as the great Chatham did, the blundering policy which lost America to the British Crown.

Though the nations are divided, the people ought to be again united in sympathy and friendship, as they are one in origin, in language, and in faith. The time is past for speaking disparagingly of American institutions. These English over the sea will be soon before us in population and in power, as they are already before us in education and in most things that make the well-being of a great commonwealth. In the troublous times that are coming upon Europe we may need the alliance of their strong power, as many may have to seek the sanctuary of their free soil amidst the calamities that are to come on the Old World " in the latter day."

Washington was almost a blank at the time of my visit, so far as political life is concerned. The Senate Chamber and Hall of Representatives were both under repair, the benches all pulled to pieces for rearrangement. Workmen were busy in other places, both outside and inside the Capitol. The White House was also in the hands of painters and decorators. The President was at the seaside, at Long Branch, and all the Cabinet and officials dispersed. Mr. Fish, the Secretary of State, was alone at his post, the only visible sign of Government of any sort. He was literally alone, living *en garçon*, his family being absent. All the foreign ministers and ambassadors were enjoying the holiday season, except Sir Edward Thornton, who was alone, like Mr. Fish, detained by his important duties. Through the private introduction of a friend, I had the privilege of a long interview with the Secretary of State. I took the opportunity of speaking of the strong and general feeling of respect and affection for America which pervaded the British people—a feeling which was not fairly represented, especially during the war, by our Government or by the Press. The *Times*, and the journals misled by it, did not then express the real state of public opinion on the Alabama claims, or on any of the great questions which continue to cause international irritation. Mr. Fish expressed himself with so much frankness and earnestness as to his desire to have a speedy settlement, that I could not help writing to our Foreign Office a memorandum of his conversation. The generous spirit shown by American statesmen, and their readiness to forget the undoubted wrong done to their country by British sympathy with the Southern rebels, required concession on our part, and with men of high honour and noble character like Lord Granville and Mr. Gladstone, this was not difficult. The Treaty of Washington, whatever may be its results in details, is honourable to both nations, and the feeling on each side the Atlantic is widely different now from what it was but a year ago. Even the British minister at Washington was at that time not sanguine as to a peaceful solution, judging by the diplomatic situation. But Government and the Press, in this as in other great questions, had to follow public opinion, which happily was pronouncing with increasing urgency for peace and goodwill between the two nations.

In reviewing the debate in the House of Lords on Earl Russell's motion on the Treaty, the *Times* admits that "the expression in the preamble of the treaty of regret at the escape of the Alabama, 'under whatever circumstances,' is 'without precedent, and eminently calculated to shock the sentiment of diplomatic propriety.' But then, we fear it is without precedent for

two nations to resolve upon making up differences so grave without resort to arms, in the
manner prescribed by Christianity, and constantly adopted in private life. If this noble
resolve be called national humiliation, let us
glory in the reproach ; and if saying now what
ought to have been said ten years ago lowers
us in the estimation of Europe, let us hope that
Europe will before long rise to a higher conception of international fellowship." These are
truly noble sentiments, and make some amends
for the evil done by the *Times* when lending its
influence to the Southern rebels during the
war.

The Young Men's Christian Association at
Washington has a handsome building and commodious rooms at the corner of Ninth and D
streets. The American Young Men's Association has its head quarters, and its finest establishment, like a London club-house, at New
York, and branches in almost every town in the
Union. It is an institution of far more influence
than the similar associations in England. An
annual meeting of representatives from the
various associations throughout the country is
held at different cities. Foreign delegates are
also present, so that the meeting is really an
international convention. The meeting of this
year (1871) at Washington has been one of the

largest and most important Christian gatherings ever held in the States.

The Association is not confined to young men, as the name might imply; at least the term, like the Irish one of "boys," covers all ages. The president of the Washington Association is a veteran soldier, Major-General Oliver Howard, from whom I had a hearty reception as a stranger from the old country. They may well be proud of having such a man at their head. He was one of the most distinguished officers during the war. He was present in many of the hardest-fought fields, and lost his right arm at the battle of Fair Oaks. It was he who received the last charge of Stonewall Jackson at Chancellorsville. Alas, that two such men should have met in hostile array! He helped materially to gain the victory at Gettysburg, which finally turned the tide of the war. And in Sherman's grand march through Georgia to the sea, it was Howard who commanded the right wing of the army. To some of my friends of the Peace Society these may seem sinister topics for praise, but if ever a war was justifiable, it was that into which the American Government was unwillingly compelled in self-defence against the armed violence of the Southern rebels—a war which preserved the Union, and brought freedom to the slave.

Happily, General Howard lived to achieve more noble triumphs on peaceful fields. Appointed chief of the Freedmen's Bureau, he conducted with admirable skill, tact, and temper the most difficult business that arose out of the war. Of the four millions and a half of coloured people suddenly emancipated by the collapse of the South, vast numbers were exposed to privation and peril. Arrangements had to be made for receiving and sheltering fugitives and exiles, for feeding the hungry, tending the sick and aged, providing work for the able-bodied, and for education. All this and more was accomplished by the Freedmen's Bureau, and the success was largely due to the energy, ability, and Christian philanthropy of General Howard.

A work so beneficent, being done in behalf of the oppressed negro race, could not escape bitter opposition from the friends of slavery. Attacks were even made on the Chief Commissioner as having engaged in the work from interested motives. A committee of Congress having been appointed to inquire into these charges, declared them to be "groundless and causeless slanders," and the House passed a resolution that "the great trust committed to General Howard had been performed wisely, disinterestedly, economically, and successfully," and that "he is deserving of the gratitude of the whole American people." "With God on its side," added the report, "the Freedmen's Bureau, though encountering the bitterest opposition and the most unrelenting hate, has triumphed ; civilization has received a new impulse, and the friends of humanity may well rejoice."

An American journalist, Sidney Andrews, thus summed up the work in behalf of the freedmen :—

"Of the thousand things that the Bureau has done, no balance-sheet can ever be made. How it helped the ministries of the church, saved the blacks from robbery and persecution, enforced respect for the negro's rights, instructed all the people in the meaning of the law, threw itself against the strongholds of intemperance, settled neighbourhood quarrels, brought about amicable relations between employer and employed, comforted the sorrowful, raised up the downhearted, corrected bad habits among whites and blacks, restored order, sustained contracts for work, compelled attention to the statute books, collected claims, furthered local educational movements, gave sanctity to the marriage relation, dignified labour, strengthened men and women in good resolutions, rooted out old prejudices, ennobled the home, assisted the freedmen to become landowners, brought offenders to justice, broke up bands of outlaws, over-turned the class-rule of ignorance, led bitter hearts into brighter ways, shamed strong hearts into charity and forgiveness, promulgated the new doctrine of equal rights, destroyed the seeds of mistrust and antagonism, cheered the despondent, set idlers at work, aided in the reorganisation of society, carried the light of the North into dark places of the South, steadied the negro in his struggle with novel ideas, in-culcated kindly feeling, checked the passion of whites and blacks, opened the blind eyes of judges and jurors, taught the gospel of forbear-ance, encouraged human sympathy, distributed the generous charities of the benevolent, up-held loyalty, assisted in creating a sentiment of nationality—how it did all this, and a hundred-fold more, who shall ever tell ? what pen shall ever record ? "

These are warm and generous words. They are eloquent. But the facts they state are still more eloquent.

The territory embraced by the operations of the Bureau comprised the States of Virginia, North Carolina, South Carolina, Georgia, Florida, Alabama, Mississippi, Louisiana, Texas, Arkansas, Tennessee, Kentucky, Missouri, Kan-sas, Delaware, Maryland, West Virginia, and the District of Columbia. The colossal proportions of the work of the Bureau will be seen at a glance. Its operations extended over 300,000 square miles of territory devastated by the greatest war of modern times, more than four millions of its people sunk in the lowest depths of ignorance by two centuries of slavery, and suddenly set free amid the fierce animosities of war—free, but poor, helpless, and starving. Here, truly, was a most appalling condition of things. Not only the destiny of the liberated race was in the balance, but the life of the nation itself depended upon the correct solution of this intricate problem. But it has been solved. At the close of the war famine looked the South in the face. There was a cry for bread throughout the southern country. It was sneeringly said by the enemies of emancipation that the negro would not labour. Satisfied by the Bureau that contracts would be enforced, that justice would be administered, with words of encouragement whispered in his ear, the negro went to work. The battle-ploughed, trampled fields of the South yielded a wealth of production that seemed not the result of human labour, but as if " earth had again grown quick with God's creating breath,'' —for the crops in the South have been larger, proportionately, since the war than at any previous time.

It was not only or chiefly the means of existence, and fields for labour, that the friends of
the freedmen sought to provide. The work of
education had to be commenced. Before the
attention of the Government or of Congress had
been called to this matter, private associations
had already been formed in the different States.
The Society of Friends, as usual, took a promi-
nent part in this good work. But it was a
cause which touched all Christian hearts. We
have pleasure in giving an extract from the
official report sent by a Frenchman, M. Hippeau, to the Minister of Public Instruction of
France :—

"It would be impossible to convey an idea of
the energy and friendly rivalry displayed by the
women of America in this truly Christian work.
In the year 1862 public meetings were held
in New York, Boston, and Philadelphia, and
soon were formed, under the double influence
of humanity and religion, the 'Association for
the Aid of Freedmen' and the 'Missionary
Association' in New York ; the 'Committee of
Education' in Boston; the 'Societies of Education' of Philadelphia, Cincinnati, and Chicago.
Several periodicals were established to publish
the results achieved by each of these societies,
to announce the voluntary donations collected
by the committees, and to publish the letters

and reports from all the different places where-
in the protectors of the blacks were exercising
their beneficent functions. In one year 1,500
schools for coloured pupils were opened. No
sooner had the Northern army captured a new
city, than a host of devoted teachers of both
sexes also entered it. In incorporating negroes
into the Northern armies, the Union generals
formed regimental schools for them ; and Sherman in Georgia, Banks in Louisiana, and
Howard in Tennessee, evinced, in forwarding
this great work of humanity, no less interest
and energy than in the prosecution of the
war.

" And it should be here stated, to the
honour of a race so long disinherited, so long
condemned to degradation, to brutality, to
ignorance (a law of the South punishing with
death any one convicted of teaching a slave to
read or write), that no spectacle could be more
touching than that offered by these helpless,
unfortunate men, old and young, women and
children, as eager to rush to the schools established for the regeneration of their minds and
souls as to the places where they were provided with food and shelter. Never did a
famished man pounce more eagerly upon food
placed before him than did these poor fugitives
upon the bread of knowledge, a sublime instinct

causing them to regard education as the first condition of their regeneration.

" The beneficent Peabody consecrated five million francs to the schools of the South. One association, the American Missionary Association, received more than 45,000 francs per month ; but this sum was insufficient to alleviate to a great extent the vast amount of physical and moral suffering which, existed. Congress gave forty-five millions of francs to the Freedmen's Bureau, the presidency of which was confided by Lincoln to General Howard. What this Bureau has accomplished since the day of his installation is incredible. The unfortunates out of whom men and citizens were to be made required all kinds of assistance. They not only needed schools, but hospitals ; and these latter were established for them. From 1861 to 1866, nearly four hundred thousand freedmen had filled the forty-eight hospitals created for them, and in which twenty thousand succumbed to misery, fatigue, and wounds received in fighting for the cause which assured to their race liberty and independence.

" Such was the devotion of the men and women occupied in the education of children, that the number of schools increased so rapidly (there were four thousand at the commencement of 1868) that more teachers were required than the North and West could supply. The generals and superintendents of the Freedmen's Bureau partially supplied this want by creating normal schools for the blacks, and by confiding to them, as soon as they acquired the rudiments of reading, writing, and arithmetic, the responsibility of communicating their knowledge to others. Admirable pupils, they became excellent professors. They themselves were then able to found schools, no one knows at the price of what sacrifices and what privations. In 1868, they supported at their own cost twelve hundred schools, and owned three hundred and ninety-one school buildings.

" One fact alone goes to show the importance attached by them to education. In 1863, Louisiana had schools enough, supported by taxation, to furnish instruction to 50,000 freed persons. Pressing needs having caused the abolishment of the tax, they were at first disheartened, but they soon regained their courage. They held meetings. Already they were paying, like the whites, a tax levied for public instruction, but which was employed entirely to sustain schools for the whites, and from which the blacks were excluded. Notwithstanding this injustice, they demanded to be authorized to furnish a special contribution for the education of their children, and, at the same time, were willing to pay the general school tax, and maintain their own schools themselves. In a few years the emancipated race had already elevated itself to the level of the civilizing race.

" Surely the American people are entitled to admiration and thanks for the generous ardour with which they have lavished their gold and employed their noble and powerful initiative in giving to their new brethren all the advantages which accrue from education."

It was in Washington that the first schools for the education of the children of freedmen were established. Not satisfied with primary schools, General Howard planned schools of higher grade, and a university, with faculties of literature, law, medicine, and other departments. The design has been carried out, and Howard University will remain as the noblest monument of its distinguished founder. The university buildings occupy a fine site two or three miles north-east of the capital. The college session had not commenced when I was at Washington, but I had the pleasure of visiting the preparatory and normal schools. The opening exercises at 8 A.M. were conducted by General Howard, who takes the most zealous and watchful supervision over the

whole course of training. The largest class-
room was crowded on every bench with happy,
healthy young "darkies." I never saw an
array of more attentive, intelligent faces, and
never heard sweeter and heartier voices than
in that school, when the hymns were sung,
after reading the Holy Scriptures, and prayer.
It was one of the brightest scenes, altogether,
that I witnessed in America, and the more so
that I knew it was but a sample of what the
Freedmen's Bureau has accomplished in hundreds of places in the Southern States.

As to the intellectual capacity of coloured
children, I prefer quoting testimonies of more
weight than my own. The Rev. Mr. Zincke
says: "I must confess my astonishment at the
intellectual acuteness displayed by a class of
coloured pupils. They had acquired, in a
short space of time, an amount of knowledge
truly remarkable ; never in any school in
England, and I have visited many, have I
found the pupils able to comprehend so readily
the sense of their lessons; never have I heard
pupils ask questions which showed a clearer
comprehension of the subject they were studying." Nor is this intelligence mere "quick-
ness at the uptake," as the Scotch call it, or
precocious acuteness in acquiring knowledge
soon to be forgotten. M. Hippeau visited

Oberlin College, and what he saw entirely confirmed the opinions formed in the schools of the South. " The coloured girls in the highest classes," he says, " appeared in no way inferior to their white companions of the same age." In 1868 the degree of B.A. was conferred upon fifteen young coloured men, and ten young coloured women. The principal of the college, in his address to the students, stated that in literary taste and ability these coloured pupils were unexcelled by any of their white fellow-graduates. The professors all gave the same testimony as to their pupils, and with regard to moral character, M. Hippeau was assured that the negro race formed a fifth of the whole population of Oberlin, and that "the most peaceable, well-behaved, and studious citizens of the place belonged to the coloured race."

Having given these testimonies, I need not express my own opinion, as formed by a visit to the Howard University. Whatever may be the inferiority from natural constitution, or from the effects of centuries of oppression and wrong, there is the same capacity in the coloured race as in the white for indefinite improvement by intellectual and moral culture. Above all, the power of Divine truth and grace can bring men of all races to the same high standard of Christian excellence, of which many noble examples are found in the United States, both in Church and State.

I have devoted a large proportion of space in my chapter on Washington to this subject of the coloured people and the Freedmen's Bureau. Mere descriptions of the city and its sights are found in every guide-book and journal of travels. The condition of the people has a far deeper and enduring interest. I found myself at Washington for the first time in a place where the coloured race forms a large proportion of the population, and had an opportunity of studying their position and prospects. If the work of the Freedmen's Schools and the Howard University is well sustained, there is no risk of weakness, but rather the certainty of increased strength and power to the Republic from the accession of the coloured race to equal civil and political rights.

CHAPTER XX.

AMERICAN POLITICS.

MY visit to Washington being at the dull season, I had no opportunity of seeing notable politicians * or hearing party debates. But I had time to make some observations on the general principles of the United States Government.

I spent one morning in looking through the published acts of Congress, the national statute law of the Republic. The whole are comprised in a series of about twenty volumes octavo. One volume is wholly occupied with Indian affairs, and the historian and ethnologist will find here ample materials for studying

---

* I heard from good sources many proofs of the corruption and venality of public men, strange anecdotes also about wire-pullers and office-seekers, not only at Washington, but in various State legislatures. But I refrain from dwelling on these abuses. They are things not peculiar to American institutions, though certainly too prevalent in the United States, owing to the strifes of party, and the leaving so much to the management of professed "politicians," a larger class than the electioneering "agents" with us.

the relations of the Red and White men from the beginning till now. Another volume records all financial transactions, including grants of money or land; and in turning over its pages I found interesting records about Washington, and Lafayette, and Kosciusko, and Kossuth, and other historical notables.

But apart from matters of curious interest, the inspection of the Acts of Congress showed me how small a part the central power holds in the actual history and life of the American nation. The basis of social and political life is the " township," or " *commune,*" with local independent government. The legislation for these communities belongs to the State governments, and the State laws represent local customs and usages, on the foundation of English Common Law. The good old Anglo-Saxon institutions thus flourish on American soil, and the hosts of immigrants, of all creeds and nationalities, have to conform in civil and municipal life to the good and free institutions of the country, a wonderful transformation to many of them.

Excluding all the legislation that has arisen out of slavery, and out of war, and out of tariffs and other interferences with free trade, the Acts of Congress shrink into small dimensions. If the good times could come of uni-

versal peace and universal freedom, including
freedom of commerce, the central government
of the Republic would have comparatively little
work to do.　For individual happiness and for
social well-being, the separate communities
and the State governments could provide, without any Congress at Washington, the elections
for which bring disturbance throughout the
Union, and must often be found a bore instead
of an advantage.

But that good time is not yet.　Besides matters of common interest, such as judicial and
postal arrangements, there are questions that
require united force, for which the separate
States would not have enough power.　For instance, the Northern free States might have
saved themselves vast expenditure of money
and of precious lives if they had left the Southern States to regulate their own institutions.
On selfish grounds many might gladly dispense
with central or federal government; but for
the welfare of the whole nation, and for the
progress of truth and right, the stronger the
national government is, the better for America
and for all the world.　There must be a central
power, and a standing army to enforce obedience to that power, whether against rebellious
States, as in the great war, or against Mormon
or Indian lawlessness, and other contingencies.

A Southern gentleman told me that the
Confederates were all surprised at the patriotic
enthusiasm evoked in defence of the national
flag when the war of secession was declared.
They thought that the advocacy of States'
rights would have neutralised this feeling.
But now more than ever Federal union is a
first principle, and the national flag has more
power than before. And well for the world
that it has. With the British Union flag may
the " Stars and Stripes" ever be in close
alliance! There may be need for their joint
action in China and the East, if nowhere else.
The alliance with France is an unnatural one
compared with this. The Crimean war, for
instance, arose out of squabbles between the
Greek Church and the Romish Church about
the Holy Places, and never had any higher
principle than maintaining the Mohammedan
empire of the Turks. We have wasted countless lives, and incurred vast debt, in vain attempts to maintain " the balance of power,"
or to uphold ungrateful dynasties in Europe.
The alliance of America and England can
never be for such miserable purposes, but for
worthy objects of freedom and civilization
through the world. Therefore, though the
predominance of States' rights over central
government might be better for the Americans

alone, for the good of the world we hope for increase of the federal power of the Union.

This leads me to say a few words about political parties in the Union. There now are really only two great political parties, the Ins and the Outs. At each quadrennial election there is a universal scramble for office, including "loaves and fishes," as well as honours. For it must be remembered that each new government implies the removal of scores of thousands of office-holders, from the highest to the lowest functionaries, at home and abroad. This is the worst and weakest point in the whole American system as now worked. It makes all people strive for party instead of the Commonwealth. It is not an essential part of the Constitution, dating only from the time of President Jackson. Nominally, the Democrats and Republicans are at present the candidates for office. But there is no sharp division between these opponents. Many Democrats hold the same principles as the Republicans on some points, and not a question can be raised that has not advocates among either side. The Republicans of the West do not like the high tariff and protection ticket of the Republicans of the East. The Democrats of the West, lovers of Union and of freedom, have nothing in common with the Democrats of

New York and the Border States, who sympathised with the slaveholders, and carried the disastrous slavery compromises. These compromises involved the free States in the calamities and "judgments" of the war. The Republican party saved the country by its high principles, and it is sad now to see it opposed by Democrats, many of whom were with it in defending the Union, merely because they must have their turn of office. If the good men of both the Republican and Democratic parties were allied, they could form a great and strong government, on a broader platform than the old "native American," comprising the best statesmen and administrators of the nation, and be able to resist the evil .influences which weaken the Commonwealth. There would be progress then in all matters of social and political welfare, whereas now there is sheer waste of power in the party strife of the Ins and Outs.

After the great fire in Chicago, the leading politicians met, and said that a party contest would be unseemly, in the presence of common calamity and danger. Why should not this principle be carried out through the nation? There are perils against which good men should unite ; and it will be a happy time in England, as well as America, when party strife is merged in patriotic coalition.

CHAPTER XXI.

PHILADELPHIA—ASSOCIATIONS OF PENN AND
FRANKLIN — THE STATE HOUSE — HOMES OF
THE WORKING CLASSES—PHILADELPHIA AND
GLASGOW COMPARED—CHURCHES—THE PRESS
—THE PHILADELPHIA LEDGER.

A T Philadelphia, as at Boston, I was upon
old classical and historical ground. The
memories of William Penn and Benjamin Franklin, of the Founders of Pennsylvania and the
Fathers of the Republic, haunt the place. The
first English settlement here was not, as elsewhere, achieved by violence and treachery, but
by amicable arrangement with the Indian pos-
sessors of the soil, and a blessing seems to have
descended upon the successors of the early
peaceful settlers. Even during the troubles of
the Revolution the city escaped the horrors of
war. Except the brief occupation by the
British troops after the battle of Germantown,
the patriots retained possession of Philadelphia,
the centre of their influence and the seat of their

Councils. It was in the State House that the Declaration of Independence was drawn up and the first Congresses held. The venerable building remains, one of the consecrated shrines of which Americans and liberal Englishmen are justly proud. I lingered long and mused much in this room, and gazed with delight on the relics which are preserved in it. It is fitted as a sort of historical museum, with portraits, and maps, and other records of the early times of the city and of the Republic. Going through the central hall, we emerge on Independence Square, to the crowd assembled in which the " Declaration " was read, from the steps of the Court House, on the 4th of July, 1776.

My first stroll in Philadelphia was in company with the ghost of Benjamin Franklin. I remembered his account of his landing in Market Street Wharf, in his working dress, " unacquainted with a single soul in the place, and not knowing where to seek for a lodging." Walking from the wharf to Market Street, " I asked," he says, " in a baker's shop for some biscuits, expecting to find such as we had at Boston ; but they made none of the sort. I then asked for a threepenny loaf. They made no loaf of that price. He gave me three large rolls. I was surprised at receiving so much. I took them, however, and having no room in my pocket, I

walked on with a roll under each arm, eating
the third.   In this manner I went through Market Street, to Fourth Street, and passed the
house of Mr. Read, the father of my future wife.
She was standing at the door, observed me, and
thought with reason that I made a very singular
and grotesque appearance."   This is the first
peep of Franklin's Deborah, whose portrait may
be seen in the State House among people more
truly great than kings and queens.   The two
spare loaves went to a poor woman on the quay,
and then, says Franklin, " I joined a number of
well-dressed people all going one way, and was
thus led to a large Quakers' meeting-house near
the market-place.   I sat down with the rest, and
after looking round me for some time, hearing
nothing, and being drowsy from my last night's
labour and want of rest, I fell into a sound sleep.
In this state I continued till the assembly dispersed, when one of the congregation had the
goodness to awake me.   This was consequently
the first house I entered, or in which I slept, in
Philadelphia."   Another kind Quaker recommended him to a house of good repute, the
" Crooked Billet " in Water Street, his first
landing-place.   The voyage had been made in
consequence of William Bradford in New York
saying his son George, the printer in Philadelphia, might probably give him employment.

George had no need then for a journeyman, and recommended him to the only other printer in the place, one Keimer, whose " printing materials consisted of an old damaged press and a small fount of worn-out English letters."

Such was Franklin's first start in Philadelphia, and such the condition of " printing and the press" a hundred and fifty years ago ! Long afterwards Franklin often referred to these days, and when prosperity began to dawn on the town he thus wrote: " When I first paraded· the streets of Philadelphia, eating my roll, the majority of houses in Walnut Street, Second Street, Fourth Street, as well as a great number in Chestnut Street, had papers in them signifying that they were to be let, which made me think at the time that the inhabitants of the town were all deserting it one after another."

How strangely this reads now! and more strange to think that this friendless printer lad rose to be not only the first man in Philadelphia, but is coupled with Washington as one of the chief founders of the Republic, and has left a name honoured through all the world among the great and good.

This is not the place to say more of Franklin's life. I suspect his writings, and especially his "Autobiography," are not known as much as

they ought to be among English working men,
although his name is so often quoted. One
thing only I must mention—above all his literary and scientific, and political fame—in his
old age he was president of two societies established in Philadelphia, one a "society for
alleviating the miseries of public prisons," and
the other a "society for promoting the abolition of slavery, the relief of free negroes unlaw-
fully held in bondage, and the improvement of
the condition of the African race." His last
public act was signing a memorial, 12th Feb.,
1789, to the House of Representatives of the
United States for discouraging the slave trade.

I need scarcely say that I beheld with vene-
ration all the scenes and localities associated
with his name. His grave, a plain, unadorned
spot, is visited with reverence by all strangers.
I went to it with a fellow-passenger in the
"Scotia," a native of Philadelphia, Mr. Scull, a
name unusual, but not new to me, his ancestor,
Nicolas Scull, surveyor-general of Pennsylvania,
being one of Franklin's early friends, and an
associate in the club called the "Junto." Mr.
Scull introduced me to the Librarian of the
Philadelphia Library, the descendant of the
secretary of William Penn, and custodian of
the Logan Library, which occupies part of the
same building with a Public Library of which

Franklin was founder and president. In this venerable place I spent a pleasant morning, examining many of the old treasures of historical and literary interest. But I must dwell no longer on the antiquarian associations of the place, but proceed to describe my own first impressions of the modern city.

It was in the gloaming of a fine autumn evening I entered Philadelphia from Baltimore. On nearing the city there were signs of busy life in the ironworks and huge factory-like buildings, among which I remember was a wall-paper factory, said to be the largest in the Union. But the sight that impressed itself most that evening was the succession of rows of clean, neat, comfortable houses in the outskirts of the city. It was a striking contrast with the dingy, squalid tenements that fringe most of our English great towns. Entering London from almost any quarter, the comfortless, cheerless aspect of the "homes of the working classes" leaves a feeling of sadness on the mind. Remembering the scenes of poverty that meet the eye as the train approaches the terminus of the Great Eastern, South-Eastern, or other of our metropolitan railways, I was struck with the bright and cheery look of the approach to Philadelphia. This first impression remained with me, and was confirmed by after-inspection of the homes of the working classes in this great American city. It is the one feature above all others which impressed me with satisfaction in Philadelphia. In traversing the city from end to end in the various street cars, and strolling in every direction, I always observed this as the marked characteristic of the place, that the operative class is better housed and lodged than in our cities. I found that this was the result of well-planned and well-carried-out " building associations." I was told by the master of one great establishment, employing about three hundred workmen, that a large majority of them belonged to a building club. In due time they would all, or nearly all, become proprietors of well-built and well-fitted four or six roomed freehold houses, with every convenience and comfort.

Much has been said about the " distressing neatness and symmetry" of the city. The streets are laid out in parallelogram blocks, forming rectangles like the squares of a chessboard. They are numbered from the Delaware River on the east, toward the Schuylkill River on the west, beginning with Front Street, Second Street, Third Street, and so on, up to Twenty-third Street. The parallel streets running from west to east are chiefly named after trees, Chestnut Street, Walnut Street, Spruce

Street, Cherry Street, and so on. Special
names occasionally intervene, such as Market
Street, Library Street, Washington Street, and
in the newer parts of the city the street nomen-
clature is more irregular.   From the centre of
the town, Market Street, the numeral streets
are divided, as into North Tenth and South
Tenth streets.   The numbering of the houses
is also irregular, odd and even on opposite
sides, a hundred in each block or square, so
that the first number, in Walnut Street, beyond
Thirteenth Street, is 1301 ; the fifth beyond
Ninth Street is 905.   All this may be very
" distressing " to artists and non-commercial
travellers ; but the inhabitants are the best
judges, and the regularity is very convenient
and useful, not only for sanitary supervision,
but for postal, police, and other civic and municipal arrangements.   As a general rule, it is
with towns as with individual houses or cottages,
the most picturesque to an artist's eye are often
the least healthy and serviceable for residence.
The flat, level site of Philadelphia has been
used to the best advantage for the health and
comfort of the vast population.   Nor are the
long rows of brick houses so monotonous-look-
ing as might be anticipated, all the windows in
the good streets having cheerful green outside
shutters, and the doorways being white, often

of beautiful marble. Many of the streets are also thickly lined with well-trained trees, and frequent squares and open places break the uniformity of brickwork. In the chief streets, especially Chestnut Street, one of the finest streets in America, the crowded pavements and magnificent shops leave little leisure for noticing the prosaic regularity of the place. The only fault is the narrowness of the roadways, admitting only a single line of tramway, the cars running up one street and returning down another. The beauty of the heights on the western and northern skirts of the town makes up for the unpicturesqueness of the older districts; compensating also (in the health returns), by their salubrious sites, for the dense and unwholesome crowding in the Northern Liberties and other parts inhabited by the Irish and by the poorer classes, native and foreign.

The Irish Roman Catholics seem to swell in undue proportion the poverty of whatever place they inhabit. I made inquiries about pauperism, and about the agencies, both public and voluntary, for its relief. Intemperance and indiscriminate charity are here as elsewhere the chief feeders of pauperism and mendicancy. Even with these drawbacks, the condition of the poor in Philadelphia is satisfactory compared with our own great cities. The whole is well under

the control of the authorities and of the benevolent societies. Except in two or three localities, I saw nothing approaching to the hopeless,
squalid poverty of our great towns—of Glasgow, for instance, the city most fairly to be
compared with Philadelphia, as Edinburgh is
with Boston.

It would be useful to institute a comparison
in detail, from the Census reports, of the relative condition of these great cities of the Old
and the New World. The comparison ought
to include sanitary and social as well as educational and religious statistics. My inquiries
were too brief to venture on details, but the
measureless superiority of Philadelphia over
Glasgow in regard to the general well-being of
the masses is evident to any observant stranger
who knows both places. The death-rate of
Glasgow in 1869 was 34, that of Philadelphia
19. Of the 82,000 families composing the
population of Glasgow, above 60,000 occupy
dwellings of one or two apartments only ! At
the census of 1861, 28,000 families lived in
single-roomed houses, and 32,000 in houses of
two rooms. In Philadelphia there is scarcely
such a thing known as a workman's family
herding in this miserable way.

It is idle to say that there is vast difference
in the conditions of cities in America, where

all is comparatively new, and where there is
plenty of room for the population. Neither
Boston nor Philadelphia are new cities, and in
the latter especially there is not much room
to spare for building improvements. If the
existing rights of ground-landlordism, or any
other legal arrangements, hinder necessary
amelioration of the working classes with us, it
might be well to alter these things before the
whole social structure is overthrown by the up-
heaval of Communism. But no violent changes
are required. It has been demonstrated, even
in crowded London, that decent and healthy
homes for the working classes will pay at least
five per cent. to builders, and far larger efforts
ought to be made in this direction. Instead of
leaving the matter to the speculation of in-
dividuals or companies, various public boards
could effect much, not only to the benefit of
the industrious poor, but to the advantage of
all classes, as the poor-rates, police-rates, and
other imposts could be lessened, and a vast
amount saved to the whole community by
improving " the domiciliary condition of the
masses." Commissioners have been sent to
foreign countries to report on far less important
subjects, and it would be a wise and truly
economical thing if some of our public bodies
in London or Glasgow or elsewhere would send

intelligent and practical men to report on the condition of Philadelphia. I repeat here my first impression, that in no city of the world have the great masses of the people, and especially the operative classes, attained a higher average of well-being, in sanitary and social as well as in educational and religious life.

Of possible disasters from Communism and other upheavals from below, such as have convulsed Paris and may threaten London, there is no fear in Philadelphia, a larger city than any in Europe, except London and Paris. The lower strata are sound there, the dregs at bottom and the froth at top forming but a small proportion of the vast mass of social life.

These two facts of the great death-rate and the overcrowded dwellings suggest all other contrasts, both of a physical and moral kind. Lord Shaftesbury, speaking of London,—and the remarks apply to Glasgow and all large towns,—said : " I maintain that the grave and leading mischief is the domiciliary condition of the large masses of the people. I have seen as many as twenty persons living in a single room ; and is it possible, I ask, when such cases not only exist, but abound, to institute purity of life, of thought, of action, or observe any of the demands of domestic duty ? This

is the besetting evil that surrounds us all ; this
is the great and overwhelming mischief that is
bringing corruption upon the population, which
is one great cause of that which is the main
curse of our country, habits of drinking and
inebriety.   The filthy physical state, the depression of the nervous system, the misery
brought on by that mode of life, drive people
to find artificial stimulants in the beerhouses
and the ginshops."   There is no doubt that
much of the prevailing intemperance is due to
these physical causes, and it is too true that
the habit, with all its deteriorating consequences, becomes hereditary in the children of
drunkards.   It is also unquestionable that to
intemperance is due a vast proportion of the
crime and the pauperism of overcrowded
cities.   Education and religion fail to effect
their due amount of good influence, in the
presence of causes tending physically and so-
cially to degrade the masses.

But really, after all, the condition of the
working classes depends less on what is done
for them than upon what they do for themselves. By the common schools, by the Sunday
schools, by the numerous churches, all voluntary, and to a large extent supported by the
working people, by the cheap press, and free
libraries, the American workmen of Philadelphia

have raised themselves as a body to a higher standard than in any great city I have ever visited.

Whether this well-being is progressive, or whether it will last, I have no idea, speaking only from what I witnessed. To the old agricultural wealth of Pennsylvania, the finest farming and breeding ground in the Union, great mineral resources—coal, iron, and oil—have now been added. The trial of people by sudden increase of wealth is always severe, and there may be a risk of Philadelphia losing its staid, sober, solid character, as compared with New York, for example. With wealth and luxury come many evils, which descend from the rich to other classes of society. If there is danger in this respect, I see equal watchfulness and activity for maintaining and extending what is good. There is no city more abundant in churches and schools, and in all useful and beneficent institutions. There are about 450 churches, though some of these can only be small stations. The Presbyterians, including Old and New Schools, Reformed and United, number 110 churches, the Episcopalians 80, the Methodist Episcopalians 70, and the Baptists 40. The Roman Catholics return 40 churches and chapels, the Lutherans 30, besides 15 German churches, 6 Dutch

Reformed, and 4 Moravian. The Friends, Hicksites, and Orthodox, between them have 15 meeting houses, and the Jews 7 synagogues. The orthodox Congregationalists are not strong as in New England, having only 4 churches. The remaining churches belong to Universalists, New Jerusalemites, Unitarians, and other sects, all of whom form an insignificant proportion of the Philadelphia worshippers.

In like force appear the other great trainers of national character—the Schools and the Press. The Common Schools are all that could be expected in a State like Pennsylvania ; and as to newspapers and journals, the number in the State is above six hundred, Philadelphia alone producing about two hundred periodicals of all kinds, class magazines and religious magazines, as well as newspapers. The book trade also of Philadelphia is flourishing—at least if I may judge by what I saw and heard at the store of Lippincott and Sons, one of the largest book firms in the Union. Messrs. Claxton, Remsen, and Haffilfinger, in Market Street, are also extensive publishers and book-dealers.

Philadelphia is the head-quarters of the Presbyterian Board of Publication. The Sunday School Union has its own large sphere of usefulness in publishing books for the young, as well as occasional works of a higher class, in the preparation of which the committee have the advantage of the aid of Dr. Allibone, (author of the "Dictionary of Authors," and other standard books,) one of the best respected literary men of America.

Of the United States Mint, of the Girard College, the Fairmount Waterworks, and other stock sights of Philadelphia, I have nothing special to say, and must refer for description of these, and of other public institutions, to the gazetteers and guide-books. The Park, three thousand acres of most varied surface, already promises to be the finest demesne of the kind in the world. Some of the buildings and establishments, both public and private, are on a scale of vastness which has given rise to a gentle Pennsylvanian joke, which speaks of "seeing the elephants," instead of "the lions," as elsewhere.

One mammoth establishment I select for notice, not only for its own attractions, but because it is full of interest, as illustrating the history of American journalism, and as showing the career open to industrial enterprise, even in these days of keen competition.

Among the most conspicuous and imposing edifices in Philadelphia is the "Public Ledger Building," at the corner of Chestnut and

Sixth Streets. I found it a common thing in the great towns for a successful newspaper to have a block of buildings bearing its name, part of the premises being occupied for its own use, and the remainder let off in offices and stores. The publicity of the site in such cases is sure to command high rents for such annexes to the main establishment. Several of these buildings in New York and Chicago I had inspected, but none of them approached in vastness and completeness that of the Philadelphia *Ledger.* I have no space to enter into details, but retain a lively impression of what is one of the largest and among the most perfect printing and publishing offices in the world. The machinery, the presses, the offices, the fittings, are all of the most perfect kind that modern skill has contrived. But beyond the mechanical wonders of the place, I was struck with the provision made for the health and the comfort of the workers. As an editor, I looked with admiration and envy at the commodious and well-furnished rooms in the editorial departments; and, as to the composing room, no compositors in England work in such comfortable and wholesome quarters. Not only is there plenty of space and air, but in the very colouring of the walls to relieve the sight, and in the providing of bath-rooms and other comforts, every care is taken of the health of the workmen. I am not surprised that the opening of such an establishment was celebrated by a public banquet at the Continental Hotel, when the Mayors of Philadelphia and New York, and many of the most distinguished public men in Church and State from all parts of the Union, assembled to do honour to the proprietor of the *Ledger*, about whom and his paper a few brief notes will be read with interest.

The *Public Ledger* has long been known in this country as one of the most remarkable papers in America, remarkable in its origin and in its history. It was started in 1836 by three working printers—Swain, Abell, and Simmons, who clubbed together their savings, and worked with their own hands. It was not the first, but it was one of the earliest experiments towards a cheap press. The "opening address to the public" had in it the ring of success. Appealing to "the intelligence and love of improvement which pervade the population of Philadelphia," stating its claims on the mercantile and manufacturing community, and affirming its freedom from partisan principles, the *Ledger* proclaimed that "the common good is its object; and in seeking this object it will have especial regard to the moral and intellectual improvement of the labouring classes

—the great sinew of all civilised communities."
A clever New England barrister, Mr. Russell
Jarvis, was engaged as editor, whose tact in
taking advantage of current topics, and able
leading articles, secured public attention. By
the end of the first year the success of the
paper was secured. The size was increased
from a sheet $15\frac{1}{2}$ by $21\frac{1}{2}$, with four columns in
the page, to 18 by 24, with five columns. The
hand-press with which the work began was
succeeded by a double-cylinder "pony" press.
Several other cheap journals were now started,
and the higher priced press was affected by
a movement at first ridiculed and despised.
The *Ledger* continued, however, to keep the
lead. In the following years some exciting
events, such as the "Abolition Riots of 1838,"
and the "Native American" movement, cul-
minating in 1844, brought the *Ledger* into
increased prominence. On both of these questions the sympathies of the paper seemed rather
on the side of the turbulent agitators, but, when
actual riots occurred, its strong support of the
supremacy of law and authority against mob
rule gained the approval of all friends of order.
Its influence at that time was so great that the
despised "penny press" took a new position
in public estimation. From this date the
prosperity of the *Ledger* was progressive.

In 1847 a four-cylinder rotary press was introduced, one of the first applications of Colonel
Hoe's wonderful invention. The size of the
paper had been gradually enlarged to four
seven-columned pages, $22\frac{1}{2}$ by 34 inches. So
it went on till 1864, when the high price of
paper and of labour during the war brought
financial trouble. Unable to agree as to increasing the price of the paper or the rates of
advertising, the two surviving partners, Messrs.
Swain and Abell, sold the property to Mr.
George W. Childs, already well known as an
enterprising book publisher. Mr. Childs proved
himself equal to the crisis. The price of the
paper was advanced to twelve cents weekly,
and reduced after a short time to ten cents, the
present price. The advertising rates were also
advanced, and though there was at first a
falling-off of subscribers, the defection was
soon repaired, new elements of strength and
popularity introduced, and the prosperity of
the paper again secured. It has now reached
a circulation of 75,000, and is acknowledged to
be one of the ablest and best conducted, as
well as the most prosperous paper in Philadelphia. Its highest merit is having mainly
helped to establish the cheap press among the
great powers of public opinion throughout the
Union.

As the *Ledger* is one of the most remarkable papers, its chief proprietor, George W.
Childs, is among the most remarkable men
in America. A native of Baltimore, he went
to Philadelphia early in his teens, without a
friend in the place, and with a few cents in his
pocket. Beginning life as a boy in a bookseller's shop, by industry and frugality he
gradually raised himself, till, before he had
reached forty years of age, he was one of the
largest publishers, and proprietor of one of the
richest newspapers, in the world. For the
goodwill, machinery, and whole "plant" of
the *Ledger* he paid down a large sum in
cash, and the property has fructified in his
hands. The character of the paper has also
improved, of which one proof may be given in
the exclusion of all doubtful advertisements,
however lucrative, and the insertion of which
defaces too many of the leading American
journals. There would be little satisfaction in
recording the success of Mr. Childs if he were
merely one of the many examples of successful
millionaires. Fortunes are rapidly made in
the States, but not often accumulated by
plodding industry and self-denying thrift. Nor
is it usual, though happily not uncommon,
for such wealth to be used for unselfish and
generous objects. One of his benefactions is

the singular but sensible and practically useful gift of a burial-ground, in Woodland Cemetery, for the printers of Philadelphia. Mr. Childs has gained for himself a good repute, and the respect of his countrymen, by his public spirit and beneficence,

CHAPTER XXII.

ON LANDSCAPE GARDENING—HORTICULTURE—
FLOWERS AND FRUIT — THE EVERGREEN
TRADE.

THE public parks in New York, Brooklyn.
Philadelphia, and other great cities, while
they are admirable specimens of landscape gardening, are still more interesting as showing advance in æsthetic culture and in provision for the
health and enjoyment of the people. The civic
rulers and authorities are displaying public
spirit and good sense in this direction. When
I was in Philadelphia, the Board of Direction
of the Public Park heard that Mr. Robinson,
author of the work on French Gardens, and a
high authority on landscape·gardening, was in
the States, and they made a very handsome
offer of securing his professional aid for improving their fine demesne. In Prospect·Park,
Brooklyn, and the Central Park, New York, no
expense is spared to improve the ground. In
the latter park, Mr. Waterhouse Hawkins was

employed in setting up some of his wonderful restorations of ancient animals, on the plan so skilfully exhibited in our Crystal Palace at Sydenham. The example of these public places will exert good influence throughout the Union, and will help to diffuse a love for landscape gardening, and the improvement of popular taste in horticulture, in its ornamental as well as useful departments.

There is ample room for such improvement. I did not think much of the gardening in those parts of the States which I visited. In many country houses and villas there are, no doubt, fine gardens and conservatories, while a few florists' and fruiterers' shops in New York, Boston, Philadelphia, and other great towns, showed that the luxuries of vegetable life are supplied for the wealthy. The market gardeners of New Jersey and Western New York must also be well up to their trade. But I speak of the culture of flowers among the people. Ornamental horticulture is an art that does not flourish in the early life of a nation. In some suburban regions, such as the upper part of Brooklyn, Philadelphia near the park, and at Mount Auburn, Cincinnati, I saw rows of villas with elegant ornamental flower-plots. The sight struck me from its rarity. In the small towns I noticed few signs of floriculture.

or even of window-gardening, and in villages
seldom a house with the cheerful adornments
of our English cottages.   The cemeteries were,
in this respect, better kept and more ornamental
than other public places; certainly better than
the parks and pleasure-grounds.   The grounds
even of the Capitol, and of the White House at
Washington, have an uncultivated look.   I was
astonished at the desolation in the grounds of
Harvard College, all overrun with weeds and
thistles. An old historical place like this might
show some æsthetic emulation of the well-kept
grounds of the English colleges.

At Washington I found a small but well-
stocked botanical garden, the superintendent,
Mr. Smith, trained at Edinburgh and at Kew.
At Boston I went to a flower and fruit show.
To the Boston Horticultural Society is due the
ornamental laying out of the Mount Auburn
Cemetery, of which the Bostonians are justly
proud.   At the show prizes were gained by
some excellent pears, melons of various sorts,
cherry tomatoes, hybrid corn, and egg plants.
The latter is a favourite fruit; but a Scotch
gardener, who kindly pointed out the notable
things in the Boston exhibition, said to me,
" When you have sliced the egg plant, and
fried it, and buttered it, what's it good for ?
Only to throw out of the window."   American

apples are too well known to be here described.
The peaches are very inferior, at least in the
Eastern States. As to grapes, the best of
them, and the varieties are now numerous, are
tough as raisins, and have a strong foxy taste.
I do not believe they can ever attain to any
worth, except by hothouse cultivation. I was
disappointed also with the Catawba wines of
Ohio, of which so much has been written. In
all departments of flower and fruit culture there
is room for improvement, and good gardeners
will yet be a class of emigrants appreciated as
America advances in the luxuries of civilised
life.

There is one branch of cultivation which has
grown to large dimensions in the Eastern States,
" the evergreen trade." The Christmas before
my visit I was told that upwards of 120,000
Christmas trees had been sold in the New York
markets, and " more than 200,000 yards of
evergreen wreathing." The German population for their homes, and the recently intro
duced fashion of decorating the churches, have
created the demand for this trade. Every German home has its Christmas tree, and the
Americans are adopting this cheerful usage.
But the expansion of the evergreen trade for
ecclesiastical uses is more remarkable. Several
churches expend 500 dollars, or above £100,

for Christmas decoration.   Nor is this confined
now to Episcopal churches, the puritanism of
other denominations relenting at this festive
season.   For a few days before Christmas the
Hudson mountain forests seem (Birnam-wood
fashion) to have migrated to Washington
market and its neighbourhood in New York.
Alleys of cypress and cedar divide spaces filled
with vines, and holly, and fir-trees, and festooned with evergreen wreathing or " rope."
This rope, made in the mountain district by
girls, is sold for about five cents a yard.   Stars,
crosses, and other devices, are formed of the
same material, and the result on the whole is a
busy and profitable industry.

CHAPTER XXIII.

RETURNING to the parks, one might expect to see there, if anywhere, American
equestrianism. But riding does not seem a
national enjoyment. On any June morning in
Hyde Park there may be seen a finer display
of well-mounted equestrians, especially of the
fair sex, than can be witnessed in all the
American parks through the whole season.
The New England people do not seem to
take kindly to the saddle. The northern
papers admitted during the late war that this
fact gave to the Southern cavalry so decided a superiority, and will always leave the
army deficient in this branch of the service.
The establishment of racing parks may give an
impulse to equestrianism in some aspects, but
these not of a kind promotive of the best
features of national character. There are now

four racing grounds within reach of New York
—Jerome, Prospect, and Monmouth* Parks, and
the track at Saratoga.   Great crowds resort to
these meetings, but few native Americans have
any special love for the races apart from their
being the occasion of an outing and holiday.
So much the better for the national taste and
for public morality.   It would be a baleful
influence for them, if this branch of sport
extended as it has in the old country.

If they do not excel in riding, the Americans
are "thunder at driving."   The popular taste
in this art has run into wild extravagance.
Four-in-hands, and even six-in-hands, with
showy harness and gay liveries, are the pride
of the vulgar rich.   In the parks and on the
roads it is amusing to behold the variety of
equipages, and pleasant also to see the number
of plebeian, square-framed "buggies" mingling
in the course.   But the greatest specialty of
American driving is the fast trotting horse,
with its spider-like iron bicycle.   Portraits of
famous trotters and pictures of trotting matches

---

* In the programme of the Monmouth Races I noticed a
curious proclamation of Lynch law : "*Resolved*, that any thief
or pickpocket caught on the grounds shall be brought before the
Board handcuffed, then taken before the Grand Stand and pub-
licly horsewhipped, and a placard placed upon his back, and
paraded around the track. *Resolved*, that any persons misbe-
having themselves on the racecourse during the meeting shall
be immediately expelled."

are common in the smoking rooms and drinking saloons, such as the celebrated match between " Hero " and " Flora Temple," when three two-mile heats were run, each heat within five minutes! Wonderful trotting horses may be seen in the morning on the roads, or in the Central Park of New York. A few well-appointed English drags, and other imported carriages of various build, may be seen ; but the great mass of the vehicles are the old-fashioned native buggy, and carts with light wooden and leather framework for shade and shelter. Even in the rural districts the American farmer rarely walks or rides, but " hitches up " his buggy for any little distance.

The American field sports do not much differ from our own, so far as " the rod and the gun " are concerned. Of the Game Laws in the State of New York I have already spoken (*ante*, p. 272), and these afford a glimpse into the public opinion on the subject in the older parts of the Union. In the Far West there is ample scope for sport of a more adventurous kind, and many Englishmen every year go to share in these adventures. The fashionable battues and matches of English amateur sportsmen are, as might be expected, held in great contempt by Americans. A leading article in one of their papers on the pigeon matches of

some of the English aristocratic gun clubs thus
concluded: " The primitive and true idea of
the chase is a direct conflict between man and
certain savage elements in the world which
must be overcome and disappear before civilization. Bear, deer, or buffalo shooting seem not
unmanly work, nor unsuited to a certain degree
of culture and enlightenment. There is at
least fatigue to be endured and danger to be
incurred. The idea, however, of unlimited members of parliament, hatted and gloved *à la mode*,
driving out to the enclosure at Hurlingham to
butcher some dozen caged frightened pigeons,
while their lady friends look on exultant, is to
us indescribably absurd. But when we consider
that out of this occupation this remarkable people hopefully assert their expectation of deriving
strength for their legislative duties and religious
enlightenment, our wonder can find no words.
We can only look on in silence and perplexity."

On one of my first mornings in New York, I
saw, among the bustling crowd in the Metropolitan Hotel Hall, a group of athletic young
fellows in light flannel dress. At first I thought
they were cricketers, but the bats and balls
were not those of our game. I was told it was
a " Base Ball Club." These clubs I afterwards
found wherever I went, Base Ball being recognised as " the national game" of America.

Throughout August and September matches were going on, and the newspapers had a column, and often several columns, headed " The National Game," and filled with reports of the play. City against city, county against county, amateurs against professionals, all sorts of matches were going on, like cricket matches among ourselves in the season. At Chicago, at the time of my visit, there was great excite- ment on account of the victory of the " White Stockings " of that city over the " Red Stockings " of Cincinnati. The " conquering heroes" were met at the railway depôt by an enormous procession, with music and banners, and paraded in carriages through the town. The " White Stockings " also beat another crack club, the " Eagles " of Louisville, and for the time were the champion players, though they had yet to meet the " Atlantics," " Athletics," and one or two other famous clubs.

After hearing and reading so much about the National Game, I was surprised to find it only a development of our own homely game of " rounders." There are nine on each side— centre field, left field, right field, first base, second base, third base, catcher, short stop, and pitcher. There is room for considerable skill in pitching, batting, catching, and fielding ; but on the whole the game appeared to me be a hobbledehoy affair compared with cricket. It is immensely popular, however, among all classes and ages, from lads at school up to "old boys" of business. I saw the report of one match between two corporations in the West, including several "aldermen"! Like too many sports, the game has got into the hands of betting and gambling fraternities, and the most celebrated clubs are now the property of "stockholders," whose speculations and arrangements are made for gain more than for honour. The grand jury of Baltimore actually reported Base Ball as "one of the gradations of crime," alluding to the temptations to gambling which it has introduced. This is the abuse of the thing, however; the love of the game is creditable to "Young America," and affords a healthy athletic out-of-door sport. Except at Baltimore and Philadelphia, I heard nothing about cricket. There is said to be a good club at Germantown, but I suspect the game is comparatively unknown in the States.

Of indoor amusements and pastimes I saw little, and therefore can say little. Public amusements, whether dramatic or musical, seem much the same as our own, with balls, concerts, and masquerades, as in Europe. The masquerades are only recognised by professed lovers of such scenes, and are mainly got up by theatrical managers and hotel proprietors. In the list of costumes in the great masquerade of last season, at Saratoga, I noticed, among various public characters from New York and other cities, the names of at least seven of a well-known hotel-keeping family, at one of whose houses the affair came off.

The amusements of "fashionable life" are very much alike in all countries, and are not worth mentioning among special features of national character or usage. The world of fashion—the world which dresses, dances, sings, plays, bets, and lives only to amuse itself—is not greatly different in New York and Paris, Newport and Scarborough, Philadelphia and Milan, Saratoga and Baden. These people count little in the estimate of what makes a nation, and in America the proportion of idle pleasure-seekers is less than in any other country I have visited.

At the same time it is to be feared that this annual resort to great watering-places will come to affect perceptibly the national life and manners. It is a new social feature, and on a scale of vastness unknown in the old country. Before the end of the season last summer, I saw an estimate in the papers that there had been above 100,000 visitors at Saratoga, 150,000 at Cape May, 150,000 at Atlantic City, 100,000 at Newport, and 200,000 at Long Branch. Now these visitors come from all parts of the country. They meet people from New York, who are far more likely to influence them for evil than to be influenced by them for good. It is not as in our great English watering-places, where the home life and home customs of the visitors, whether grave or gay, for health or recreation, can be maintained at choice. The monster-hotel system of America compels all classes to intermingle. The whole life of these places is public, and not of the best sort of publicity. Of course there are quiet boarding-houses and homes, even in the most crowded summer resorts ; but the general tone of life is a tone of relaxation—not relaxation in the good sense of relaxation from hard work, but relaxation of good habits and homely ways, and relaxation of good morals too often. The rich American paterfamilias takes his wife and daughters into scenes from which an English gentleman with his family would shrink. " Life at Saratoga" will not improve the national character any more than " Life in Paris," which many Americans regard as the acme of felicity. In fact, the word has become pro-verbial that such Americans expect to go when they die to the Champs Elysées ! There is too much of the Parisian influence apparent at Saratoga, not improved by filtering through New York. At the marine watering-places there is less of stagey-looking life, but there is also there too much publicity for those who wish to see the best features of the national character retained. Last season at Newport it was the fashion rather to affect "cottage" life instead of the hotels, though not with less gaiety of public amusements. I remained at Boston, finding more to see there than I could overtake, when some friends preferred to have a look at Newport. They came back open-mouthed about the gaiety of the place, and es-pecially at the beauty of the women. It was sad to read a few weeks after of the death of the acknowledged belle of the Ocean House. She died of a low but rapid fever—a scourge which will make itself terribly felt in these watering-places, with their huge caravanserais and crowded population. The difficulty is already felt with us in England, some of our watering-places being nests of fever during summer, and yet drainage sparingly used for fear of polluting the sea for bathing. The practical conclusion of all which is, that it would be better both for health and morals to diminish the rush to huge watering-places, and occupy more numerous summer stations,

whether inland or on the coast.   As with hospitals for the sick, so with resorts for health,
the detached system has many advantages over
the crowding into great hospitals or hotels.

CHAPTER XXIV.

SPORTS AND AMUSEMENTS (*continued*)—IN THE
COUNTRY—ON THE SEA—YACHTING.

THE Americans have various rural sports and
amusements handed down from generation
to generation among the rustic folk. The reader
will be pleased with the following extract from
a genial book on "American Society," by Mr.
G. M. Towle, of Boston, formerly U.S. Consul
at Nantes, and at Bradford.

"In the autumn, at harvest time, there are
numerous merry gatherings, in which useful
tasks are joined with hearty amusement. When
the Indian corn is gathered, it is the custom to
have, at many of the farmhouses, what is called
a 'husking.' The object is, to get the corn
husked : the neighbours are invited to assemble
on a certain afternoon at the barn of the farmer
whose corn is to be husked. Here are great
piles of the just-gathered ears. The guests
sit about on the barn floor and the haymows,
and proceed to strip the husks and silk from

the corn and deposit it clean and bare at one side. Meanwhile there is plenty of talking and laughing; the farmer's home-brewed cider and ale are passed frequently about, and dough-nuts, pies, and cakes of all sorts are plentifully provided. After a while the husking is sus-pended, the barn floor cleared of the rubbish; one of the boys mounts the haymow and strikes up a lively tune on his fiddle, and the barn fairly shakes with the rollicking dance or the lusty game which ensues. Whatever young man finds in his pile a *red* ear of corn, is entitled to kiss any girl he chooses; if a lass finds one, she must submit to be kissed, and must choose the lad whom she prefers to per-form the operation. Another autumn custom is called an 'apple bee.' Several barrels of apples are collected in the farmhouse, the neighbours are invited in, and all set to work paring them. After the outer skin is taken off, the apples are divided into small sections, the core taken out, and the pieces are hung on a string. These are afterwards put in the sun to dry, and are then laid away, with which to make 'apple sauce' or dried apple pies in the ensuing winter.

"The people reciprocate with each other in doing these tasks. When a farm dame needs an additional quilt for one of her beds, she calls in her neighbours, and they set to work making one, patching it together with odd pieces of cloth ; this is a party at first confined to the women ; tea-drinking and gossip comprise the pleasures which relieve the task ; in the evening the ' men-folks ' drop in.

" A famous time in some of the Northern States is that when the maple-trees are tapped, and the delicious maple sugar made. The sugar maple-trees are very profitable, and often add materially to the income of the farmer. Early in the spring these are tapped ; the sweet juice is collected in tubs ; great fires are built ; huge iron kettles are hung over them ; the maple sap poured in, and boiled down to a thick syrup. It is of a rich brown colour, and nothing can be nicer, especially if eaten on hot cakes or waffles. In the evening, when the syrup has grown quite thick and ready for the ' sugaring off,' the lasses and lads gather at the ' camps,' in the wood, to partake of it. A favourite method is to dip snowballs into the yet warm syrup, and, thus coated, to eat them ; these are very delicious. The froth, or ' wat,' of the syrup is also very palatable. The festivities end with dances, games, and ditties.

" In the Fall, almost every town has its Agricultural Fair, which is, to the rustic population, one of the great events of the year. It is held

not seldom in the spacious airy town-hall; the
farmers for miles round have been preparing
for it the summer long; the farmer who takes
a prize for the heaviest pig or the biggest pears
is like the politician who has won an election,
like an author whose book is a ' success,' like a
lawyer who has gained a famous case, like a
parson made a bishop. These Agricultural
Fairs are truly interesting and curious shows.
Within the hall long tables have been set
against the walls and in the middle of the
floor; the walls have been decorated by the
young women with all varieties of evergreen
festoons, fantastic flower designs, pictures, and
deftly-fashioned embroidery or worsted work.
The tables display every kind of fruit and vegetable, all of the largest, ripest, and most lus-
cious, with little cards on the plates, informing
the uninitiated of the particular species, and
the name of its contributor. Pyramids of
pears, peaches, and apples are followed by
monster pumpkins and cabbages, mammoth
beets, melons, and turnips, great tempting
clusters of grapes, wonderful potatoes, beans,
and tomatoes. Farther on you will see specimens of the women's handiwork—wax flowers,
pictures made of hair, embroidery, crochet
work, odd examples of aptitude with the needle,
pen, or penknife. On other tables appear

specimens of domestic cookery—specimen loaves of bread and cake, preserves, pickles, hams, and pies. Outside the building are rows of pens where are kept the oxen, cows, sheep, pigs, chickens, goats—the dumb competitors for the prizes ; placards announcing the various kinds are tacked to the pens, and groups of farmers are gathered about them, discussing the merits of this hog or that big-headed bull.

" On the open spaces round about are all sorts of small shows and pedlars' waggons drawn up in eligible places. Tents, covered with large gaudy pictures of giantesses and bearded women, wonderful dwarfs and living skeletons, are thickly set on the sward ; and the showmen at the tent openings are talking themselves hoarse, jingling their money boxes the while, and describing with oratorical flourishes the wonders to be seen for a trifle within. The pedlars are driving brisk bargains with their astonishingly cheap penknives, their patent knife-sharpeners and axe-grinders, their little bottled balms for every human ill, their marvellous writing apparatus, making half-a-dozen simultaneous copies, their soaps, confectionery, and imposing silver ware. A perambulating photographer has drawn up his portable saloon in a convenient corner, and offers to produce perfect likenesses of loving couples and rough old farmers for small prices. The country people are there in multitudes, dressed primly, and deeply interested in all that is going on ; the city people, too, have driven out, and mingle in the concourse which is grouped about the tables and on the green. The fair usually lasts two days; the second day is the best attended. In one of the upper rooms a bountiful collation is spread ; on the platform at the farther end is a table, at which sit the dignitaries—the president of the agricultural society, the orator of the day, and any notable visitors who are present. Just below them is a table for the reporters, who have come out from the city to take notes for the 'evening edition.' A fee of fifty cents or a dollar is demanded of those who wish to partake of the collation ; it consists of cold meats, vegetables, pies, and fruits. The repast over, the orator of the day is introduced, and, rising behind the platform table, he proceeds to deliver an address on some agricultural subject. Other speeches are made ; the prizes are announced by a committee appointed for the purpose; and then the productions on exhibition are taken away by their various owners. Sometimes, in the evening, a dance at the town hotel concludes the affair. Every one competes for the prizes who so chooses, these being offered by the agricultural societies.

" The country people practise many robust out-door games. There are shooting matches and quoit matches, base-ball contests and foot races. Nearly every boy has his gun, and early becomes an adept in shooting at targets and hunting in the free forests. Every boy, too, learns to swim and to row ; for everywhere in rural America, there are, near by the farms, lakes and rivers where aquatic sports may be enjoyed without fear of molestation. Of course the country boy sits on his horse, without a saddle, as easily as if he had grown there ; and when he is very young, is sent to mill with a load of corn, or wheat, sometimes several miles distant from home, returning with the flour after it has been ground.

" In the winter time, the farmers having little to do—their fields being thickly covered with layer after layer of crusted snow—they stay much at home, attending to the cattle in the sheds, reading, and leisurely lounging about. Then it is that the sleighs—long processions of them—may be seen gliding over the roads, full of hilarious parties. The young men of the neighbourhood get together, and arrange to give their sweethearts *en masse* the treat of a sleigh ride. The village tavern is doubtless

supplied with a bouncing great sleigh, a barge-
like vehicle on runners, which the landlord is
readily induced, for a modest sum, to lend ; and
there is besides a general muster of all the
farm sleighs for miles around.   The horses are
decked with bells, and after the accidental
slippings and fallings-down, screaming and
joking, the party starts off, echoing some
familiar song.   The broad landscape is everywhere white and shining ; the fences and walls
are half concealed beneath the high drifts, the
rails and stones peeping out here and there at
intervals ; the farmhouses seem imbedded in
the flaky mounds ; the narrow beaten paths
from the doors leads through snow walls often
five or six feet high ; the road is crusted with a
coat of snow frozen into ice ; the tree-boughs
bend low beneath their accumulated burden ;
everywhere the snow-particles glisten and
glitter ; as far as eye can reach, hill-top and
valley, house and tree are shrouded in the
monotonous and long-enduring robe of white.
The procession of sleighs glides rapidly
over the frozen roads ; the joyous jingling of
hundreds of little bells mingles with the shouts
and laughter of the happy-hearted party, who
are wrapt and bundled almost out of sight by
capacious blankets, quilts, shawls.

       " To relieve the desolate monotony of winter,

'sociables' are often formed. Once a fort-
night gatherings take place at the houses in
turn, which are all the jollier because the
people have so few chances to see each other.
In many of the villages concerts are given by
choral societies, and lectures, either by the
parson or schoolmaster, or some neighbouring
notability. The boys and girls have as much
skating as they please. The lakes and rivers
remain frozen for several months, and moon-
light skating parties are among the pleasantest
of the winter season."

The taste for yachting has grown recently,
and the number of yachtsmen on the eastern
coast increases every year. Of some of the
crack American yachts we have heard much of
late years, and the international races across
the ocean have become renowned. But, apart
from these public displays and competitions,
the passion for yachting is on the increase.
And no wonder, with so splendid a coast, from
New York up to New Brunswick, a stretch of
seven hundred miles, or the length of the
British Islands. For those who like quiet
water there is Long Island Sound, a lovely
sheet of sheltered water, with many pleasant
ports of call. Many families spend the most
of the summer months on board these Long

Island Sound yachts, and cheery healthful homes they are for men of business. Then there is the run to Portland and Boston, round Cape Cod, the great part open ocean, and with safe harbours and anchorages at various intervals. Except the Mediterranean, no cruising ground can compare with this, however it may be in winter, or in the poetic description by Mrs. Hemans of " the stern and rock-bound coast." There are no better sailors in the world than the pilots and fishermen and yachtsmen of the New England seas. In the love of the ocean, both for work and pleasure, the Americans are " true chips of the old block."

CHAPTER XXV.

BEFORE passing from the subject of American sports and pastimes, I must set down my impressions on two subjects, which may seem odd in such connection, but which, in addition to their original and higher uses, have come to be regarded very much in the light of amusements. Few readers would guess that I mean "Camp Meetings" and "Fire Brigades." *

The Methodist Camp Meetings, which originated in religious uses, when population was

---

* Before the war I might have added "soldiering," the militia of the different States being analogous to "volunteers" among us ; but the terrible realities of that struggle, the greatest war of modern times, great beyond any European war, forbid the least reference to vanity and display in wearing uniforms. Unprepared and undisciplined at the opening of the war, before its close the youth and manhood of the Northern States displayed a heroism and endurance which compelled the admiration of the world. The South were better prepared at first and better commanded, and at last were moved by the strength of despair, but the issue of the contest was never doubtful to those who knew the history and resources of the Free and the Slave States.

sparse, and ordinances few and far between, have greatly altered their character in later times. In some places it is true that the chief object is to encourage the " revival" spirit, by meetings for prayer and preaching. In out-of-the-way new districts this may be still the main purpose. But I am uttering no scandal in saying that the camp meetings in the older States have come to be merely or chiefly pleasant annual rural gatherings. At Martha's Vineyard, Massachusetts, one of the most noted and important, the newspaper report says that " there was nothing ascetic or gloomy, but, on the other hand, a great deal that was cheerful and enlivening. If there was no dancing, there was at least croquet. The cottages, occupied by their owners, are pleasant residences, although the affair seems to have taken the shape of a serious rural fête. What John Wesley would have said to all this it is needless to inquire." We should think so ; nor should we be surprised to find the camp meeting, as an institution, become the theme of satire akin to that of Robert Burns in his " Holy Fair."

Much has been said by travellers in praise of the American fire establishments, the pride of the young men in American cities. I have already described the excellent system of watching, and of signalling by electric communica-

tions between the stations. But when we pass
from these arrangements to the *matériel* and
personnel of the force, I think the efficiency of
the American system has been exaggerated.
Their engines are splendid constructions, but
too ponderous to manage, except on great
occasions. They are almost wholly steam-power
engines, hand-engines being disused in the
large towns. The brigades have as thorough
organisation as the militia or the army, and are
constantly parading and marching through the
streets in showy uniform, with music and decorated engines. All this looks very imposing,
and the young men take pride in belonging to
a fire brigade. The officers, moreover, are
appointed by election, and it is said that political influence largely enters into the affairs of
the force. Social vanity and political feeling
thus combine to lessen the efficiency of what
ought to be purely a department of public
safety and of civic police.

Two or three years ago, Captain Shaw, the
able and energetic chief officer of the London
Fire Brigade, visited the States on purpose to
study the American system. His report was
reassuring as to the greater efficiency of our
own fire establishment. While admitting the
merit of the signalling system, and admiring
the beauty and power of the engines, Captain

Shaw decidedly objects to the semi-military discipline of the force in the States, the result of which is to foster public display at the expense of individual skill and self-reliance. The occasions are few when firemen have to attack a conflagration in parade order of companies and regiments. Every fireman must be trained to perform any part of the duty of the department, and ample scope must be left to personal skill, daring, and endurance. Our English system effects this, and is therefore on the whole more useful, though less showy, than the American system. Captain Shaw also thinks it is a mistake to allow hand-engines to get into disuse. A manual can be got into play in thirty seconds, whilst a steamer requires four or five minutes. I saw the engines at work in Chicago, and witnessed magnificent processions of firemen in Boston and New York; but with all my admiration of many things American, I think they are far behind our own " Metropolitan Fire Brigade."

CHAPTER XXVI.

TRADE AND LABOUR UNIONS—CONFLICT OF
LABOUR AND CAPITAL—STRIKES—CO-OPE-
RATIVE LABOUR.

UNTIL recent years, the questions which
most agitate the working classes in Europe
have been little mooted in America. When
all kind of industrial work was abundant, labourers comparatively few, and wages high,
the workmen were prosperous and contented.
It is so in the new and thinly-peopled regions
still. But in the older States and in the cities,
where the population presses on the means of
subsistence, and where the cost of living is
high, the relations of employer and employed,
of capital and labour, are less harmonious, and
trades unions, or " labour unions " as they are
termed, interfere with the ordinary conditions
of work and wages. The principle of labour
unions is sound enough. If men can obtain by
combination advantages not to be obtained by
individual effort, they are right to combine.

23

They may unite in order to obtain increase of
wages or decrease of working time, as well as
for any other purpose of mutual benefit. But
the power of law and of public opinion is too
strong in America to admit of the alarm which
trades unions in England have exhibited.

When I was at Boston there was a strike
among the operatives at the Fall River factories.
An attempt was made to coerce, at the instiga-
tion, it was said, of some English trade unionists
of the Sheffield type. The militia was promptly
called out, and the unionists were told that
"whatever they might do in England, interference with the right of free labour would not for
an hour be tolerated in America." There was
a strike some time afterwards among the col-
liers in Pennsylvania. This also was traced to
foreign workmen, few of the native Americans
taking part in it. The combinations of working
men, however, are increasing throughout the
Union, and may cause political as well as social
troubles. We have heard already of a labour
league threatening to make a separate organi-
zation in view of the next presidential election.
The prospect of political influences from such
combination is small, the mass of the people
being well leavened with sound views of political economy through the press. In illustration
of this, and as presenting a clear and forcible

statement of truths worthy of being weighed by working men in England as well as America, I quote a leading article which appeared in the *Cincinnati Gazette* when a "Labour Convention" was being held in that city.

" The Labour Convention descended a moment from the airy height of perfecting the condition of the labourer by using him for a political party, and by making money of paper, to resolve in favour of two things which seem to have a direct and practical bearing on the conditions of labour ; these were eight hours for a day's work, and the co-operation of labourers to carry on business without the medium of the capitalist.   Passing by for the present the eight-hour question with the general remark that we have an abiding faith that whatever is good for the labourer is good for the whole, we may say of co-operative industrial enterprise that it is a thing to which all will bid good speed, save perhaps a few owners of great establishments who have possession of some monopoly by combination of capital and by government favouritism.   The influence of these, though strong, in affecting legislation bearing on their privileges, would be small in any case where it was plain that they were in opposition to the labourer ; therefore we may say that practically the sympathies of the whole com-

munity will be in favour of intelligent co-operative industrial enterprises.

" These enterprises require in the co-operative workmen the same steadiness in the pursuit, the same self-denial, the same willingness
to forego present indulgence to lay up capital,
which have enabled the labourer to become the
capitalist and employer; and the same patience
and pluck under the adversities which occasionally come upon all industries that the single
capitalist must have to carry the business
through these periods of depression and loss.
In times of prosperity these co-operative workmen must have the providence to forego large
dividends and an expanded scale of family expenditure, in order to accumulate ready capital
to carry them through the intervals of adver-
sity. From the beginning they must be content
to allow a part of their earnings to accumulate
in stock. Like the capitalists, they must be
content to receive for their work only their food
and clothes, while their savings go to increase
their capital and their stock of machinery and
materials. And they must have the patience
to continue the same industrious co-operation
in the periods when there are no profits, and
when they have to see the savings of their
former earnings diminished.

" This is no more than to say that the co

operative workmen who are their own capitalists must have the same qualities of providence, steadiness, patience, and pluck, that the single capitalist and employer must have. Co-operation, therefore, requires workmen of the best qualities ; such qualities as will generally raise the single workman to the employer and capitalist. Society in general will bid good speed to co-operation which fosters these qualities in the workmen, and to all efforts to elevate the qualities of the labourers so as to make co-operation practicable. For to say that the improvident, indolent, and unskilful labourers, who are content to live from hand to mouth, and whose highest aim is a contest with employers to cheat them out of a fair return for their wages, can carry on any co-operative enterprise, is to say what no workman will believe. These are drones who abuse the present labour unions, and tend to drag down all workmen to their level. Co-operative industry would find them its worst competitors, because in time of industrial depression their improvidence would leave them subject to any terms that capital might impose.

" As, for successful co-operative enterprise, each individual workman will need to have the provident and stable qualities of the successful capitalist employer, so the interest of the co-operative workmen becomes the same as the single capitalist employer. Therefore, when the Labour Convention assumes that labour is in conflict with capital, and then resolves in favour of co-operation, it simply resolves that the workmen of the best qualities shall go over to the enemy. This is an inconsistency, however, which can be removed by correcting the erroneous notion that labour is in conflict with capital. We will instance some of the things in which the interests of co-operative establishments will be in conflict with what the labour unions assume to be the interests of labourers, and will be on the side of what they call the hostile interests of capital.

" Co-operative enterprise will at once make a breach in the eight-hour system, which the Labour Convention assumes to be the interest of the labourer against the employer. The object of the eight hours scheme is to get as much wages for eight hours' work as for a whole day. Workmen who have the ordinary ambition to improve their condition will not be limited to eight hours' work in a day, if they can get pay in proportion for working ten or twelve. The profit of co-operative industry will be in proportion to its productiveness ; therefore the co-operative can make more by working ten or twelve hours, and he will do it ;

and therefore all co-operative enterprises are breaches in the eight-hour system.

" The eight-hour scheme also expects to square the results of paying ten hours' wages for eight hours' work by making the consumer pay the increased cost, and by limiting production so as to compel him to. But it becomes the interest of the co-operative workmen to cheapen the cost of materials and subsistence and production in every way, to increase the consumption and their own profits. Thus generally the interests of the co-operative workmen become antagonistic to the interests of the labourer in general, if it be true, as seemed to be assumed by the Labour Convention, that labour is in conflict with capital.

" When the co-operative workmen become interested in all the results of the manufacture of a particular article, it becomes their interest to have all other processes cheapened which in any way enter into the cost of their production ; and to have its market increase by increasing consumption. For example, the co-operative enterprise may be engaged in the manufacture of furniture. It then becomes the interest of the co-operative workmen to have all things that enter into their expenses furnished as cheaply as possible, in order that by reducing the cost of production they may extend their

market and increase their profits. It becomes
their interest to have all their materials, and
their dwellings, subsistence, and clothes, at a
low cost. To this end they want cheap lumber,
shops, machinery, paints, varnishes, etc., cheap
building materials, cheap transportation, cheap
building, cheap fuel, cheap provisions, and so
on through all the articles of living and all the
materials and elements of the cost of the article
they are producing.

"Therefore the co-operative workmen will
find all combinations to raise the price of materials, machinery, lumber, brick, brick-laying,
plastering, carpentering, painting, plumbing,
food, fuel, clothes, and so on, by raising the
wages of workmen in all these things, contrary
to his own interest, which is to buy cheaply
everything that he has to buy, and to sell dearly
everything he has to sell. Thus a resolution to
encourage co-operative industrial enterprise is
a resolution to create among workmen an interest hostile to the leading policy of labour
unions, namely, to raise all wages and the cost
of all production. One of these, therefore,
must be an erroneous view of the interests of
labourers. But this conflict of inconsiderate
declarations brings into view the fact which is
palpable to every workman who ever thinks,
namely, that combinations to raise wages uni-

versally, neutralise themselves by raising every
workman's cost of living in proportion to the
advance of wages, and that no labour protective
association can be effectual except when partial.
When these protective associations become extended so as to embrace all labourers, then the
protection is neutralised, and the result is that
all have raised their expenses of living in proportion to their wages. This is the natural law
to which all schemes of labour protection are
subject.

" The working of this interest of co-operative
industry may enable us to come at a clearer
view of the true interests of labour, and its relation to capital. The Labour Convention does
not see that it declares for an interest antagonistic to the labourer, when it declares for co-
operative enterprise, and we maintain that it
does not. But it is· plain that co-operative
workmen are simply combined capitalists, and
that their interests are identical with those of
all capital engaged in that branch of industry.
This seems to show that the notion of an irre-
pressible conflict between capital and labour is
an error. If we look at the thing, we shall see
that capital is the savings of labour, and that
in general the capitalist, like the provident co-
operative workman, has little but his food and
clothes for his share, while the increase of his

capital from further savings goes to extend his enterprises and thus to furnish more employment to labour.

" If there be no increase of capital, there can be no increase of employment, and thus the increase of labourers would steadily depress their condition. A warfare upon capital, therefore, which aims to prevent its increase, and to restrict production, is a direct warfare on the labourer's employment. Thus it will be seen that the interests of capital invested in industrial enterprise and the interests of the labourer are identical. If the employer gets ten per cent. increase on his capital, his workmen have all the use and benefit of his capital, save the fraction of ten per cent. If he invests this increase in extending his enterprise, the workmen have the use and benefit of all his capital. He has only his board and clothes. He may live in a little better style than they, but he dies and carries nothing away with him; and if his capital remains in the industrial enterprise, the workmen enjoy it, while he has gone where it cannot follow him.

" And this will make plain that combinations to raise universally the cost of production, and to restrict production, are simply combinations of labourers against themselves. We will suppose that the labourer is as successful and provident as the average capitalist and employer, and that he saves ten per cent. of his wages— a saving which will put him on the road to become a capitalist and employer. Then 90 per cent. of his wages goes for his consumption, to pay for dwelling, fuel, food, clothes comforts, and so on ; all of which are products of labour. Therefore, all the combinations he enters into to raise the wages of the work that produces these things are combinations to raise the cost of his own consumption and diminish the portion that he can save.

" The same benevolence that exhorts the labourer to co-operative enterprise will exhort him also to the skill, energy, stability, and frugality that enable workmen to become capitalists and employers. The notion that there is an antagonism between capital and labour assumes that the line between the capitalist and the labourer is fixed and impassable, and that the object of each class is to plunder the other. But co-operative workmen become capitalists, with interests the same as single capitalists and employers ; therefore, when the Labour Convention declares for co-operation it virtually admits that it is wrong in the notion that capitalists and workmen are in antagonism. And the skilled, industrious, and frugal workman becomes singly a capitalist and employer ;

therefore, the just compensation of capital, instead of being antagonistic to him, holds out to him an object of ambition, and a chance to better his condition. The theory that labour is at war with capital assumes that capitalists and labourers are two distinct and fixed classes. It throws away the opportunities of superior individual skill, energy, and economy, and consents to accept the position and destiny of the average of all sorts, including the indolent, ignorant, and improvident, and to be held down by them, instead of rising by superior qualities. It consents to forego the individual ambition that is the right of all men, and to be tied down to the improvident masses ; and then it joins them in combinations to raise the cost of their own consumption, in the foolish notion that it is waging warfare on capital."

CHAPTER XXVII.

I T has been a puzzle to some minds, and has even been used as a sceptical argument against the Bible, that sacred prophecy seems not to include in its range the history of the New World. The field of view is there so large, and the development of events so great, that it is strange to find America occupying little, if any, place in what purports to be a vision of human history to the end of time.

I once mentioned this difficulty to the greatest student and expositor of prophecy, Dr. Keith, and his reply was prompt and satisfactory. The brief prophecies of the latter day refer to principles, operating alike in the Old World and the New. In America the principles of Popery and Infidelity, and whatever opposes the truth of God, are at work in the same way as in Europe. The same spiritual conflicts are waged on both continents. Prophecy deals with political events and with human developments only as these bear upon the great history of the kingdom of Christ. That kingdom has no geographical scenes or limits, but reaches from sea to sea, and from the river to the ends of the earth.

We call it the New World, but we find there only new forms and new illustrations of old-world religions, as well as of social and political life. The negro is there with his charms and Fetish worship, the "heathen Chinee" with his joss-house. The Hebrew synagogue is there, and the Popish mass-house. There is nothing new in any of the wild sects that have sprung up: the wonder is that wilder and more numerous forms of free thought and free living have not appeared in a land where liberty passes into licence. By public opinion, more than by law or force, are extravagances of creed and conduct kept within bounds. I have already stated that these are only slight specks on the broad surface of American life. Sensational bookmakers give the impression that the country is overrun by Shakers and Spiritualists, and all sorts of fanatical sects. The whole of these combined form an insignificant fraction in the religious census. The vast mass of the population profess the same creeds, and belong to the same communions

known among ourselves—Episcopal, Methodist
(Episcopal), Presbyterian, Congregational, and
Baptist. With differences of organisation, all
these hold in common the leading truths of
Protestant Christianity. The Roman Catholics
number between four and five millions, the
vast majority Irish. Among the Southern
Germans and other continental emigrants there
are also many Roman Catholics, but the great
body of the North German and Scandinavian
emigrants are Protestants. It was pleasant to
see together in many a German home in the
West the portraits of Luther and Washington.

I have given the relative statistics of churches
and denominations in several of the large
cities. In the smaller towns, and throughout
the country, the great bulk of the people belong
to the leading Protestant denominations already
enumerated. The Methodists and Baptists are
the most numerous, taking the whole Union ;
but the Presbyterians prevail in some of the
older States, both of the North and South. It
would be difficult to say which of the denominations includes the largest number of the educated
and wealthy classes. In the large cities it is
very probable that the Episcopal communion
will increase in a larger ratio among the rich,
and that it will become the church of the
higher social grades, as in England. It is said

that this is because discipline is laxer, and the members of the Episcopal churches are less under the control of such public opinion as the church membership of other communities maintains. This may be partly true, but it is not the whole truth. It is certainly not true of the large masses of good people who belong to the communion of such men as McIlvaine, Tyng, and others, whose names are honoured in all Evangelical churches. It may be well for the leading men in Presbyterian and other churches to consider how far the spiritual instincts and educated tastes of their people can be met, without driving many to find elsewhere what is lacking in their own services. I am afraid to say more, in case of treading on the toes of any one behind me; but it is vexing to an overlooker to witness the strange vagaries of those who are in the thick of ecclesiastical controversies having no reference to things essential. The same questions also appear so different under different circumstances. For instance, one of the leading clergymen of Scotland wrote a book to prove that the use of instrumental music is a denial of the Gospel system, and a return to the Jewish dispensation of types and bondage! In America nearly all the churches have organs and choirs. On the other hand, G. H. Stuart, of Philadelphia, the

President of the Christian Commission during the war, one of the best and most respected citizens of America, has been excommunicated by the " Reformed Presbyterian Synod" for singing Christian hymns, instead of Rouse's old version of the Psalms of David, "the only fit medium for tuneful praise "!

The greatest contrast that strikes a stranger from the old country is the absence of an Established Church. There are no such names known as Churchmen and Dissenters, with all the unseemly divisions of social and religious life associated with the names among ourselves. There is no union of Church and State as in Europe,—whether, as in England, by one denomination being established, or, as in France, by all denominations receiving State pay. All denominations are equal before the law in the United States; all are free from State control, and obtain no State assistance. The idea of one denomination being selected from others for establishment or endowment, and the others being *tolerated*, is inconceivable in America. The whole circumstances and conditions of civil and religious life are different there, and the statement of this fact of the separation of Church and State may be made, without any reference to our own ecclesiastical arrangements in England, which date from a time

24

when the Church had visible unity, and which
were continued at the Reformation, when sepa-
ratists from the Established Church were few
in number and of little influence.

Some who have not visited America may
imagine that the absence of an Established
Church implies a low state of public religious
feeling. There could not be a greater mistake.
Religion pervades the nation to a far greater
extent than in any country of the Old World,
and Christianity is far more honoured and influential in every department of public and
social as well as domestic life. Not only are
the sessions of Congress opened with prayer,
as are our Houses of Parliament; but all courts
of law are also opened by prayer. In legislation and government, whether of the Republic or of the separate States, there is more
frequent reference to religion than with ourselves. But most of all is this manifest in the
system of common school education, which is
the pride and strength, *decus et tutamen*, of the
American Commonwealth. Notwithstanding
diversities of sects and of opinions in minor
matters, it was a grand sight to see the children
of all denominations meeting in the same
schools, opened every day by prayer or praise
and reading the Bible. I could not but think,
with sorrow and humiliation, of the miserable

squabbles and jealousies of our School Board constituencies, and the inefficient patchwork educational system alone possible with us.

If any other illustration is needed of the prevalent national respect for religion, I might refer to the appointment of days of humiliation or of thanksgiving on special occasions. No authority is recognised as compulsory in such matters, but the issuing of a recommendation, signed by the President and the Secretary of State, is responded to heartily throughout the nation. Every year " Thanksgiving Day " is a time of special assembly for public worship, when national mercies are devoutly acknow- ledged in fifty thousand churches, and the in- cense of praise rises from millions of thankful, reverential hearts.

Sabbath observance is another fair test of the amount of religious feeling pervading a nation. The day is far better kept than in England, or even in Scotland. I remember hearing the late Robert Chambers, a man not very sensitive or very demonstrative on such subjects, speaking with the warmest admiration of the way in which the day of rest was ob- served. He was surprised at the extent to which labour and traffic were suspended, and at the large attendance at churches and Sunday schools. The scene struck him the more from

his knowledge of the " traditions " of Scotland
on this matter.   In the large cities of America,
in some of which the native population is
actually in the minority, the observance of the
Sabbath may be expected to be more lax; but
taking the whole Union, town and country
together, " the Lord's day," whether as a day
of rest or a season of Christian worship, is
better observed and more honoured than anywhere in the Old World.   I may add that the
increase of churches and church members is
far beyond even the rapid ratio of the increase
of population.

   I am glad to confirm my statements as to
the influence of religion among the masses
of the people, by the testimony of an English
clergyman, well known for his shrewdness and
liberality—the Rev. Harry Jones—who thus
wrote to the *Guardian* newspaper: " I was
not prepared to find such strong evidences of
popular respect for religion, as met me everywhere during my tour.   I found them not only
in the city and the country, but in the forest,
the steamboat, and the railway station. . . . .
There is little in America corresponding to the
provision of the means of divine worship for
the ' poor ' of which we hear in England.   I
have heard this brought as a charge against
American Churches.   But the real answer, to

speak generally, is that there are few poor, as we understand the word. Large numbers of the working classes who might be loosely classed as 'poor' with us, are in the habit of attending some place of worship. Moreover, we are ready to form an opinion on the general religious provision for the 'masses' in America from what we see in the cities. The city poor are mainly Irish Roman Catholics, who are looked after by their own priests. The bulk of the real American working people are found in the country. Look at the little wooden church in every village. See how the spire or tower, staring with paint and æsthetically ugly as possible, shows itself in a new settlement, and ask who build these—who attend them? The real 'working men' of America.

"The people have reversed the process with which we are familiar in England. Instead of having money begged for them by others for a church, they build it themselves; and instead of having a parson set among them, they look about, and call some one to be their minister. It is the same in education."

I observed little that was special in the preaching of American ministers. My Sundays were not many, but I made the most of them for observation, if not for edification. The majority of the sermons, or parts of sermons,

which I heard were very much like what would
be preached in our English pulpits, whether
church or chapel. The Presbyterians pay more
attention than other communities to the theological training of their ministers; and in their
churches, I heard expository and textual
preaching more than in other churches, where
the customary text was given out chiefly as a
motto or peg upon which to hang the discourse.
It may partly have been from the heat of the
weather, and the absence of stated ministers
from their posts; but I confess that the
majority of preachers were of the heavy-and-
dry sort. Men of genius and eloquence are
wondered after and wandered after there as
with us. Ministers of solid learning and sober
speech abound as with us. A minister of
great spiritual fervour and earnest feeling—
one who preaches "as a dying man to dying
men"—is rare there as here. There is much
that is conventional and professional in all the
churches, but there must be a large amount of
true spiritual life to sustain the active and
energetic Christian work everywhere apparent.
In the Episcopal church Ritualism is not often
obtrusive, though there are full-blown specimens
of it. New York has a St. Alban's as London
has, and there are clergymen who believe
baptism to be regeneration, as indeed it is the

only regeneration they know or understand.
The Roman Catholic churches into which I
went were crowded with zealous worshippers,
and I found the pew-rent system among them
thoroughly worked; plans of the church, with
the prices of sittings, being suspended in the
lobbies.

The clergy of all denominations are, on the
whole, treated with great respect. It is a
common thing to make deduction in prices of
travelling, hotel charges, and even trade
purchases to ministers. It is also a common
thing for congregations to present their pastors with a purse to defray the cost of a trip
in the summer, which partly accounts for the
large proportion of ministers met with among
American tourists in Europe.

As to the regular stipends, there are a few
" pets " and popular preachers who have
salaries like English bishops. Below them there
are large numbers with sufficient salaries; but
below these, again, a vast number can barely
subsist and rear their families in the position to
which their services entitle them. There is no
" Common Fund," as with the Free Church of
Scotland or the Wesleyans of England, to
secure a competency for all, leaving the few
in richer stations to be supplemented by local
gifts. A very large proportion of ministers

seem to be "unattached," and to take engagements by the year, or even shorter terms.   An
unpopular preacher, or incompetent minister,
has no provision made for him ; still less can
he obtain a living by purchase as with us.
The " Voluntary " system thus is pushed to
its extreme development, though one advantage is that many are prevented entering the
ministry from mere worldly motives.   Some
change is wanted, similar to the system of the
Free Church Sustentation Fund, to secure the
ministers from too direct dependence on the
tyranny of deacons or managers, or the caprice
and temper of the people.   But the real
spiritual work of " Home Missions " to new
or poor districts is not practically hindered,
the missionary Boards of the several churches
guaranteeing salaries for a certain time to the
agents who undertake to break up waste or
fallow ground.   Hence new settlements in the
remotest regions are gladdened by the Gospel
sound, and blessed with the civilising and
saving influence of Christianity.

In a former article I gave a detailed notice
of the Sabbath services at Plymouth Church of
which the Rev. Henry Ward Beecher is the
minister.   The only other sermon that I heard
of an unusual kind was in a Methodist Episcopal Church at Washington.   The preacher,

Dr. Gibson, is a man of some mark in that community, and has reputation as an eloquent preacher. The subject was the parable of the prodigal son, and when the text was given out, my first passing thought was one of satisfaction at hearing the old Bible truths in every land, having heard the same text not long before given out by good Mr. Müller, at Bristol. But in two minutes I was wakened up to a surprise. Whether the preacher took for granted the usual exposition of the parable as accepted by his hearers, or whether he rejected the spiritual interpretation commonly given, there was not a word about the wandering of the soul from God, and its sins and sorrows; not a word about its awaking and return to the merciful and forgiving Father. The younger son wished to leave home, to see the world and make his way in the world. "If his motive was enterprise and independence, and not merely a desire to be free from the wholesome restraints of the parental roof, his desire was laudable and exemplary. Shame upon the young man who remains tied to his mother's apron-strings, and a burden upon his father, when able to go out into the world, and in a spirit of enterprise and independence make for himself a living and a home! The younger son is far more worthy of honour and imitation than the stay-at-home, selfish, idle, elder brother. He said to his father, divide the living. There is nothing of the abominable law of primogeniture here, as in some countries of the Old World. Equal rights and fair division for freemen!" And so on, in racy and original style, the commentary proceeded, the preacher giving an eloquent and effective description of the perils from intemperance and evil company that beset a young man's path in life, and the nobility of overcoming temptation by industry and temperance, and good principle. Of the corruption of the heart, and the necessity of restoring grace, little was said, and little about the divine and spiritual lessons of the parable. I do not say that the preacher rejected these, nor do I refer to his sermon as a representative one of the country or of the denomination to which he belongs, but it proved that " broad " views are not unknown in the Evangelical churches of the States, and the whole discourse was racy of the soil, and could have been delivered to none but an American audience. The sermon, I should say, was specially addressed " to young men."

Is Popery on the increase in America? Counting heads, and counting priests, churches, chapels, seminaries, convents, and the other " plant " of the Roman Catholic Church in the United States, there seems at first glance a wonderful increase at each successive census. Cathedrals of imposing magnitude are rising in all the great cities, and the churches equal in numbers those of the largest Protestant denominations. But this is only in places where the Irish and other Popish immigrants are congregated. Compared with the general increase of population in the States, the increase of Roman Catholics is of little account, and is really of no account among the native Americans. And if we extend the survey to the whole of the New World, the decline of the Papacy is far more marked than in the Old World. A century ago, with the exception of the New England colonies, the Roman Catholic Church bore supreme sway in the New World, from Canada down to Cape Horn. All the lands under French, Spanish, and Portuguese rule were covered with gross spiritual darkness. The progress of the great American Republic, as of free States everywhere, means the progress of Protestantism, and the steady and sure decline of Popery.

CHAPTER XXVIII.

THERE is a remarkable letter on emigration, written by George Washington in 1796, which contains information as correct, and advice as valuable, at the present time as it was then. It was written in reply to a letter of inquiry from Sir John Sinclair, Bart., the well-known political economist, and author of " The Statistical Survey of Scotland." Depressed by the gloomy aspect of public affairs towards the close of the eighteenth century, Sir John had thoughts of seeking a refuge and a home in the New World. The circumstances out of which the correspondence arose were narrated by him in publishing the letters as long afterwards as 1821. In the quarter of a century which had elapsed, Great Britain had passed safely through all her perils, and peace had been restored to Europe. The power of France, which had culminated under Napoleon, was no longer a terror and menace. The home administration of England was as tyrannical and impolitic as ever; but the safety and honour of Great Britain had been restored by the victories of Nelson and Wellington, and the other gallant defenders of our country. Sir John Sinclair lived to a good old age in peace and quietness, and his sons and sons' sons have seen England greater and more influential than ever.

Though no danger from abroad, not even a Teutonic invasion and "Battle of Dorking," may ever compel the rich to seek a transatlantic sanctuary, there may be social revolutions in the future that may raise similar alarms; and always the pressure of increased population must compel the relief which emigration alone can afford. Domestic anxieties, the *res angusta domi*, still prompt the inquiries which Sir John Sinclair made under the foreboding of public calamities. Here is an extract from his explanation of the correspondence with General Washington: "At the commencement of the year 1796, the aspect of affairs in Great Britain became of the gloomiest description. Such was the success of the arms of France, and such the terror which they inspired, that the Continent seemed to be completely subdued, while the affairs of Great Britain itself were so unsuccessfully conducted as to give rise to the

most serious apprehension in the minds of
many that it could not much longer continue
the contest." After expressing his strong dissatisfaction with Pitt for his course and policy,
feeling that it would ruin the country, Sir John
Sinclair says : " Seeing but little prospect
that the country would be extricated from the
difficulties in which it was involved, unless a
different course was pursued, which was not
probable, I naturally thought it necessary to
look out for an asylum for myself and family,
where we might live at a distance from the
calamities of Europe, which seemed more likely
to increase than to diminish. I was thus induced to apply to a most respectable corre-
spondent, the President of the United States,
to know what part of America was the most
desirable place for a British emigrant."

The whole of General Washington's letters
have been republished in a little book by Elihu
Burritt,* well worthy of being studied by intending emigrants. A few sentences will suffice
in this place :—

" The United States, as you well know, are
very extensive—more than 1,500 miles between

* " Washington's Words to Intending English Emigrants to
America," with Introduction and Appendix by Elihu Burritt :
Sampson Low, Son, and Marston. (The Appendix contains
useful information about all the States of the Union, and their
inducements for various classes of emigrants.)

the north-eastern and south-western extremities,
—all parts of which, from the seaboard to the
Appalachian Mountains (which divide the
eastern from the western waters), are entirely
settled, though not as completely as they are
capable of, and settlements are rapidly pro-
gressing beyond them. Within so great a
space, you are not to be told that there is a
great variety of climates; and you will readily
suppose, too, that there are all sorts of land,
differently improved and of various prices,
according to the quality of the soil, its con-
tiguity to or remoteness from navigation, the
nature of improvements, and other local circumstances.

"The rise in the value of landed property in
this country has been progressive ever since
my attention has been turned to the subject,
now more than forty years; but for the last
three or four years of that period it has increased beyond all calculation, owing in part
to the attachment to, and the confidence which
the people are beginning to place in, their
form of government, and to the prosperity of
the country from a variety of causes, none
more than to the high prices of its produce."

After giving details about the New England
States, Pennsylvania, and other Northern and
Eastern States, and Virginia, he says: "The

uplands of North and South Carolina and Georgia are not dissimilar in soil, but as they approach the lower latitudes, are less congenial to wheat, and are supposed to be proportionately unhealthy. Toward the seaboard of all the Southern States (and the farther south the more so) the country is low, sandy, and unhealthy, for which reason I shall say little concerning them; for *as I should not choose to be an inhabitant of them myself, I ought not to say anything that would induce others to be so.*"

"If all," says Elihu Burritt, "who have written glowing descriptions of certain sections of the country had followed this conscientious rule and principle, thousands of credulous and honest emigrants from Old England would have been saved a sad and bitter experience. Persons who have a special interest in some particular district may truthfully set forth the cheapness, the fertility, and the rich and varied productions of the soil. All they say may be true; but, withholding one vital fact from the description, it may be delusive and disastrous to those who trust to its statements."

Following this principle, and keeping in view a certain health-line as the southern boundary for English emigration, Mr. Burritt goes over the whole of the Republic, including the vast regions of the West, which in Washington's days were unexplored, or only traversed by wandering Indians. For details we must refer to his little volume, or to other more extended works, only mentioning that the emigrant will obtain from any of the Government land offices* reports, with maps of any unsold lands in the district which that special office represents. A large proportion of emigrants are determined in their choice of locality by the communications of friends who have already settled there, and those who leave the decision till their arrival in America will receive every help and advice at the offices of the Emigration Commissioners, and at the "Labour Exchange" at the landing-place in New York.

Of this landing-place, and the arrangements for the reception and disposal of emigrants, a brief notice may now be given. Until a few years ago, the arrival of emigrants of the poorer classes was a scene of painful confusion and misery. Those who had no relatives or

---

* There are in England various American agencies where information can be obtained, especially " The International Land and Labour Agency," Town Hall Chambers, Birmingham. This agency was established by Elihu Burritt, late U. S. Consul, and other gentlemen, and is worthy of confidence. Lists are kept of all investments in land and other property, and the Labour Department undertakes to find situations and employment for persons of any trade or occupation for a moderate commission. The secretary of the agency will furnish every information.

25

friends waiting to welcome them, were at the mercy of the New York land-sharks and other devourers of body and soul, as well as of what little substance they brought with them. The hapless and helpless state of the large propor- tion of emigrants induced many benevolent people to form an association for their assist- ance, and the Government was induced to establish a Board of Emigration Commis- sioners. The old Fort, with the surrounding area known as the Castle Gardens, was given over for their use as a receiving-house. Off this the emigrant ships lie, sending their freight ashore in steam tenders to the landing-stage, from which there is a passage to the interior of the Castle, or " the Rotunda," a place of which we used to hear as the scene of great public assemblages, such as political meetings, and entertainments. It was here that Jenny Lind's concerts, for example, were given. The space is now fitted up with various offices or counters, at which all sorts of entries are made and in- formation given. On the arrival of a cargo of emigrants, the names and places of birth, em- barkation, and so on, are entered in a registry. The place of destination is asked, and those who know this, and have money to pay for their passage, are furnished with tickets for the cheap emigrant trains. All being registered, a clerk reads out the names of those who had letters or money-orders addressed to them, which they receive; and of those who have friends waiting for them, to whom they are taken.

Of the remainder, without friends or fixed destination, but with sufficient money, those who choose to remain in New York are introduced to lodging-house keepers licensed by the authorities, so as to protect the new comers from the places of plunder, and taverns for drinking and gambling near the water-side. Others, who are anxious for employment at once and anywhere, are taken to the "Labour Exchange," where clerks are ready to engage labour of every kind, a record being kept of all the engagements. The wages appear high, but to quote examples would be useless, as they vary constantly, and as the value of money depends on the expense of the locality. Rent in the towns is high, and clothing, and all manner of provisions beyond bread and water.

Those emigrants without friends, letters, or money, and not capable of being employed by the labour agents, remain at the Rotunda a night or two, till they can be forwarded to Ward's Island, up the River Hudson, where are buildings for their reception, with hospitals

for the sick, schools for the young, and other
establishments, under charge of the Commissioners.   From ten to fifteen thousand may be
thus stranded on Ward's Island each season, the
largest number of whom are disposed of before
the close of the year.   A few are permanently
employed on a farm and in work on the island;
the hospital and lunatic asylum retain others;
and the death-rate is large after all the able-
bodied and healthy have been drafted off.

The Commissioners are bound to keep registries, and to have supervision of emigrants for
five years, maintaining correspondence for this
purpose with distant branches and agencies.
The necessary funds are obtained from the
owners of the emigrant ships, who have to pay
five shillings a head for every passenger, so
that virtually the fund comes from the passage money, and is in fact a mutual insurance
fee paid by the emigrants themselves.

Besides the official Board of Commissioners,
there is an association of benevolent persons,
including clergy of all denominations, for the
assistance of friendless emigrants arriving at
New York.   There need, therefore, be little
anxiety about the welfare of those who arrive
there, and it is no uncommon thing for unprotected females, and invalids, and little children
to be consigned to the New Word, with or

without labels and directions, in the certainty that all care will be taken of them that Christian philanthropy can devise.

The total arrivals of emigrants in the United States in 1870 was 353,287. In 1869 the number was 385,287, being the largest in any year except 1854, when 427,833 landed in the New World. Taking several years, the average may have been 365,000, or a thousand a day. It is estimated that the average value to the country of every immigrant is a thousand dollars, so that this is no unimportant element in the increase of national wealth as well as of population.

The great majority of the immigrants are from Europe, and New York is the chief place of arrival. The chief port of embarkation is Liverpool, from which, in round numbers, about 200,000 annually are shipped. Of the nationalities, Germany and Ireland are most largely represented, then England and the Scandinavian races. Many thousand Chinese land every year at San Francisco, a flow of emigration having commenced from Asia as well as from Europe. The influence of this new disturbing element in the labour market, when the "celestials" make their way east of the Mississippi, as they have already begun to do, is one of the difficult and troublesome political

problems with which the Americans will have
to deal.   They are not regarded with the same
favour as other emigrants, though their labour
is invaluable in developing the wealth of the
States on the Pacific side.   It will be long,
however, before they interfere with the European emigrants.   For the present most of them
come with no intention of settling, but only
to make money by their industrial labour, and
return with it to their own land.   The European
emigrants go to find permanent homes in the
New World, and most of them become citizens
of the United States.

I have before me an official pamphlet or
Circular from the General Land Office, issued
from the Department at Washington a few
weeks before I was there last autumn.   It contains the various Acts of Congress as to the
sale and occupation of public lands, and describes the manner of proceeding (with forms
and schedules) in order to obtain title to possession.   Some of the Acts are of a special
kind, such as giving privileges, or relaxing
rules, in the case of those who have served in
the United States army or navy ; but the main
enactment of interest to emigrants is " the
Homestead Act," which gives to every citizen
of the States, or to those who declare their intention to become such, the right to a home-

stead on surveyed lands. An affidavit has to be made before the Registrar or Receiver at a land office, that the applicant is over twenty-one years of age, or is the head of a family, and that the land is for actual settlement and cultivation. The right of purchase is then conceded to the extent of one quarter section, or 160 acres, at 1 dollar 25 cents per acre, or 80 acres at 2 dollars 50 cents. There are two classes of public lands, the one class at 1 dollar 25 cents, which is designated as *minimum*, and the other at 2 dollars 50 cents per acre, or *double minimum*.

The circular, which contains directions and regulations as to the required forms of application, fees, commissions, and other charges, can be obtained at any of the public land offices in various parts of the Union, where also maps are exhibited of the surveyed lands in sections.

In regard to naturalisation the law differs in different States. The usual law is that the alien shall be able to read a clause in the constitution of the State, and declare his intention of becoming a citizen, taking at the same time an oath to support the constitution of that State, aud the constitution of the United States. One year after this declaration and oath, the settler is entitled to vote for State officers, and in five

years to vote in the election for President of
the Republic.

Without naturalisation, any alien can hold
property, and is entitled to all rights and protection under the laws, unless found bearing
arms against the State. Almost every new
comer so soon becomes interested in the political and social and still more in the educational
matters of his neighbourhood, that it is very
rare to meet with a person who has resided
one year in any community who has not been
naturalised.

What has been said hitherto only relates to
public lands. Those who have money to go
into the open market have a wider range.
" There are farms always and everywhere for
sale," Washington wrote to Sir John Sinclair ;
" if, therefore, events should induce you to cast
an eye toward America, there need be no apprehension of your being accommodated to
your liking." The same is true now, not of
farms and land only, but of all manner of real
property, in town or country, in every part of
the Union. In the Middle and Southern States
the collapse of the Confederate rebellion, and
the ruin of many of the old slave-holding proprietors, have thrown great tracts of land into
the market, which are rapidly being taken up by
Northern colonists and speculators. Abundant

choice remains for English purchasers, who are hailed as more welcome neighbours by the Southerners than the still hateful " Yankees." Professor Goldwin Smith visited Virginia last summer, and after speaking of the magnificence of that State in point of resources, and capabilities, and climate, says: " The people are the most English of all Americans. They are very friendly to the mother-country, and very anxious that their States should be filled up by English emigrants." Labour is cheap, coloured labourers being hired at £2 a month, with provisions supplied. All local taxes do not exceed about twopence in the pound, the direct income tax being two and a half per cent. all over the Union. Even in the Old States east of the Hudson, the flow of native emigration to the West has left ample choice of cultivated farms, which can now be bought for from £3 to £12 an acre, including house, barns, and all other buildings necessary for such an estate. " In New England," says Elihu Burritt, "a man with £400 or £500 may buy a farm of one hundred acres, and be able to stock it, and bring his tools, and set to work, within an hour's·ride of the capital of the State. His £500 English gold, turned into United States or Massachusetts bonds in England, and then into American paper money at the current exchange, will yield him 3,500 dollars of lawful tender for the purchase at 25 dollars per acre, leaving him 1,000 dollars for stocking the farm. If he is a married man, and has already furniture sufficient for his new house, he may take it with him free of duty. If his farm should be nearer a large market town, or more valuable in soil or building, so that 50 dollars per acre should be demanded for the hundred, he might obtain it by giving his note, payable at the end of one or two years, with interest at six per cent., for the balance. In this case, also, he would have 1,000 dollars left out of his 3,500 dollars for stocking his farm and other expenses."

This case is supposed in the older Eastern States. In the Middle and Western States the purchase-money is at a lower rate ; labour, also, is cheaper, and expenses less. In Virginia, for instance, there were last year more than a thousand cultivated farms for sale, at prices from £2 to £12 an acre. A hundred may be bought within two or three hours from Washington City, at an average of £3 per acre. The residences, indeed, are only old-fashioned log houses, but an English farmer and his family could live comfortably in them till he had time to build a house more in accordance with his habits. Then there is Missouri, which aspires to be the central empire State of the Union,

and to make its great city of St. Louis the
capital of the Republic. Missouri contains
forty-three millions of acres, an area as large
as all England, with fertile soil and splendid
climate, rich in mineral as well as agricultural
wealth. Hundreds of farms may here be
bought from 10s. to 40s. an acre, and millions
of acres of Government lands may also be
entered under the Homestead Act by those
capable of the rougher work of clearing the
land. Every State has its special claims, its
advantages and drawbacks, all of which must
be well weighed by the intending emigrant.

One point is worthy of separate and special
notice in regard to the possession of land or
other real property in America, the cost of con-
veyancing. The legal expense of getting good
deeds or titles is merely nominal. For the safe
transfer of an ordinary farm the cost will not
exceed a dollar in almost any of the States.
And in fact in all matters of legal expense the
customs of America form a striking contrast to
the heavy amounts of " lawyers' bills " in England, where the people seem to exist for the
benefit of lawyers, rather than lawyers for the
benefit of the people.

There remains the essential practical question, Who ought to emigrate ? Leaving out of
view what may be called involuntary or com-

pulsory emigration, which applies to the poorest
classes, as in the time of the Irish famine, and
in the case of Highland "clearings," or the
decline of special branches of manufacture and
industry, there is always a large and yearly increasing multitude, from pressure of over-popu-
lation and competition, who are straitened in
the means of subsistence. Some who can support themselves have anxiety about the up-
bringing of their families in the same social
position. Others are dissatisfied at spending
their strength and passing their years in a bare
struggle for existence, with little prospect of
laying by provision for infirmity or old age.
These, and many other cases, arising out of the
simple motive of "the means of living," may
turn to emigration as a ready remedy. If willing and able to work, none need be disappointed if they decide on going to the United
States. There is room for millions of homes to
all who can handle the axe and plough, the hoe
and spade. There is also employment for men
of every handicraft in all departments of mechanical labour. The mineral wealth of the
Union is waiting for workers. One thing we
may be sure of, that so many States would not
clamorously invite and compete for emigrants,
if they feared that any number of them would
be thrown on their hands as helpless paupers.

As long, therefore, as the Americans invite emigrants to come, those who have a struggle for
life at home may feel it safe and advisable to go.

In what is here said about the United States,
there is no intention of disparaging Canada, or
any of our own colonies, as fields of emigration.
They may offer the same, or even stronger inducements, but my present object is to convey
the impressions formed by what I saw and
heard in the States.

But over and above the advantages as to
" means of living," there are inducements of
no unimportant kind to settling in the United
States. Not, indeed, for the wealthy and well-
to-do classes, " the upper ten thousand," to
whom emigration is only known as a way of
getting rid of the surplusage of " the lower
orders." People accustomed to the amenities
and amusements of aristocratic and plutocratic
life in the Old Country would be like fish out
of water in America. Jeames de la Plush and
Carolina Wilhelmina Amelia Skeggs would
think it a 'orrid place. Lord Dundreary would
wonder what a fellow could do there. Yet even
among the highest orders of rank and intellect
there are many who would enjoy life in the
States ; whether men like Goldwin Smith, who
admire the political institutions of the country,
or like Principal M'Cosh, in sympathy with the

academic culture and high moral tone of the seats of learning, or like the late accomplished and lamented Earl of Aberdeen, who regretted having to leave what he called a "land of freedom and common sense." But for the great middle class of Englishmen, and for the operative classes, whether in town or country, there are many points which they would admire and enjoy in the States more than even in England. Always excepting New York and the slavery-blighted States, there is as high social and moral tone throughout the Union as in the best parts of the Old Country. Education is more diffused, religion is more influential, the Sabbath is better observed, and Christian ordinances more honoured among the whole body of the people. There is a spirit of manly self-reliance and sturdy independence, which although at first repulsive from the brusqueness of manner which it induces, comes to be respected. The poor serf-like clodhopper of our English counties soon holds his head erect as a well-paid and free labourer. And the farmers remind one of the yeomen freeholders who once formed an influential portion of the British Commonwealth. Now that slavery is extinguished—the last legacy of misrule bequeathed by the mother-country—the emigrants as well as the native population more than ever exhibit what Washington described as "attachment to and confidence in their form of government and the prosperity of the country." And this applies to the manufacturing as well as agricultural classes of emigrants; they are as a rule better paid, better housed, better clothed, better fed, better educated, more contented, and more independent; in short, in moral as well as physical condition superior to the same class in the Old Country. It is certainly not true, as has been said, that decreasing means and an increasing family are the only conceivable inducements to think of settling in America.

We must not conclude, however, without saying a few words as to who ought not to emigrate to the United States. All classes of professional men, those who work chiefly with the head rather than with the hands, will find few openings. Commercial men and speculators of all sorts, with little or no capital, are not wanted. Capitalists can make their profitable American investments at home. Mercantile clerks are in no request. An advertisement in any American newspaper will bring as great a crowd of applicants as one in the *Times* or any English paper. Even of the operative classes, none but the industrious, frugal and temperate can expect to prosper in America. The chief engineer of one of the large steamers told me that he seldom made a return voyage without some disappointed emigrants working their passage home as stokers and cindermen. I saw some of these poor fellows, and their experience is that of many. The only occupation that could be obtained by them was in-agricultural work, for which health and strength are essential.* There are very few of the clerks or shop assistants in England who could stand the fatigue and climate of backwoods life in the West, or of common agricultural life in any other part of the Union, any more than they would be fit for it at home.

Even to farmers, Elihu Burritt says, " I would advise all of them who are over forty years of age, and can command £500 capital, to settle down in some of the old States of the Union, where a century of cultivation has not only subdued the soil to their hands, but subdued those raw conditions of its wild nature that generate ailments of a serious character to its first occupants. Not only for their physical comfort, but for their social enjoyment, would I commend to them this choice of residence. Young, vigorous

* Here is a sample advertisement : " WANTED. *Live* men everywhere. Permanent employment. Able-bodied men to go into the country. Prompt pay, and plenty to eat. Also reliable girls for household work." At the " Intelligence Offices," as servants registries are called, the rawest Irish girls are offered twelve dollars a month.

men can more safely and comfortably run the hazards not only of "the bush," but of the rich and level prairie, as yet unbroken by the plough. The febrile affections, the chills or bilious tendencies of such a region of country, and all the other discomforts which they will at first experience, do not sap the vigour of their constitutions, as in those past middle life. Such may go to any of the New States of the Great West, and make homes for themselves and their children, which they may all the more enjoy for the rough experience of the first few years."

Nor is there any opening for female emigration, except for domestic service. The native supply exceeds the demand for teachers, shop assistants, and workwomen of all grades. The "employment of females" question is quite as pressing there as with us. The post-office, telegraph service, and other public institutions employ many, but the proportion of unemployed and unprotected females, above the servile grade, is as great as at home, at least in the old, settled States.

Beyond the emigration question there are others at which I can only glance, but must not touch, as they lead to political ground. It is clear that the vast majority of emigrants leave their native land not by choice, but from necessity. Few are attracted by anything in the in-

26

stitutions of America, and fewer still from any
motive so lofty as the Pilgrim Fathers had.
Most go because they cannot subsist at home.
Is it then a necessity that so many should thus
be unwilling exiles? Does Great Britain support all the population of which she is easily
capable? The question will one day become a
practical one. The time must come when other
countries· may decline to take an unlimited
number of emigrants. The people also may
not always remain content to be jostled out of
the country into the towns, or thrust forth from
the land of their birth, if they think it is able to
support them. It is the part of a good government to render social revolution impossible, by
timely legislation for the many as well as for
the few, on the safe principle that " property
has its duties as well as its rights."

A special commission for the United States
is now in Europe, with instructions to examine
the whole subject, and to report, with a view to
legislation by Congress, upon existing abuses
of emigration and their remedies.

CHAPTER XXIX.

PRINCETON, NEW JERSEY—BACK TO NEW YORK —FARRAGUT'S FUNERAL.

AT Philadelphia I received a note from Dr. M'Cosh, President of Princeton College, New Jersey, inviting me to visit " the noble institution " over which he presides. It lay in my way back to New York, and was reached by a small branch railway from the main line. The winter session at the college was just commencing, and I was the more glad of the opportunity of having this peep at American academic life that I had passed Yale and Harvard during the vacation.

I must confess, however, that my chief interest in Princeton was not educational, and that I longed to see it most for its historical associations. It was connected in my mind with great names, above all with the name of the greatest thinker, and one of the greatest writers, that America has produced, Jonathan Edwards. It was at Princeton he died and

was buried.   The college has no higher historical distinction than having had him for its
President. I remembered what Dugald Stewart
said : " In the New World the state of society
and of manners has not hitherto been so
favourable to abstract science as to pursuits
which come home directly to the business of
human life.   There is, however, *one* metaphysician of whom America has to boast, who in
logical acuteness and subtlety does not yield to
any disputant bred in the universities of Europe.   I need not say that I allude to Jonathan
Edwards." I remembered, too, what Sir James
Mackintosh said, in his celebrated sketch of
the " History of Ethical Philosophy," of " this
remarkable man, the metaphysician of America."   " His power of subtle argument—perhaps unmatched, certainly unsurpassed, among
men—was joined, as in some of the ancient
Mystics, with a character which raised his
piety to fervour."   I remembered also the
enthusiasm with which Dr. Chalmers, in his
lectures, used to comment on the great works
of President Edwards, " On the Freedom of the
Will," on " Original Sin," and on the " Religious Affections."   The story of his life was
familiar to me ;—the ministry at Northampton,
with its remarkable seasons of revival, and its
long years of trial, amidst a people who could

not appreciate the divine seer who was among them;—the retirement to Stockbridge, where he went to be pastor of a few scattered settlers, and missionary to the Indians still residing in these regions. He seemed to be thrown away in such a place, like a broken potsherd, but it was the good providence of God that sent him there to have leisure for preparing the works which have made his name immortal. These being completed, he was summoned to preside over Princeton College, on the death of his son-in-law, President Aaron Burr. Soon after his arrival, he died from the consequences of being inoculated for protection from smallpox. He was only in his fifty-fourth year when he died, March 22, 1758. The scenes of his life were vividly recalled as I sat in his study and stood by his grave.

There is another great name associated with Princeton, and whose influence in the early history of the American Republic has not been duly estimated—John Witherspoon. In the history of literature he is known as the author of "Ecclesiastical Characteristics," a work which for keen wit, racy humour, and delicate satire, applied to the noblest uses, ranks with the "Provincial Letters" of Pascal. It was written when Witherspoon was a minister of the Kirk of Scotland, and was directed against the growing scepticism and "moderatism" of the eighteenth century. Bishop Warburton was delighted with the book, and only wished the English Church had such a counsellor and corrector. The publication of the "Characteristics" raised a host of enemies ; and, saddened by the hopeless state of affairs at home, the author emigrated to the New World. The College of Princeton was proud to obtain such a man as its President, in which office he continued till the outbreak of war with the mother-country. Many of the men who took the leading part in public affairs at that crisis had been trained as his pupils at Princeton. The citizens of New Jersey appointed him a delegate to the Convention which formed their State Constitution. In 1776 he was sent as representative of New Jersey to the first Congress of United America. He served for seven years in Congress, and though less known than some others of the fathers of the Republic, there was no one whose advice was more weighty, and whose influence was more felt. In face of danger he was always firm, and in the gloomiest times always hopeful and cheerful. He lived to see the Republic safe and prosperous, dying in 1794, in his seventy-third year. Many abuses were removed through his influence, and good measures carried. His political sagacity appeared in the warnings he gave as to the internal dangers that might arise from the conflicting interests of the separate States of the Union, and he urgently advocated the strengthening of the authority of the Central Government.

I have dwelt on these old names the more because they are not much noticed by common historians, or by travellers who describe only what they see. It is not by increase of population and growth of material wealth alone that America has attained its greatness. " What constitutes a State ?" Soemthing more than broad acres and steam-power, dollars and ballot-boxes. It is not easy to estimate the influence on national life and character exerted by such men as Jonathan Edwards and John Witherspoon. They worthily maintained in the eighteenth century the cause of religion and truth, of freedom and virtue, established in the seventeenth century on the shores of New England by the Pilgrim Fathers. I am delighted to find the same idea expressed by a recent traveller in the States, the Rev. W. G. Blaikie, who says " Edwards had eleven children, and their descendants now count by thousands. There can be little doubt that as his descendants penetrated the various strata of New England society, and carried with them much of the vigour of mind and fervour of spirit which belonged to both parents, they contributed to give it a considerable share of the tone or stamp which it now bears." There was a gathering last summer at Stockbridge of above two hundred of the descendants and connections of the family, including names of high mark, and the speeches showed how the old traditions are kept up to our own day.

The influence of President Witherspoon was greater than even that of Jonathan Edwards in the direction given to American national life and character. The part taken by himself and those who had been his pupils in the foundation of the Republic has already been noted. The spirit of his teaching has been preserved in the Princeton College, and is worthily sustained by the distinguished President who now fills his chair. It was a pity to allow a man like Dr. M'Cosh, the first of our metaphysicians since Sir William Hamilton, to leave his native land; but he holds an office second to none in the New World for moral and social as well as intellectual influence. I do not know the number of students at Princeton; but there are among them, even in greater proportion than at Yale or Harvard, the sons of senators, judges, and highest public men in the Union. If ever Dr. M'Cosh turns a look of regret towards the old country, of which I saw no sign, he may rather glory in the office he fills, training the minds and forming the characters of those who will hereafter guide the destinies of the great Republic.

I have little to report about the College or its studies. I saw the students assembled in the Chapel for worship, conducted by the President, and remember their devout demeanour and hearty volume of praise. I saw them at gymnastics in a hall fitted for indoor sports, and at base-ball in the grounds, and thought them a fine athletic set of fellows. I examined their course of study, and found it as thorough as in our own universities. I was witness to the quietness and order of the College and the town, giving proof of good discipline on the side of the governors, and high character in the governed. In fact, the discipline seemed almost overstrained, and the tone such as could not be easily kept up. But altogether, my impressions of Princeton as a place of study, and of the learning and ability of its professors, were of the most gratifying kind. But I carried away with still deeper feeling the impressions of the hallowed memories of the place. I went in the evening with the President to the cemetery of Princeton, and lingered there till light failed to read the inscriptions. It is a true *Campo Santo*, enclosing

the remains of more great and good men than
any burying-place of the size in America. The
graves of Aaron Burr and of Jonathan Edwards, two of the first Presidents, are side by
side, and there is the tomb of another Aaron
Burr, whose life brought dishonour to the name
he bore, but in whose tardy penitence there
was hope, and who desired that his body might
be laid at the feet of his father and grandfather.
Near at hand are the tombs of the other Presidents whose portraits I had seen in the College
Library and Hall, which, like the cemetery,
contains many precious relics and records of
past times.

The College is not the only great institution
at Princeton.   Here, too, is the chief seminary
and training school for the ministry of the Presbyterian Church, one of the most numerous,
and certainly the most influential, Christian
denomination in the States. Among my pleasant
recollections of the place is the hour spent
under the roof of the venerable Dr. Hodge,
President of the Seminary, long the editor of
the *Princeton Review*, and author of writings
which have made his name honoured in all the
churches.   Whatever truth there may be as
to the stern and repulsive tone of Calvinism
on paper, I seldom have seen a man more
genial and attractive than this representative

of the American Presbyterians. Clear light
does not interfere with warm love in good old
Dr. Hodge; and I remember his parlour-study
as one of the cheeriest glimpses I had of an
American interior.

It was with regret I left quiet, studious
Princeton to return to the bustle and crowd
of New York. In my second visit I saw
little that is worth reporting to my patient
reader. One memorable event I was fortunate
in witnessing, the public obsequies of Admiral
Farragut, a pageant more imposing than any
that has been seen since the funeral of our
Wellington. He died at Portsmouth Navy
Yard, but his embalmed body was removed to
New York for interment in Woodlawn Cemetery. The occasion was seized for a great
public ceremony, and I saw, in the words of
the newspaper placards, "THE EMPIRE CITY
IN MOURNING FOR THE DEAD SEA-KING." A
few sentences from the *New York Herald*
will explain why Farragut was thus honoured,
while affording a parting example of the
spread-eagle style which too much characterises
American journalism :—

"It was exceedingly appropriate that the
Empire State should receive the nation's Admiral into her bosom, and that New York city
should bear him to his tomb. An empire in

herself, resplendent with battle-fields won in
the cause of independence and liberty, glorified
by the heroism of four hundred thousand men
who fought in defence of the Union, queenly in
commerce and science and art, the grand old
State is a proper mausoleum for so grand a
hero. New York city, throned upon the
islands of the sea, crowned with intelligence,
wealth, and splendour, whose brain conceives
the progress of the New World, whose heart
throbs with every pulsation of the nation, whose
ships whiten every ocean, and whose skill has
given so many frigates to the battle and the
breeze, was the best, the only Commonwealth
to take him whose only flag had so long and
gloriously defended her prosperity and happiness, and lay him away to his last long sleep.
As the minute guns boomed, and the magnificent pageant moved along through the sorrowful city, what thoughts and memories were
stirred up!   How the mind went back through
the darkness and smoke of the rebellion far
down a beautiful vista of peace and grandeur
to the conflict of 1812, and lingered about that
scene on the gallant Essex's deck in her death
struggle with overpowering numbers, where
Farragut's name first began to shine.   It
followed the young officer as he rose step by
step in the navy, until it found him, in 1861,

at Norfolk, steadfast to his country in the midst
of desertion and treason.   On through doubts
and disasters the retrospect accompanied him,
ever finding him true and brave, until at New
Orleans he leaped into the full stature of his
being, and emerged from the appalling scene
a calm, victorious hero.   Again he looms up,
lashed to the masthead, in the cetnre of shot
and shell and flames, and ramming iron-clads
at Mobile; and, following him across the seas,
memory revisited the fleets that hailed him
great, and the palaces where royalty loaded
him with favours.   Through all these grand
vicissitudes those who yesterday followed him
to his grave chiefly ·recognised the noble
qualities of the man, Farragut.   To them he
was not only all that is heroic—the peer of
Nelson and the Admiral of the present age—
but he was the model and pride of America,
the type of everything that is frank and genial
and generous."

The day of the funeral was the last of September, a day of rain and storm.   The miserable weather interfered with ·the splendour of
the pageant, but did not prevent almost the
whole of the population from witnessing the
scene.   The houses all along the line were
festooned with strips of black and white cotton,
many of the public buildings having mottoes

and sentiments, or transparencies to be illuminated at night. One of these, at Niblo's Theatre, had a portrait with the words " D. Farragut, born 1801, died August 14, 1870," and on either side inscriptions, " The noblest Roman of them all," and " After life's fitful fever he sleeps well." On each side of the street were unbroken lines of people, patiently waiting, with or without umbrellas. At the crossings there were dense blocks of vehicles of all sorts; but the police kept good order, and the mounted troopers stationed at long intervals had no trouble in keeping the centre of the streets clear. The windows and balconies of the houses were crowded with spectators. Had the weather been fine, the spectacle would have been more interesting; but the long array of carriages, containing the most distinguished notables, from the President of the United States down to the Mayor of New York, were all closed. Besides the public functionaries of New York City and State, many other cities and public bodies sent representatives, even from the Ohio and the Mississipi. For the first time I saw a detachment of the Federal Army. The Navy and Marines were also represented. Many thousands of the National Guards of the City and State were conspicuous, the passing of certain crack regiments, at the head of one of which rode the notorious "Colonel Jim Fisk," being greeted by instructive comments from the crowd. I had also a good opportunity of seeing the police of New York, and the fire brigades, who turned out in full array with their engines and accoutrements. The booming of minute guns, and the strains of the successive bands of music, made solemn sound; but the whole pageant had an artificial air, and was a patriotic rather than a personal tribute. As the Admiral had been dead rather more than six weeks, few but his comrades in arms and friends could feel much more than I did, as a stranger witnessing a great national spectacle.

I must not conclude my notes on New York without expressing the satisfaction which many feel at the movement, too tardily made, to throw off the yoke which has burdened and disgraced the city. The organised gang of robbers which has long controlled the civic institutions and political influence of the Empire City, has at length been arraigned at the bar of public opinion, and the Government of New York, it is to be hoped, will now be more in keeping with the honour and credit of American institutions.

CHAPTER XXX.

TO the reader who has followed me thus far it is scarcely necessary to give any general result of my observations; yet I cannot conclude without stating in few words the sum of my impressions. In spite of the difficulties of a new country into which the stream of European emigration is constantly flowing, in spite of political disadvantages which none are so ready to admit as intelligent Americans, they are in advance of us in many of the things that constitute the true welfare of a nation. They have solved problems that baffle the rulers and philanthropists of Europe. In the education of the people by their Common School system, in the management of pauperism, in the home comfort of the working classes, in the relations of capital and labour, and in many points of civic and municipal government, the legislators and magistrates of England could learn much from the great towns of the United States. New York may be excepted, but this is because the government there is so much under the control, not of Americans, but of Irish.

In the highest of all elements in national welfare, the contrast is in favour of America. The number of churches and of Sunday-schools is far in advance of the proportion with us. Lord Shaftesbury stated lately that the number of working men in England who belong to any church can scarcely be reckoned at fifteen per cent. In America I believe that the great majority of working men do attend public worship and contribute to its support. Education and the general diffusion of Bible teaching have so leavened the nation, that it has been able, up to this time, to bring under the institutions of the land the vast hordes of foreign immigrants, and to maintain the position of a great Christian and Protestant state. Attempts to overturn the Common School system have been made in New York and Cincinnati, and, having proved unsuccessful there, are not likely to succeed elsewhere. The curse of slavery and of slave institutions being removed from the Southern States, education and evangelisation will now have free course throughout the Union, and there is nothing to hinder the unlimited progress of the nation in

27

all that marks the highest Christian civilisation. The prophetic words of good Bishop Berkeley have fair prospect of being realized:

> "Westward the course of empire takes its way :
> The four first acts already past,
> A fifth shall close the drama of the day :
> Time's noblest offspring is the last."

I must say that my admiration does not extend to the distinctive political system of America. The suffrage is too extended even for a country of such widely diffused education. The effect is that in some places the American voters are swamped by the hordes of easily naturalized immigrants. In other places men of the highest position and character keep aloof from all public affairs. Then the chief magistrate of the state has more power than is fitting in a country professing to be ruled by public opinion. He is like an autocrat during his term of office. By his veto he can obstruct good measures, and at his will can involve the nation in trouble. In talking with Americans I always affirmed that ours is a truer republic. Ours is only a monarchy in name, not an autocracy, the Queen having comparatively little political power, and being the head of institutions which are absent in America, where there is no court, no established church, no titled aristocracy, and no hereditary legislature.

The real comparison should be between their President and our Premier. A vote of the House of Commons, expressing the popular voice, can control or displace the government, which is not the case in America. It is an admitted disadvantage, too, in the United States, that at every change of government the whole administration of the country, from ambassadors down to village postmasters, may have to vacate their posts. The change affects the position and income of hundreds of thousands of the population. The effect is that no sooner is one government established than agitation and plotting commence for the next term of office. The judges of the Supreme Court alone are free from this perpetual political agitation. I never met an American, not a placeman, or aspiring to be a placeman, who did not acknowledge the fault of this part of their system. The loss of time, the disturbance of trade, the unsettlement of credit caused by every Presidential election, makes the real cost of the Republic tenfold the expense of any monarchy. Were it only the saving to the nation by the quiet constitutional way in which a change of government is effected, the superiority of the English over the American system is apparent. Yet, I repeat, in spite of these political disadvantages, such is the healthy

power of public opinion, and such the love of
law and order diffused through the nation, that
the machinery of State and Municipal legislation and government works wonderful results.
Public opinion, trained by the school, the press,
and the pulpit, is everywhere in advance of
the law. When a thing is seen to be for the
public weal it is done, promptly and effectually.
Some may think that these local measures are
carried to an extreme, as in the case of the
Maine Liquor Law. But on such questions
the people themselves are the best judges, and
legislation is easy when it is in harmony with
educated public opinion.

True of every government, emphatically true
in America, is the sentiment beautifully expressed by Goldsmith in the " Traveller" :—

" How small, of all that human hearts endure,
  That part which laws or kings can cause or cure !
  Still to ourselves in every place consigned
  Our own felicity we make or find :
  With secret course, which no loud storms annoy,
  Glides the smooth current of domestic joy."

Frederika Bremer, the amiable and intelligent Swedish writer, entitled her book on
America, " Homes in the New World." This
was to me the one best and most satisfying
impression received as to America, its limitless
capacity for the multiplying of free, peaceful,

and comfortable homes. There are millions of acres of surveyed lands yet unoccupied, and above a thousand million of acres remain unsurveyed. Nor do the emigrants settle down in mere animal existence in these wild regions. Far away in the forest clearings, often as soon as twenty or thirty log houses have been set up, a wooden schoolhouse is built, and used for Divine service on Sundays. When two or three hundred homes are made, there is sure to be seen the spire of a wooden church, or even two churches. A newspaper soon follows, and all the appliances of Anglo-Saxon civilisation. If the first settlers are not such as carry religion with them, they are soon followed by Christian and benevolent agencies, home missionary societies sending their colporteurs and evangelists to the remotest settlements. There may be personal hardships, and the absence of some social privileges, in the vast new regions yet thinly peopled; but in the old settled parts of the country, life is the same as with us, and for the labouring classes better. No industrious working man need be without employment, or without protection of law for himself and his labour. No child is without the means of good secular and religious education. Poverty there may be, but pauperism is almost unknown, except as the fruit of idleness,

intemperance, or vice.   The boundless regions
of the West are ready to receive the super-
fluous working population.   The same regions
are open to us, as well as Canada and our own
colonies, as fields of emigration ; and, helped
by the experience of America, the sad condition
of our great towns might surely be amelio-
rated.   The majority of Englishmen who have
been in America have gone for amusement or
for gain.   I only wish that more would go in
order to gather useful hints for the improvement of our own country.   There is more to
get than to give by increased intercourse with
America, which can hardly be said of travel on
the Continent, or in any other country of the
world.

Here I adopt the language of a distinguished
Englishman, whose ' unpublished journal of a
recent visit to the States I have seen : " Thus
ended our American tour—the most interesting
and instructive one I ever made, and which I
heartily recommend to any of my friends who
may care more to speculate on the future destinies of our race than to ruminate on the past.
America must be seen to be understood ; and
those who visit it will probably return with
mixed feelings—of pride, at the thought that
the great work of civilisation which is rapidly
overspreading that continent is being carried

on by men of our own race and language ; and
of grave reflection, I will not say of sorrow, at
the thought that half a century hence America
will be the most powerful country on the face
of the earth, and that, as all greatness is relative, our own star will be on the decline." I
too returned with these mixed feelings, but with
pride far prevailing over sadness. The interest
felt in the prosperity and progress of America
is utterly different from the superficial cosmo-
politanism which makes light of one's own
country. I never felt as if among strangers in
America, and I believe that many Americans
share this feeling. They rejoice in the welfare
of the island home of the common race, the
birthplace of great thoughts and glorious deeds
of which both nations are alike proud.

I am aware that I saw only a small portion
of the most prosperous part of the United
States. I did not see that part of the Union
so lately overrun by contending armies, reduced
to poverty by the war, and by the sudden
emancipation of the slaves. The country is
still in a transition state, and it will take years
for the nation thoroughly to accommodate
itself to the new state of affairs. But this
revolution was essential to the future welfare
and safety of the Republic. The influence of
the better elements of the Commonwealth had

been kept out of those States impoverished and degraded by slave institutions. The South must now follow where the North leads, and will no longer be a drag on the nation's advance.

It is a great problem whether the influence of the New England States will be able to assimilate the vast immigrant population, or how far the social and political as well as religious life of America will be overborne or modified. I have no doubt of the result. I believe that the common school system everywhere extended, and the influence of the old common law of England, and of the English Bible, will leaven the whole nation, and that a glorious future is destined for the Great Republic. There is no peril possible so great as has been successfully passed through in the civil war; and now that the Washington Treaty has restored the fulness of international good feeling, England and America, united in friendship, will secure the world's progress in freedom and good government.